FARRAR
STRAUS
GIROUX

BLUE

Mondays

BLUE

Mondays

ARNON GRUNBERG

Translated by Arnold and Erica Pomerans

Farrar, Straus and Giroux   NEW YORK

Published simultaneously in Canada by HarperCollins*CanadaLtd*

Printed in the United States of America

Designed by Abby Kagan

First published in Dutch in 1994 as *Blauwe maandagen* by Nijgh & Van Ditmar, Amsterdam

Publication of this book has been made possible through financial support from the Foundation for the Production and Translation of Dutch Literature, Amsterdam

First American edition, 1997

NOTE

A guilder is worth approximately fifty cents (American).

LIBRARY OF CONGRESS CATALOGING-IN-PUBLICATION DATA

Grunberg, Arnon.
 [Blauwe maandagen. English]
 Blue Mondays / Arnon Grunberg ; translated by Arnold and Erica Pomerans. — 1st ed.
  p. cm.
 ISBN 0-374-11485-4 (alk. paper)
 I. Pomerans, Arnold. II. Pomerans, Erica. III. Title.
PT5881.17.R96B5513 1996
839.3'1364—dc20   96-17252
                   CIP

CONTENTS

Part One
I STILL OWN TWENTY HORSES IN BERLIN   3

Part Two
ROSIE   9

MARTINIMARTIN   11
THE OYSTER BAR   19
MARIAHOEVE STATION   26
THE PHARMACY   34
THE APOLLO HOTEL   41
ANTWERP   47
UNDER THE PINE TREE   58
4,320 MINUTES   65
FUCKING   71
WATCHING *SHOAH*   85

Part Three
WALK LIKE AN EGYPTIAN   95

Part Four
THE GIRLS   123

CARPENTER'S GLUE   125
TINA   129
A PRAYER FOR MARCELLA (PRONOUNCED MARSHALLA)   145
NATASHA   159
HAVE YOU COME FOR AN ANAL? NO, FOR ASTRID   189
SANDRA   227

Part Five
IN THE EMPLOY OF THE BLUE MOON   265

Part One

I STILL OWN TWENTY HORSES IN BERLIN

*M*y father was a stamp dealer, or at least that's what we assumed, my mother and I. I'd been told by my mother that his father had owned a drugstore. A drugstore on a cart. He used to push this cart through Berlin all day long. "One day they found him lying dead on top of his cart," she said, "but it wasn't on account of the storm troopers. It was on account of the Neunundneunziger vodka." A little later she said, "But my parents had a furniture store, in fact two in the end, and we didn't get a single cent for either, not a single cent."

We were living in a hotel in Düsseldorf, where there was a memorial plaque fixed to the wall: "As a young poet, Heinrich Heine spent many happy years here." We had to take a photograph of that, of course, with me in front of it. Heine the young poet used to drive me nuts.

When I was still in elementary school, my father would sometimes take me along on his travels. He never stayed away for long, just a day or two. On the train we would eat kosher sausage rolls he had filled himself. But we ate nonkosher sausage as well, and lots of pancakes and pastries. In his opinion, that sort of food was every bit as good as a hot meal. He would meet people in cafés. The weather was hot. I wore my short pants.

My father was bald. People took him for my grandfather. They would ask, "Do you like going out with your grandpa?" We would go into some café where the man he had arranged to meet would be sitting. He'd be old and bald too. They would have a few vodkas. I'd get ice cream, never anything but ice cream. They would talk for hours. My father never told me what he talked about with all those bald men. When we had finished in the café, we would go to the fairground and eat pork sausage. He said that God didn't care about one pork sausage more or less. God might not, but my mother did. In the evening we'd go to another café, where we'd meet yet another old man, the kind who might have played God in a B movie. More vodkas would be drunk. My father would get excited. His hair looked like straw. That was because he let it grow very long to cover the bald spot on his head, and when he got excited it would fall over his eyes. "To better times!" they would shout. My father would thump the table. No one paid any attention to him. They all thumped the table in there. The talk would be about the Majdanek trial. Or maybe about the young poet Heine again, who knows. It was all pretty much the same thing. My mother thought I'd gone with him to sell stamps, but I never saw a single one. I'd ask him if he'd sold any. He'd refuse to say. Not even to my mother. If you pressed him, all he'd say was, "I could tell you a tale or two—any fool could."

For breakfast I would get hot chocolate, something I never got at home. Once we stood for a whole hour in a shopping mall listening to a man playing the accordion.

Another time we went to Brussels. We saw an accident there. An old man with a cane was run over by a truck at a traffic light.

It happened very slowly. The driver began to accelerate but didn't see him. My father waved his arms in the air and shouted, "Hey! Hey!" The driver paid no attention to my father and the truck drove right over the old man. We couldn't stay and watch because we were due in a café where another old man was waiting for my father. The cafés were always the kind where old men were the only people who ever came, and not too many of them either. Even the waiters were ancient. And the fans turned too slowly to be any use.

Brussels didn't have a fairground. In any case, I was never allowed to go on a roller coaster because my father was too scared to go on one himself. He let me try the shooting, but I was never any good. My father always hit the target. Once he won a teddy bear for me, but what was I supposed to do with a teddy bear? He always took along a plastic shopping bag from the Albert Heijn grocery stores when we went to those cafés. He said, "It's best to carry important things in plastic bags." Sometimes we'd have to wait for the other old men, who always stank of garlic just like my father. I would refuse to sit on their laps, because I wore short pants and their own pants tickled like mad, the same as their cheeks.

Once we had to take some herring to an old man in Düsseldorf. We got up early to lay in a stock of ten herrings from my father's herring man next to the stock exchange building. It was the kind of day when most people would rather be lying in a tub of ice-cold beer. My father was wearing sunglasses, and later on in the train he joked with two girls who were sitting with us in the compartment. Just past Oberhausen the compartment began to stink of herring. My father had put the herring in the baggage rack. He always carried a small black bottle with a gold top on his travels. It was filled with eau de cologne or something that looked like it. He pulled the black bottle out of his inside pocket and began to sprinkle the walls of the compartment with the cologne, to the great amusement of the girls, who slapped their knees. My father seemed to be enjoying himself, too. Besides the bottle he always brought along a book, the same book each time, an English textbook. It was the most well-thumbed book I have ever seen, and it's a mystery to me why he never lost it, since he lost almost everything else on his travels. He even lost me a few times. Just before Düsseldorf, the air in our compartment became unbearable, despite the cologne. He pulled the chopped onions and the cucumber pickles and the herring out of his bag. He let the girls take a whiff, he sniffed it himself, and then he flung the herring out of the moving train onto the track. That compartment must have reeked like the inside of a herring barrel for days afterwards.

My father told us, "In the old days our family would all eat out of a single pan, and they'd turn out the light before they began so that everyone could start on equal terms. Some days they had to make soup from the smell of last week's meat."

When I was twelve, the travels suddenly stopped, or perhaps I wasn't welcome on them anymore.

After my father died, we did indeed find a safe full of stamps, although not as many as we had expected. We won't have to buy any for the rest of our lives, no matter what country we're in. My mother has forbidden me to use them, though. It seems they may be worth quite a lot. I'll believe that when I see it. He also turned out to be the owner of twenty horses. In Berlin. A riding school for the disabled. Acquired in 1965. It occurred to me that my father probably bought the horses so we could all get some exercise. That was an odd idea, since I couldn't really see my father, my mother, me, or my sister on a horse. My mother was terribly upset. "What am I supposed to do with twenty horses?" she cried. "Aren't the stamps enough?"

We managed to get rid of the riding school. A lawyer fixed it all up. "It had been losing money for years," he told us. "Not a soul went there anymore, not a single solitary soul. It beats me why he hung on to it for so long." We got next to nothing for it. No one wanted the horses. Later it turned out that a lot of them were ponies. It's easier for the disabled to get up onto them or something. I said to my mother, "You could sing a song: 'I still own twenty horses in Berlin.'" I didn't get much of a laugh with that.

In the old days we used to go to Berlin quite often. We had an aunt in an old age home there. We went to see her just about every summer, and we'd stay in the old age home ourselves. A whole summer in an old age home! Summers in Berlin can be hot. The people in that home dropped like flies. In the afternoon we would all go to the cake shop and eat like pigs. Me too. As far as I was concerned we could have stayed in Berlin forever, just for the cakes. Now and again we'd go to Wannsee beach. When my mother wasn't looking, my father and I would get some pork sausage and potato salad from huge tubs. Dripping with fat, but the most delicious I've ever eaten. My aunt would be there, too, with her parasol, because she was afraid of the sun.

We all had to go to Israel, where my sister lives, for my father's funeral. We couldn't bury him in Amsterdam, because my sister wasn't allowed to fly. She was nine months pregnant. The baby was due any minute. So we took the body to her. Via Rome, because it had to be done quickly and there was no direct flight that day.

Finally we arrived at Ben-Gurion airport, having spent all day traveling. My mother never stopped moaning the whole time: "I killed him, I killed him." Until I said, "Shut up, or I'll kill you."

We waited in Arrivals. "Where is my husband's coffin?" my mother asked. "It'll be here in a moment," they said. "You un-derstand—we can't send it down with the ordinary baggage."

We waited with my sister. One hour, two hours. They brought

us coffee. Another hour. The whole plane must have been cleared by that time. They brought us more coffee. They called Rome. The coffin was still in Rome. "No panic, nothing's wrong, it's simply been left behind in Rome. That can happen, what with all the transfers. It'll be here on the very next plane."

My mother burst into tears. I thought, Now my sister's going to give birth, right here in Ben-Gurion.

I shouted, "We'll all go to Rome. We'll bury him in Rome. Rome, here we come." All that crying was making me nervous. And my sister's labor pains.

He arrived the next morning. We buried him right away. They hurtled to Jerusalem with him because it was Friday and you're not allowed to bury people on a Saturday.

Then we sat on boxes for a week eating bean soup. That was because my sister's friends were under the mistaken impression that we were crazy about bean soup. You are not allowed to do your own cooking when you are in mourning, but actually I'd rather eat nothing at all than eat bean soup every day.

A week later I flew back to Amsterdam, and with my mother's power of attorney in my pocket I sold the horses.

Part Two

ROSIE

MARTINIMARTIN

I had had my hair cut short and combed straight back, and
every morning I rubbed in half a jar of gel. I wanted to look
like that actor whose name I've forgotten. All I remember is that
he was in the TV version of *Tender Is the Night*. I left my glasses
at home, too, whenever I went out. I couldn't see a thing and
crashed into parked cars a few times at night. Finally I gave up
riding my bicycle altogether.

Our class went to Someren for a week. We had to swim a lot
and bring our parents back asparagus, which we had to wrap in
wet dish towels. The World Cup was being held in Mexico. I was
Maradona. That was a whole lot better than picking asparagus
and wrapping it in dish towels. The third day we were taken to
some clock museum. On the way there I fell off my bike. It was
all the bike's fault, because we had rented the bikes from a farmer
who must have had them rusting away in his barn for the past
ten years. There was a big hole in my pants, and in my knee as

well. "You can say good-bye to those pants," said Mr. Diels, our Greek and Latin teacher. My knee was a gory mess with little bits of gravel stuck all over it. The trip leaders didn't want to take them out and I was too scared to. Then Rosie picked them out one by one. It must have taken her at least two hours, and it hurt quite a bit, all that fussing around with my knee. My bandage had to be changed every evening. Otherwise I would have to be sent back home, they said. Changing the bandage was pretty disgusting, too, because there was still a lot of pus in the wound. First Rosie did it, then Mrs. Haaseveld, our class teacher, and in the end I had to do it myself.

When we played soccer and I couldn't get past someone on the other team, I'd grab hold of his hair until I could. With the girls on the other team I'd pinch their breasts. Some of them acted outraged, but I'd suffered a serious injury and I was Maradona, after all.

Then it was our last evening. We took bets as to who'd be able to drink the most of the huge stock of Martini we'd laid in from the Someren supermarket. After half a bottle I had to give up. One boy managed a bottle and a half. He won, but we didn't see him again that night. His name was Martin, and after that we all called him Martinimartin.

We were upstairs in the dormitory and could hear Diels and the other two getting loaded downstairs just like us. They had had more practice than we had, though, and also had more reason than we did, since all we wanted was to be like the men we idolized, with their husky voices and their faces deeply etched by life. As far as we could gather from what Diels and the others were talking about, what they wanted was to be the way they used to be or the way they hoped to be one day, and they had long since stopped idolizing anybody.

We talked about what we'd be doing in ten years. Deborah said she wanted to adopt ten children. A few months earlier she'd asked me to her birthday party, even though I never spoke to her.

She had three sisters and a mother with a small moustache who served us soup and couscous in vast quantities. An older boy was sitting at the table who went on at length about saxophones, as if they were eggs he'd laid himself. When I left, it turned out he was her father. Her kid brother lay sleeping on the sofa. Later in the evening he turned to me. "We're poor—are you poor too?" he said.

We tried to persuade Deborah that adopting ten children would be an act of supreme folly. Rosie said she'd rather die than have a baby, since there's practically nothing as ugly as a pregnant woman. So the night passed, and at six in the morning we went swimming in a small lake. I stayed standing in the reeds, because if there's one thing I hate it's swimming. After an hour or so we saw Mr. Koenraads, our German teacher, bike past. A little later Mr. Diels rode by as well. Diels never bothered us much, because he spent virtually the entire day drinking Dutch gin and, from about four o'clock on, beer as well. "One for thirst and one for taste," he would say. After a while all of us said, "Mr. Diels, one for thirst and one for taste."

We began each day with morning exercises at seven o'clock. We had to line up in the youth hostel courtyard, where Mr. Diels would stand waiting for us in his shorts. He had said during assembly that he'd be leading the exercises.

He spent most of the time telling us how he used to earn his living repairing refrigerators. He even took us all into the kitchen after betting us that he could take the refrigerator apart and put it together again in less than an hour. Koenraads overheard him and said he didn't think dismantling the youth hostel refrigerator was a good idea. In any case, Diels could have been a whole lot worse. The next time, of course, none of us showed up for his exercises and the trip leaders immediately split up into into search parties. If there was even one person still missing by suppertime, everyone would have to get onto their bicycles and comb the village.

In the end they found us in the little lake. They were soaked through from bicycling. There was no time left for exercises. We were immediately packed into the bus. Martinimartin was beat. I didn't think he would make it to Amsterdam. Then Koenraads asked me, "Where's *your* asparagus?" Because everybody else was going around with a bunch in a wet dish towel. I said that I didn't have any. I said that my parents were quite capable of getting their own asparagus. Koenraads didn't like that at all. He probably wouldn't have dared turn up at his own parents' without any asparagus.

It was too hot in Amsterdam to do anything either, but we still had another month of school. That's why we went to Zandvoort that Monday and played soccer until Martinimartin was sent sprawling by a man who apparently came to the beach for the sole purpose of sending other people sprawling. That was the day we still talked about later, all of us insisting that we had had nothing to do with it and that we'd said from the beginning that the whole thing was a crazy idea. That we had gone on warning him even when everyone realized that it wasn't any use anymore.

Thomas was taller than any of the rest of us. He had draped cans of beer over his girlfriend Natasha's shoulders. Like the cans, her breasts bobbed up and down in time with her steps. Thomas was so tall that all he had to do was to stretch out his arm to drop the ball into the basket. His hair was long as well, like his fingers and toes, and his pimples were without number and deep red in color, like small, ripe raspberries. Every now and then, as he walked with Natasha, who came up to his Adam's apple, he would place his hand on the back of her neck. When we finally found some room on the beach, he lifted Natasha off her feet. By then she was in her bathing suit, which she must have had on under her clothes. We noticed that she had shaved her legs, because we remembered her legs from the exercises.

They made the bet at just about the hottest part of the day. We said to Martinimartin, "Don't do it," because he'd been sick the whole weekend after that night in Someren. He looked a little like Johnny Bosman, the soccer star, the same kind of small head on a long neck. He was very good at heading the ball too. When he heard what Thomas said, he went to a store and bought two bottles, which were lukewarm since it was nearly ninety degrees that day. We looked at Natasha, who was sunbathing on a towel and didn't so much as give him a glance. Martinimartin opened the first bottle, and I have to admit that Natasha looked awfully nice in her red bathing suit. Perhaps he was afraid to call it off once he'd started, or perhaps the heat and the first few swigs and the sight of Natasha aroused a sudden upsurge of lust in him. Maybe that was it, for lust, like death, passes no one by. Anyway, he emptied the first bottle and we could see that Thomas was beginning to have second thoughts. Some of us egged Martinimartin on to open the second bottle, so he did. It must have been about three o'clock by then. Natasha was still lying in the sun, seemingly oblivious to everything. As far as we were concerned she was getting more beautiful by the hour, and Martinimartin, with his bony body and his colorless lank hair, more repulsive by the minute. By about four o'clock the second bottle was half gone.

He was sitting down, and we were standing around him. Maybe he spat a sip out every now and then, but he managed to empty the other half of the bottle. Thomas was standing next to him, watching him like a hawk. A few of us shouted that he should stop, but others urged him to go on. When he'd almost reached the end and some of the drink had spilled out over his chin and onto the sand, Thomas shoved the dribbled-on sand back into Martinimartin's mouth. Then Martinimartin downed the last two gulps as if he hadn't drunk anything for a week. He walked up to Natasha.

She gave him a look. Then she held up a towel and took off her bathing suit and put on her jeans and her T-shirt, saying nothing to us the whole time. She put her wet things into her plastic bag and the two of them walked off toward the village. Natasha first, with her hair still wet from the sea, followed by Martinimartin in his shorts and his flapping shirt. Martinimartin turned around and gestured to us a few times, but he was too far away for us to see what he meant. Still, we all swore that he didn't look like someone who wasn't feeling perfectly all right. Deborah was the only one to say we were all crazy.

We sat down in the sand again and waited for them to come back. When they weren't back by nine o'clock, we used the two bottles as goalposts and I scored the best goal of my life. I was at least twenty yards out, and I volleyed the ball, something I was normally unable to do. All I was good at was kicking hard and running hard. But that evening I took the ball in the air, right on my instep, and shot it straight at one of the two empty bottles. That the goal was disallowed is totally unimportant, because I know without the shadow of a doubt that I hit the inner side of that bottle and not the outer side.

If I should ever meet Martinimartin again, I'll tell him that when he and Natasha disappeared among the dunes I scored the best goal of my life. And that it was disallowed only because the sun and all that beer had made Thomas a little nearsighted. I'll also tell him that that very night I solemnly resolved to sleep with all the beautiful women in the world. That was when we were still standing there, saying nothing, just looking at Natasha, who was walking at least twenty yards ahead of him, swinging her plastic bag with the wet bathing suit inside. I still remember her Amsterdam-South rs and her big chest. Today I know that even the Amsterdam-South r can wear off. As for her chest, it's quite possible that her body was still too small for her breasts, the way my head was too small for my nose, which it still is, according to some.

When they were out of sight we began playing soccer and went on until Thomas suddenly picked up the ball and said, "That's enough." He was up 3–0 and he thought, just as we all did, that we'd be seeing them back any moment, up there on the dune by the fish stall. We had seen them disappear forty-five minutes ago into the white, clammy air.

I had nothing to do with it, of course. I was no friend of Martinimartin's or of Natasha's. She came from a nice family, had chubby little cheeks, and to this day I don't know why she didn't go on lying on her towel, why she didn't just say, "You bunch of idiots." She was no Spider Woman and was unlikely ever to turn into one. At the time, we all went on about Spider Women, but I forget exactly what a girl had to look like or exactly what she had to do to be called a Spider Woman.

Her parents must have given her warnings about everything, about the sun, about fatty foods and who knows what else, but she'd probably spent the whole day doing her best to forget all that, and if I'd looked at her more closely and listened to her more carefully, perhaps I'd have been less surprised. Less surprised, anyway, than the others, who also failed to understand why she hadn't just tapped her finger against her forehead. Later they asked some of us why we hadn't called after her. I always considered that a ridiculous question. There was nothing we needed to ask her and absolutely nothing we needed to call after her since we knew she wouldn't answer. Not that evening or in the days that followed.

As for the questions they put to me, the only answer I gave was that like everyone else I had kept shouting, "Go on, have some more, finish it up."

Just before it grew dark we walked to the train station. The girls held their arms out, then their legs, to compare their tans, and we bought ice cream. But we didn't find the two of them.

In the end each of us had a different story to tell about that evening, and finally there were so many stories that no one was any wiser. What's certain is that after that evening Natasha would have nothing more to do with Thomas or, for that matter, with Martinimartin.

Before the class trip no one had noticed Martin, but when he was suddenly revealed as Martinimartin there was more talk about him in a single day than there had been in the three years before. I often wondered what made Natasha appear more and more beautiful to us that day, and why we all ended up thinking nothing of drinking two bottles of Martini. When I look now at photographs taken at the time, all I see is an ordinary blond girl with a rather coarse face.

After I came back home that evening, I went with my father to the restaurant we ate in every night. My mother was staying in Israel with my sister, who had just had her first baby. We didn't say much. It was a good thing my mother was away, because that meant I didn't have to go to my tennis lesson. She always came along and told the coach, "He never gets a ball over the net, but he's only doing that to spite us."

That week I began to get letters. In English. From someone called Yasma, and I didn't know any Yasmas. My English was terrible, so I didn't understand half of what I read. I asked my friend Eric, but he wasn't interested in my letters. His parents were in the process of breaking up. They'd been in the process for the past ten years, so that didn't interest me either. Everyone still thought I was going to study law or Dutch at the time.

All that June, I went to only about ten classes. At the eleven o'clock recess we'd arrange to meet in fifteen minutes at the sidewalk café called Le Berry. We'd spend the rest of the day sitting outside Le Berry drinking black-currant gin with ice. Iced black-currant gin was my first favorite drink. Sometimes we'd go to a movie in the evening, but usually our money was all gone by six o'clock. Then we'd go and sit on the jetty opposite Dikker and Thijs.

THE OYSTER BAR

*O*ne of the girls in our class came from a titled family, another
was a Jehovah's Witness, and there were a few Jewish girls
as well. The titled girl gave a party. In her parents' garden. A
class-trip reunion. She invited Koenraads, Diels, and Haaseveld
too.

Diels was drunk by the time he arrived. He sat in a corner
and rolled a cigarette with shaking hands. The only tobacco he
smoked was Javaanse Jongens. He told the story of how his
mother sent him out to repair refrigerators when he was only
twelve. He told that story all the time at parties. He used to have
to cover almost the whole of north Amsterdam, ringing every
doorbell. "Do you happen to own a broken refrigerator?" If you
ask me, the experience left him with an obsession about repairs,
because everywhere he went he repaired things.

We were sitting there under the trees. They had a giant-sized
garden. I listened to Diels's stories dragging on, like the turtle's

story in *Alice in Wonderland*. Luckily we were called inside just then, to look at slides of the class trip. Everyone walked around with faces that said, "See how well we got along with one another?" Even Martinimartin. That's what depressed me the most. That they all kept going on about how well they'd hit it off with one another and that they'd sooner cut their tongues out than tell you how it really was.

Next morning Diels had a new aftershave on and Rosie said she wanted to go to the zoo.

I told the caretaker that it was an important Jewish holiday. At school they had a lot of respect for Jewish holidays. The zoo turned out to be much more expensive than we'd thought. We'd arranged to meet a couple of other people from our class in front of the lions' cage, but we just left them to wait and went for something to eat in one of the tourist pizza parlors on Leidseplein. We talked about all sorts of things, about Diels's refrigerators and Martinimartin and Natasha, and then Rosie said there weren't just the two of us. I thought she meant that she was having a baby or something, that I was about to hear some dramatic news. She said that she was Yasma, or rather she wrote it down on a coaster. It occurred to me that this sort of thing was going to happen to me quite often in life, that it would really be nothing out of the ordinary for people suddenly to confess to me that they were the ones who had been sending me letters for weeks.

The evening before examination week began, Rosie and I decided to have a meal out. I was to pick her up at the ice cream parlor in Van Woustraat where she worked. Rosie called it the Vermicelli Bar because the boss was an Italian. I had to wait outside because they said I kept her from working. She'd told me that it wasn't at all easy to serve good ice cream, to make nice round scoops. A few days before I'd read in *Avenue* at the dentist's that famous and important people ate at the Oyster Bar. So I said to her, "Let's go to the Oyster Bar. I eat there quite a lot."

We were shown to a table next to an aquarium full of lobsters. We ordered sole and two glasses of wine and then another two and after that another two. Only then did it occur to us that we would have done better to have ordered a bottle in the first place.

The waiter was nice to us. Just as we'd come in I'd heard him say to the other waiter, "They're making them prettier and prettier these days, aren't they?"

I couldn't finish the sole, and she couldn't either. They were enormous fish, and we found out later that they charged you by the quarter pound. We told each other which cocktails we'd already tried and which ones we still had to try. She was wearing an OshKosh outfit and had put her hair up in a little ponytail, which she called her "shaving brush." Then the waiter came over and said, "Will you be wanting any dessert? Otherwise you'll have to vacate your table."

We asked for the menu and she sat there gazing at it. I felt awfully hot. She grabbed hold of my hand, which was all wet. It was the first time a woman had grabbed hold of my hand like that, but I didn't take much notice. Everything she did with my hand, in fact, passed me by, because I couldn't stop thinking of the waiter who had said they're making them prettier and prettier these days.

"Let's order dessert," she said, "because while we're eating we don't have to pay."

I thought that was a brilliant idea. The waiter came sauntering over to us again. It was obvious that he, too, was feeling hot. Both of us ordered sorbets. Very large sorbets to cool us down.

"What's that?" she asked the man. She pointed to the menu.

"That is *champenoise*."

"Let's have some of that too," she said.

"Spanish or French?"

"Make it Spanish," she said. She did that very well, saying "Make it Spanish" as if she said it every day.

After the sorbet we ordered ice cream, because there was nothing to do now but carry on, and we finished the Spanish bottle slowly, and then she said, "I think I'm getting a pimple, I can feel my skin getting really tight." By then it was ten o'clock and the place was filling up fast. There were lots of families on holiday, and businessmen. She took out her fountain pen and started to write on her white napkin. I saw the waiter looking, but he said nothing. I didn't say anything either. There aren't that many moments in your life when you're sure you can do anything you want, but I hadn't yet realized that. I probably didn't say anything because I was thinking the same thing she was. She covered the whole linen napkin with writing. She wanted us to sign an agreement never to become grown-ups. Later I signed a few other agreements like that, but never again on a napkin.

I signed it in the Oyster Bar on July 3, 1986, with her fountain pen. She wanted to take it home, and I could see that they were starting to mop up in back. I looked at her, with her narrow face with those slightly projecting cheekbones, and the small mouth with the large lips, and her eyes that sometimes looked green and then went brown again, and her eyebrows, which she had put on with a whole collection of pencils from the case she always carried with her. I remembered that it was exam week, that we had done no work, that they couldn't hold me back a grade, but they could do it to her. I remembered her telling me in Beatrix Park that she might easily go on serving ice cream for the rest of her life. At the moment, that did not seem to me the worst of all possible fates.

"We'd like to go home now," said the man, and placed a dish with four peppermints and the check on the table.

I remembered the teacher telling her one day, "Just write that down in your homework book." Then she'd said, "I don't have a homework book." It had fallen out of her case. Later a lot more seemed to have fallen out of her case—books and notepads and dictionaries.

"Where do you live?" asked the waiter. Rosie refused to tell him and she wouldn't let them call her parents, so they called mine. There were three of them by now. They weren't yelling at us. They just stood around our table. "That's all we needed," said one, "walking our legs off all night for nothing."

Then the manager came out to join them. We had eaten and drunk to the tune of nearly three hundred guilders. She looked at the lobsters and so did I. They went to call my father, and we had to wait. Most of the lights had been turned out by then and everything cleared except for our table, which still had a cloth on it, with the dirty glasses and the empty *champenoise* bottle. Nobody said a word, except every so often she'd say, "What a bummer."

The waiters had to keep hanging around too. I felt sorry for them because the manager bawled them out. "Couldn't you have told the moment they came in?" he kept asking. "Couldn't you have told?"

One of them was bald and didn't reply, and it was only when the manager had gone that he said, "Bullshitting, that's all he's good for." To us he said, "He's one hell of a bullshitter, you know. He can bullshit everyone under the table." He was the man who'd said they're making them prettier and prettier these days. We were given a glass of water because the ventilation had been turned off, and we were quite thirsty from all that *champenoise*.

Finally my father turned up, in a taxi. He had obviously just gotten out of bed, because his hair was a mess, his shirt was all over the place, and he had a red nose from the wine he'd been drinking that night. He wrote two checks. He was much calmer than I'd expected. Then he turned to us and said, "Are you out of your minds, you two? Don't you know anything about money?" To me he said in German, "You're just a bum," and he said to the man from the Oyster Bar, "The last time I was here was ten years ago, with my wife's family, and you were all crooks even then, and if my son ever comes back I'm telling you right now you'd better not serve him, because I won't get out of bed for you a second time."

"You go straight home now," he said to me, "but not in my taxi." Then he was gone. They cleared our table and wished us a good night.

My parents had not yet gone to bed when I got home. They were sitting in the living room. Or rather my father was asleep on the sofa and my mother was sitting at the table drinking tea. I can't remember anymore exactly what happened then, but it ended with my mother smashing half the tea service. That was nothing special. When my sister was still living with us, dishes were smashed on an even more regular basis. We had a white porcelain service, I think it was called Rosenthal—anyhow they had a name, those dishes. My mother flung them to the floor. First she shouted, "I'll never cook for any of you ever again." Then she started on the dishes. My father shouted, "Finish them off then—you've promised to a hundred times. Why don't you keep a promise for once in your life?"

She shouted at me, "You're vermin just like your father, your father's whole family is vermin, and vermin eat off the floor." After that she threw the food, a beef sandwich she'd kept for me, all over the Persian rug. Then all hell broke loose. The woman from next door called to say that she didn't wish to interfere, all she wanted was to be allowed to sleep. I heard my mother yell at her over the telephone, "Then take a sleeping pill. I've taken sleeping pills all my life. You think it would kill you if you took a sleeping pill just one night?"

At three-thirty in the morning things became a little quieter, and then they decided I would have to go stay with my sister in Israel for a few weeks. That was the first time they decided that, and afterwards they decided it a few more times. So I could calm down there. I thought it more likely that they wanted to calm down themselves. That was ridiculous, though. They never calmed down.

The whole week before I was supposed to go to Israel we arranged to meet every day at a table outside Le Berry. We drank iced black-currant gin and took turns getting french fries. It was so hot that the little packets of mayonnaise turned porous in the sun and burst open all by themselves. I even had to buy drinks all around for a Frenchman and his family one afternoon because I was accused of squirting mayonnaise onto his shirt. After that we couldn't buy any more drinks for the rest of the day.

The night Argentina played Germany in the final we couldn't sit outside the café, because they'd put up a huge screen on the wall of the municipal theater to show the game. The place was so crowded that I thought we'd never find each other, but Rosie found me all right. She said, "I could smell you." I had bought some cologne a few days earlier and had sprinkled it liberally all over myself. Even so, I didn't believe her. That night we drank iced black-currant gin at a café near Central Station. When Argentina won I just had to kiss her.

MARIAHOEVE STATION

The day before I was due to leave for my sister's, Rosie and I went to The Hague. We sat outside at various sidewalk cafés there too. She wanted to borrow my sweater because it wasn't nearly as warm as we'd thought it would be. That's why my sweater smelled of her that night. I still remember that very clearly, because I took it with me to Israel, but even though I didn't wash it, it started to smell less and less of her.

She talked about her previous boyfriends. The one before me had been Jewish and very fat, she said; before that she had had an Italian, but it hadn't lasted long. All they'd done was roll around a little one evening in a deck chair on the beach. We bought picture postcards of Queen Beatrix and mailed them to almost everyone in our class. "Your nose has shrunk," she said suddenly. She repeated that a lot afterwards. In the middle of some conversation, suddenly, "Your nose has shrunk again. Honestly, it's shrinking all the time." It would always make us laugh, but never as much as that time in The Hague. I'm glad that after her no one else has ever said that to me. People can say almost anything else to you so often that you don't even remember any-more who said it or exactly why and when.

We sat all afternoon at a table outside an ice cream parlor and Rosie said, "Toothpaste is good for pimples and mosquito bites, but it's also good for runs in your panty hose. You can stop a run with toothpaste, did you know that? It's really kind of all-purpose."

I had never realized that it was all-purpose. After that I would smear it over my face from time to time, though I can't honestly say that it produced spectacular results.

"Do you ever read girlie magazines?" she asked.

"No. Why?"

"My last boyfriend read nothing but girlie magazines. I know because I went on vacation with him once."

"Oh, I see," I said.

Then she started going on about some pop group or other. She knew much more about music than I did. She often wrote lyrics and sent them to me. At first I thought they were all her own work. I didn't understand them very well either. Later I began to understand them a bit better because she explained what she thought they actually meant. What those groups were singing was always pretty incomprehensible, but then, my English was useless. We were taught English by Mrs. De Wilde. Of course, my ignorance wasn't all due to her.

Mrs. De Wilde had a few books on tape, and last period on Thursdays she would play us a tape. Every few minutes she would stop the tape and shout that we had to shut up and that what she'd really like to do would be to throw a few of us out the window. I was generally among those few she wanted to throw out the window. We'd been doing "Bananafish" for three whole months, and it was slowly driving me crazy. On top of that she had the nasty habit of locking the classroom door halfway through the lesson so that at least some of us would stay in. Then she'd hold the key up and screech, "This key is staying right here, with me, and we're all going to carry on for an extra twenty minutes." During those twenty minutes we'd do nothing, absolutely nothing. All right, a few of the girls would start their homework and every so often we would stage an orange fight. She said nothing about those either, about the orange fights. She just sat there with a smirk on her face, and by the end she'd be looking at us more and more drowsily. In the beginning she would join in the fights sometimes by throwing a wet sponge at us, but after a few weeks she stopped doing even that. Presumably she had realized by then that we were better at throwing wet sponges around than she was. The principal walked into our class and said, "All those who have thrown a wet sponge in Mrs. De Wilde's classroom will spend a week picking up litter."

I said, "Excuse me, but Mrs. De Wilde started it with the wet sponge."

"I'll see you in my office right away," he said pleasantly.

They were always pleasant. And they didn't hate me; at the time they were just starting to get worried about me. One after the other. The economics teacher held out the longest; he refused to worry about me for six whole months. Until he, too, said to me one afternoon, "I really am worried about you." To this day I hate people who worry about me.

I gathered that Mrs. De Wilde had had an accident once. There seems to have been one Mrs. De Wilde from before the accident and one from after the accident. I knew only the Mrs. De Wilde from after the accident. She had lost her sense of smell, as she told us more than once, and something had happened inside her head as well. After the accident she moved to Amstelveen. I also have to admit that she once took our class to the Amstelveen Cultural Center to see a play by Shakespeare, but I can't say anything about it, because I wasn't allowed to go. The fact of the matter is that, a few days before, I'd had to retake a test. The three of us were sitting in the classroom, where, incidentally, it was always tropically hot. That, too, seemed to be a necessity after her accident. No one knew the exact details. Suddenly she had to go to the bathroom. I went up to one of the girls and asked, "Is it 6A or 6B, and what on earth is 7?"

"You ought to have done some studying," the girl whispered. I tried to catch a quick glimpse of her paper, but she made a great show of covering it with her big chest. She was a real cow. The next girl wasn't much better. I still don't understand why I didn't just sit there checking any old answer or, come to think of it, no answer at all. Instead I went up to the window with those yellow curtains. I stood on a chair and hung from one of the curtains, which tore. I don't know why I did it. Sometimes you do things and then you think later, Why did I do that? I think it was because I wanted to do something to those girls but was afraid to hit them. I stood there on the chair with the torn yellow curtain in my hand, and Mrs. De Wilde came back and all she could say was, "It's beyond belief. I've never seen anything like it. It's beyond belief." She didn't even throw a wet sponge at me. She ran out, to get help, I think. I just stayed where I was. I don't remember anymore exactly what happened next. The worst thing, I thought, was that those two cows just went on with their test. That's what I thought was the worst. You pull a curtain down, you make Mrs. De Wilde run hysterically all over Vossius High School, and those two cows just carry on answering questions on *Bananafish*. As if nothing had happened, as if curtains got torn down every day of the week.

Then two teachers came in and took me off the chair. Not too roughly, though they were obviously in a bit of a panic. I had to go with them, of course, but the curtain came as well. I managed to say, "Why don't we leave the curtain here?" But that wasn't allowed. I had to walk between them and they sort of dragged me along. We charged down the corridors like that, the curtain behind us. It was a pretty long curtain, so we were a pretty unusual sight. "It's getting filthy," I said. "Why couldn't it have stayed with Mrs. De Wilde? It isn't a mop, is it?"

"You'll be mopping the whole school with that curtain in a moment," said one of the teachers.

They were full of ideas like that at Vossius. Mopping the school with a curtain, picking up chewing gum wrappers with a pointed stick, sweeping up leaves with a broom.

The two of them sat waiting for me in the principal's office. The principal said very solemnly, "We have always thought of you as a pleasant boy, but our view of you is gradually beginning to change." The deputy principal nodded her head. I was sorry about that because she was quite nice. She gave me the poet Piet Paaltjens to read when I was suspended one day.

"That's ridiculous," I said. "I pull a curtain down a little way for a split second, and suddenly your view of me has changed."

"You know very well it takes only a single second to destroy the view everyone has of you," said the deputy principal.

"But just by pulling down a curtain?"

The principal said, "A few days ago it was a wet sponge, today it's a curtain. We can only wait and see what it will be tomorrow. If you carry on like this."

"But we still believe in you," said the deputy principal. "Please don't dash our hopes."

I think she went on saying that she had hopes for me right to the end. Until the day arrived when she, too, said that she had lost all hope and that all her trouble had been for nothing. I've always been very good at dashing the hopes and betraying the trust of others. I'm still very good at it. What sort of hope was it, in any case? When two cows carry on as if nothing is happening while you pull a curtain down before their very eyes? Perhaps I ought to have jumped out the window?

"We are suspending you for two days because of the curtain," said the principal. But by that time Rosie had long since left school.

...

The day we spent in The Hague we discovered the latest type of candy store, where you can buy all different kinds of candy by the pound. We took a bag each and filled them to the top, mainly with those tiny raspberries. I could easily eat a pound of those all by myself. They put ribbons around our bags and we paid with our last money.

We ended up at Mariahoeve Station. It was completely deserted. We sat on a bench on an empty platform and ate what was in our bags because that was all we had with us. Rosie said, "We could have gone somewhere to eat, some sidewalk café. This is really shitty. It always ends up really shitty."

That was typical. Often when we'd spent the whole day together she'd end up saying that everything was really shitty. She snatched my bag out of my hand and emptied it onto the rails. That sort of thing was a shame, I felt. She could see nothing shameful about it; she found other things far more shameful, she said. We went to look for a restroom but couldn't find one. Mariahoeve Station was an absolutely useless station; there was nothing there, not even a restroom.

Then she walked to the end of the platform and I walked behind her. When she got there she threw up. I didn't really want to look, because I thought she might be embarrassed. But she said, "Hold my head." I didn't know exactly how you hold someone's head when they're throwing up. I held it anyway and looked across at the enormous offices on the other side of the tracks.

When she had finished, we sat down again and let a few trains go by. The ribbons were all we had left of the bags, and she put them in her hair. She used those ribbons until September. For tying her ponytail.

She said, "My last boyfriend jerked off into a condom."

"Really," I said.

"Yes," she said. "I was at a party once, and they had bets on who could come the quickest. I thought the whole thing was awfully childish."

She lit a cigarette. I didn't smoke. Then she opened her purse and showed me a lipstick she had just bought. She wanted to know if I thought it was a nice color. I didn't know much about things like that—to me all lipsticks were just red. But I said, "Lovely." Then she took about thirty beer coasters out of her purse.

"Notes from the Mazzo Correspondence Club," she said.

She didn't want me to read them, coasters that had been used for writing down conversations at the Mazzo Club, where the rock music is much too loud for talk. In the end she passed one to me. I still have it and it says, " 'Physically: hot, deaf, thirsty. What's the first thing you're going to buy tomorrow?'

" 'I don't know. Maybe a pencil.'

" 'What for?'

" 'To chew.'

" 'Are you nervous or something?'

" 'No, I'm desperate. (Joke, ha ha!)' "

She threw the other coasters onto the tracks. It occurred to me that she might throw more things out of her purse onto the tracks that evening. Luckily she didn't, because in the meantime we were no longer the only people on the platform. "Trash, fucking useless trash," she said, "the whole Mazzo Correspondence Club."

Then we sat down again, and I didn't know what to say. We took the first train. We even quarreled a bit, but not for long, only on the stretch between Leiden and Nieuw-Vennep. After that we started a story in which we took turns writing three lines, with the other person allowed to read only the third line. I had to get off one station before her, which is why I promised her all those things on the train, all those idiotic things.

. . .

My sister's house was overrun with cockroaches when I arrived. Whenever a cockroach died, millions of ants would descend on it and eat it up. A column of ants marched along the passage day and night. "They're burying the cockroaches," my sister said. As for me, I lay on the bed in a pool of yogurt. I'd gotten sunburned and they said I had to be rubbed all over with cold yogurt.

When I couldn't sleep in the afternoon because her baby was screaming, I tried to count the cockroaches on the walls. Outside, beyond the blinds I was very careful to keep shut, it was ninety-five degrees in the shade. In the room next door my little niece was crying. Every day out on the square the same two men played backgammon under a faded umbrella. Like me, they drank Goldstar all day, and I wondered why I wasn't writing any of the letters I had promised to write.

When I was allowed out again, I went to the café around the corner in the evening and looked for a place at the bar right under the fan. You could change shekels for dollars there and buy tape recorders. The backgammon players went there too. Apart from them there were a lot of soldiers, who taught me to play darts. There was also a girl who had been working at the café for a year. She was from Liège. She told me that she'd been very drunk one night. A few months earlier. The night she'd decided to lose her virginity.

THE PHARMACY

*A*fter my vacation I took a job in a pharmacy owned by a
man I knew from the synagogue. His name was Mr. Hausmann and he collected Smurfs. My parents thought it was a good
idea for me to have a job. So that I'd come to realize what time
and money really meant, my father said. I had to deliver prescriptions to people who couldn't walk anymore or who could still
walk but couldn't see.

They tipped me everywhere, especially in the old age home.
One woman there gave me at least ten guilders. She wanted me
to eat her food. I didn't have the slightest intention of eating her
food, because it was all chopped up and mushy. All she had to
do was to swallow it. Once she whispered in my ear, "I don't want
to eat ever again. I've eaten more than enough." I absolutely did
not want to be told that sort of thing.

"You must do what you think is best for you," I said. Then I
ate her custard anyway. I got twenty guilders for that, for that

little bit of custard. "Just have it," she said. "I can't take it with me." So I ate it and then I looked at the cold hamburger lying on her plate and I thought to myself, No, I'm not going to eat that, too, not for twenty guilders—it looks too greasy. They had warned me not to accept excessive tips, but I thought, I've worked for this one. So I thanked her and said, "Enjoy your meal, ma'am." And she said, "God will reward you."

A few days later Mr. Hausmann told me to get a bicycle. My work was taking too long. Before me they had had a boy who did it three times as fast. It wasn't much quicker on the bicycle. There were always people who kept me. There was an old bald man with two birds in a cage. He had to be supplied with those large diapers for adults. He said, "They can sing. Hang on there, boy, they'll sing in a minute." I knew I couldn't leave until they'd sung something. Or rather I could leave, but then I'd have to go without a tip. I made five and a half guilders at the pharmacy, and if the birds sang the man gave me three times that. It took longer and longer before there was a peep out of the birds, and often I felt like picking them up and hissing, "Sing or I'll squeeze the living daylights out of you."

The worst thing was when he tried to lead the singing. He'd sing a few notes and then have a coughing fit that went on for half an hour. I'd have to slap him on the back and he'd fill the room with his spluttering. When he had one of those coughing fits he'd also mess his pants. The whole room would stink of it. When it was all over, he would start again from scratch. "Let's give them a bit more of that mixed bird seed," he'd say. Then I would have to look for the bird seed. Everything in the room was sticky—the closets, the doors, the floor, the cage, the chairs, the bird seed, the newspapers, even the money he gave me. The place always stank of urine. Even the light in the room was the color of urine.

When I finally got outside, I'd have to stop and catch my breath before doing anything else. Then one of the birds died.

There was no more singing. The man just sat in his chair, a cloth over the cage. The dead bird still lay on the table. It began to stink. "Shouldn't it be taken away?" I asked.

"Leave it alone," he yelled. I no longer got my ten guilders. It was up to him if he wanted to rot away with that bird of his. When I rang the bell I would shove the diapers into his hand and take off.

Then there was old Mrs. Cohn, who hated me. I always had to go right inside when I went to her place in Roerstraat. I wasn't allowed to hang around on the doorstep in case she caught a cold. Even when it was almost ninety degrees out she could catch a cold at the door. Once inside, I had to sit down and eat a cookie. She only made me do that so that she could ask, "And where is your *kippa?*" She wouldn't wait for an answer, because she knew what it would be. She would hurry to the closet, since she was much more spry than she let on, and pull one of her dead husband's skullcaps out of a drawer. I would have to put it on, a large black yarmulke, and then she'd say, "Right, now we'll say the *beracha* together." The two of us would say the blessing together and I would eat the cookie. With difficulty, because when you picked it up it crumbled, that's how old it was. Finally she would slip me a quarter. "But," she would say, "that's not for you to keep. Put it in the blue box." Then she would come hobbling up with her blue Jewish National Fund collection box. I'm sure she extracted that quarter from the box every time I left. It would have been a true act of charity if I'd bashed her brains in with that JNF collection box.

A few days later the woman whose custard I always ate died. "She passed away peacefully," said the nurse when I turned up the next time. How could she possibly tell it had been peaceful? Anyway, the news was a blow. I was just starting to earn a reasonable amount of money from her. For twenty guilders I would gladly have finished off five helpings of custard. "Give those prescriptions to me," said the nurse. She was going to sell them, of course. I understood the nurses. There were some real stinkers among their patients. Mrs. Saenredam, for instance, who complained every day that I was late, that she was dying from pain because I was so late. But she didn't look as if she was. People who die from pain can't swear like Mrs. Saenredam. Not just at me but at everyone. Even at the cook. Even at the cleaning ladies, although they couldn't understand a word she said. That didn't bother her at all, she just went on swearing anyway. She never gave me so much as a ten-cent piece, although she was rolling in money. Mrs. Saenredam couldn't hear all that well anymore either. I know that sort of person. When the tax collector comes around they suddenly can't hear a word. If you hang around a little waiting for a tip they suddenly go blind or they have a heart attack. That's because people like Mrs. Saenredam would sooner have a heart attack than tip you even a single cent.

Then you had people who didn't live in the old age home. You might have to yell four times up some huge staircase, "The boy from the pharmacy. I've come with your medicine, your heart pills, the nose drops, and the ointment for your bedsores." Then some of them would call back, "I'm not opening the door, I'm not expecting anybody." Others even had the nerve to call down, "I'm having my afternoon nap. Come back in an hour's time."

Mr. Hendriks always opened the door half naked and called me his "medicine man." He was never convinced that he wasn't going to have an emergency. That's why he'd placed almost all his chairs near the toilet and why he never kept the bathroom door closed either. He was good for at least two and a half guilders.

I always finished off my rounds at Anita's. She was an old lady but she said right from the start, "Just call me Anita." She lived surrounded by all sorts of plants, so it reminded you of a greenhouse in there. She looked better than any of the others, but we had the same conversation every day.

"Please take me to my husband," she would say when I was ready to leave.

"Where is your husband?" I would ask.

"Far away," she would say, "very far away."

"I have a job to do," I would say. "I have to earn a living."

"But I'll pay you if you come with me," she would say. She'd sit there in that dress—she always wore the same dress, a purple one with polka dots. Often she'd wear a hat too. Once she clung to me and wouldn't let go. She was incredibly strong for such a small person. She said, "Please take me to my husband. You won't regret it."

"Where does your husband live?" I asked again.

"Far away, very far away."

I said, "I can't, I really can't. I still have hundreds of prescriptions in my bag I have to deliver."

She blocked the way, refused to let me out the door. "Please take me to my husband," she said, "just take me away from here." I telephoned for the nurse. The nurse shoved her straight into a chair and said she'd be in for it if she ever bothered me again. From then on she never dared say a word to me. She didn't have a penny to her name anyway.

The day before I was fired by the pharmacy, Rosie left a letter for me there. I only worked in the afternoons. First I always had to make tea for the ladies. One of them asked me, "Do you ever play in a band?"

"What do you mean?" I asked.

"A letter was left here for you this morning, by a girl." They started to giggle. They used to giggle all day long.

I saw at once that the letter was from Rosie and put it in my pocket. I hadn't called her since I'd gotten back from Israel, although I'd promised to. Nor had I answered any of her letters.

When I returned to the pharmacy later that afternoon, Mr.

Hausmann was waiting for me. He looked very pale, but that was nothing unusual. He had something wrong with his nose. He said, "Everybody has been calling to say their medicine hasn't been delivered. Things can't go on like this. They really can't go on like this." I said nothing, because what could I say? I had called Rosie from a telephone booth and had fed all the change Mr. Hausmann had given me into the telephone. If I could have, I would have fed all the medicines in as well. I thought of that man with his one bird left, and the stench that had been filling his house for a whole week now.

"Here's your pay for this week, but don't come back tomorrow," he said. He looked awfully sad. He said, "Nothing personal."

"Right," I said.

My parents were sitting in the garden eating cake. My mother said, "You want to bring shame on us in front of the whole synagogue—you're a nail in my coffin."

Then she poured me some coffee and asked, "Why have you done this to me? Do you want to kill me?"

Naturally a few dishes got smashed again that evening. As a matter of fact it was just before the fall when a record number of dishes were smashed in our house. I bet a thousand guilders' worth of bone china was destroyed that fall.

I had arranged to meet Rosie outside the movie theater that evening.

"Stop him," my mother shouted. "Stop him."

"I can't stop him," said my father. He'd already had a bottle and a half of wine by then and quite a few Dutch gins, and he was sitting there reading *Der Rabbi von Bacherach* again. He must have read it at least ten thousand times. He was sitting under his trees again, which he looked at every day as if he had made them himself. He said, "What a sinner I am, what a miserable sinner."

My mother had told me more than once, "Your father is a turd, a turd who think's he's Heinrich Heine."

One evening my father was reading the paper. My mother came in with a pot of spaghetti. Then she tipped the pot of spaghetti all over his paper. The whole pot.

"Why did you do that?" I asked.

"Just to show what a drunk your father is," she said.

My father stayed where he was, sitting there with the spaghetti all over his newspaper. He said, "The world has gone mad, the world has gone stark raving mad." To me he said, "Alcohol destroys the brain. Watch out." Then he turned to his crossword puzzle and my mother began to clear the table, and I went into the kitchen to get something to eat.

THE APOLLO HOTEL

*E*very Monday evening at seven o'clock Rosie and I had a date to meet in the bar of the Apollo Hotel. We had moved on from iced black-currant gin to Dubonnet. The Apollo Hotel was close to Vossius and also exactly halfway between our houses. We didn't sit at the bar as a rule but at a little table by the window overlooking the canal.

On one of those evenings at the Apollo Hotel Rosie told me about Mr. Eisenring, the science teacher who had been asked to sing something at the show put on at Vossius every year. At first he had refused, but they had gone on nagging him until he gave in.

Mr. Eisenring was a tall man with brown hair that was beginning to recede at the temples. He could roll his eyes. At recess he would walk to the staff lounge carrying his briefcase. The briefcase was ancient, and he admitted that he had used it when he was a schoolboy. I don't know if it was a matter of principle with him but Mr. Eisenring never learned our names. He always said, "That one over there," or "You there," or "That girl by the window," or "The one with the big mouth."

Once he said, "If you've stuck any chewing gum under your desk, sonny, I'll stick you under the desk too." Another time he asked, "Do any of you know what a teenybopper is?" We waited. "That girl at the back there by the window is a teenybopper," said Mr. Eisenring, "and because that teenybopper obviously doesn't have anything in particular to do at the moment, she'd better go and get me a cup of coffee." After that he drank his coffee and ate his sandwiches in silence.

Everyone knew Rosie had a good voice, so it wasn't surprising that Mr. Eisenring asked her to sing with him. He'd come up with the idea of singing a Marlene Dietrich song because nobody sang songs like that anymore. According to him. The song he decided on was *"Johnny, wenn Du Geburtstag hast, bin ich bei Dir zu Gast, die ganze Nacht."* Rosie had to provide backup by repeating the refrain. When rehearsals began, her feelings of affection suddenly changed into what she called an "all-consuming passion." I didn't doubt her word, because when you're fourteen all passions are all-consuming. When you're fifteen, too, and even sixteen.

The rehearsals were slowed slightly by her passion, but the two of them made steady progress even so, and one night they decided to go out to dinner to celebrate their achievement. Or rather, Mr. Eisenring invited her out. He didn't say much during the meal. Over dessert, though, he did tell her something about his first marriage. He said, "She ran off when we were on vacation in France, but I thought it would be a pity to cut my vacation short because of that." He wouldn't say any more, no matter how hard she pressed him. After the meal he took her home in his little yellow car, Rosie told me, and in the car he kissed her and she kissed him back.

After the next rehearsal they went out to dinner again, even though this time they'd made no further progress. Apparently Mr.

Eisenring had by now developed certain feelings for Rosie, because that night he invited her up for coffee. "He showed me his whole house," said Rosie, "but first he kissed me again in his car."

The house was exceptionally neat and tidy. Even the kitchen. He told her that he did his cooking for the whole week on Saturday and that he considered seven different menus a year quite enough. Then he opened the door to his bedroom, where there was a double bed. One side of the bed was covered with the stuff trash bags are made from. "I sleep here, and over there is where my cats sleep," said Mr. Eisenring.

In the living room he drank coffee and she had water because he had no tea in the house.

Then Mr. Eisenring said, "Well, you'd better go home now or else things might get out of hand." He tried to call a cab, but there were none available. So they started kissing again. "Everyone is trying to get a cab," he said. A little later she went home by streetcar.

Rosie told me about how they'd sung *"Johnny, wenn Du Geburtstag hast."* Shortly before the performance Mr. Eisenring had sat smoking in silence in the dressing room. For the occasion he had worn not the jeans and casual shirt he normally wore but a black suit. He had dressed as if he were going to a funeral. Their act had been announced just before the break. Mr. Eisenring went up to the microphone at the front. He said, "Ladies and gentlemen, I am going to sing you a song by Marlene Dietrich."

When Rosie launched into the refrain for the second time, the audience joined in. They didn't know the words so they just sang "Johnny, Johnny" and clapped their hands, and at the back of the auditorium, where Mr. Eisenring's words were completely lost, they sang, "Were you drunk again tonight?" When it was all over, everyone shouted, "More, more!" Some girls sitting on the windowsill threw yogurt containers and empty soda cans onto the stage, but no one was seriously hurt. Mr. Eisenring had already gone off but the orchestra struck up again, so he came back and sang the whole song once more. During the applause, the audience in the packed auditorium chanted his name.

"Thank you all very much," he said through the microphone, but it had already been turned off because it was the break.

Mr. Eisenring was given a bottle of wine for his performance, and apparently he drank it in the dressing room with Rosie. Right after that he had to leave. He had his old briefcase with him and his newspaper and he waved his long arm in the air to say goodbye to his public. When he walked past the little smoking room, a couple of the girls shouted, "We want to have your baby!" Rosie said she would never be able to look at Mr. Eisenring without thinking of his cats. Their relationship faded as quickly as it had blossomed and Mr. Eisenring soon treated her again with the same reserve with which he treated the whole class. We did try now and then to remind him of his legendary stage appearance, but he never sang in the show again.

It was Indian summer and we sometimes sat on a bench in Beatrix Park after school. She would say nothing and just sit there smoking. That was great. Sitting next to her, watching her smoke, and looking at her lipstick.

Once she said, "Come on, say something."

For the past two hours I had had gym class and Thomas had squeezed the pimples on his legs. He did that whenever we had gym. The pus would shoot high into the air.

"Aren't you ashamed of yourself?" I would ask him every so often.

He said, "No, they'll go away by themselves eventually." And pop, he'd squeeze another pimple. He did nothing the whole gym class except squeeze the pimples on his legs. I don't know how he managed that, to get them on his legs too. The last fifteen minutes, when we were allowed to play soccer, was the only time he stopped.

Rosie said nothing. Nor did I. After a while, as on every Monday evening, we went to drink Dubonnet at the Apollo Hotel. That was always the best part of the whole day.

We sat surrounded by all these old people with their heavy perfume and their wheezing and that junk they hung around their necks. We promised that we'd never get like that, that we'd do things differently. We pledged it pretty solemnly, because we hadn't yet realized that once upon a time all those old bores had also said that they'd do things differently. They'd all said it, and they'd all believed what they said.

We tried to get drunk, only we didn't have enough money on us. But Rosie had a way of looking at the bartender that made him come over and say, "Go on, have another on me."

After her I knew a few women who had the same way of looking. Then one of them told me it was a very old, cheap trick. You can run anything down, of course, until there's nothing left to run down.

When almost everyone in the bar of the Apollo Hotel was drunk except for us, Rosie asked me what sort of baby I'd been. I looked at all the drunk people and over at the canal—there wasn't much else to look at—and I remembered that my mother had told me I'd been pulled out with forceps by a Nazi. That's what my mother called the man who had pulled me out of her, and according to her he was one of the worst doctors she'd ever met because he'd given her a prolapse. Apparently the doctor had said to her, "Well, he's a real clown." My mother had also kept a report by a pediatrician. It stated, "I observed a pale baby with scaly skin and a nervous mother."

I said nothing, and then Rosie said she thought we were seeing too little of each other and ought to go on a trip during the fall vacation. She was prepared to spend all the money she had earned at the ice cream parlor. All of it. First we thought of Madrid, then of Stockholm, Paris, and Budapest, then of Naples. When we figured out how much money we had, it was clear that it would have to be Antwerp or somewhere like that. At the end of the evening she gave me a photograph of herself, with a poem written on the back.

I asked who had taken the photograph. I thought it was a little on the stark side and I didn't understand the poem. That didn't surprise me, because by then I realized that all her poems came out of books and the only thing that was hers was the name she put at the bottom.

When we'd finally managed to get a little bit drunk, she opened her purse and showed me several letters she'd received from other men. I couldn't have cared less about the letters. I just promised that I'd write her a letter too. I assumed that I'd always be with her, because I was fifteen and I knew everything there was to know about the world.

ANTWERP

*M*y mother and I spent the whole Day of Atonement in a
synagogue off Albert Cuypmarkt, as we did every year,
waiting for the day to end, much as my father waited each night
for the eight o'clock Radio Deutsche Welle financial news. The
Deutsche Welle was subject to interference from pirate stations.
We had a TV and fourteen radios on which my father tried to
receive all sorts of stations that refused to be received properly.
A radio stood next to his place at the dinner table, and he often
forgot to eat because he was too busy tuning it. Now and then
he would receive a stray stock exchange quotation which he
would jot down on the first scrap of paper he could lay his hands
on. "Thieves!" he'd shout over and over again.

My mother always said that she had fasted enough to last her
a lifetime, but she made an exception for the Day of Atonement.
When we finally came home from synagogue, I said that I was off
on a trip the next day, with a girl. My mother started to pace

back and forth through the house. My father turned up the radio so as not to hear my mother yelling. She threw the pan with the herring salad on the floor. We always had herring salad at the end of the Day of Atonement. She ran out into the garden and shouted, "You're scum, every one of you. You're all scum!"

My father disappeared into the bathroom, where he'd sit for entire evenings. He had laid in a supply of wine there. He'd begun locking himself in the bathroom a long time ago, after the business with the gardener we had whom my mother called "the Indian." God knows why she did, but after a while everyone called him that. It was just before my bar mitzvah, and I was taking lessons three times a week from Mrs. Mohnstein. Mrs. Mohnstein tried to teach me Hebrew for six years. She never managed to impart any Hebrew, but she did teach me what it's like to hate someone like poison. That's something, anyway.

For my father my bar mitzvah was even greater torture than it was for me. He hadn't been to synagogue for something like fifty years and he was going to have to go that day. I bet he had nightmares for weeks.

A few days before my bar mitzvah—I had already been bought a blue suit and been sent to the barber—my father learned that the Indian had been invited. I had seen him in a rage often enough before, but never anything like that. I think the Indian must have been the last straw. He went on shouting over and over, "It's the Indian or me—it's up to you." He went into the bathroom and went on shouting from there and refused to come out until we had chosen between the two of them. My mother had to call the Indian to tell him that he had better not come, which must have been a relief for the Indian as well.

The night before my bar mitzvah my father hardly slept a wink. In the synagogue he looked like Prince Claus or, if anything, worse, all drawn and pale. After the service there was a reception, and for some reason there was no vodka, only Dutch gin. So my father had tossed back quite a few little glasses of Dutch gin even before he started to shake people's hands. With every hand he shook he would ask my mother, who was standing beside him, "Who's that?"

Now and then my mother would hiss, "That bunch could have brought a bigger present." My father was hard of hearing even then.

At night there was a dinner. My mother had composed a drinking song, believe it or not. And she didn't stop there. When she'd finished composing my drinking song, she went on to compose drinking songs for other people too—for octogenarians giving dinner parties, for newlyweds, for lots of other people. That evening my father sat next to me in a gray suit that had been specially made for the occasion. He didn't open his mouth. But in the middle of a speech by some rabbi he suddenly pulled me toward him by my jacket and whispered, "No more gin for me ever again. It makes me go all to pieces."

The other guests celebrated the rest of my bar mitzvah in a high state of merriment. My mother in particular joined in with gusto. At the end she called out, "Shall we sing the drinking song one more time?" But by then almost everybody had gone. My father stood up slowly, wiped the sweat from his face with his handkerchief, and said, "Well, that's set us back five thousand guilders, but don't let anybody say that the Lord isn't righteous."

Then we all went home in a taxi, and from that time on my father would lock himself in the bathroom on a regular basis. The Indian, incidentally, went out of our lives, just as most other people would cease to play a part in our lives from one day to the next.

Shortly before midnight my father finally emerged from the bathroom. He started looking for Belgian francs in his closet. His shirt was hanging open and he was breathing heavily. He asked to see Rosie's photograph. He barely looked at it. "A pretty girl," he said. "You aren't her first and you won't be her last."

My mother started to wash the kitchen floor, something she preferred doing in the middle of the night in any case.

"When I was at school I always kept my coat on," she said.

"I refused to take it off. Because I was scared they would steal it. Until they started hitting me. 'Take your coat off,' they shouted, 'or you'll catch cold.' Little Karl also refused to take his coat off. We were the only ones who refused to take our coats off. That's why they sat us next to each other. He was very skinny. He was forever whispering in my ear, 'I've got a knife in my coat. That's why I keep it on.' But I didn't have a knife in my coat, I was just afraid someone would steal it. I wanted to marry him. I wanted the two of us to show everything to each other. I showed him everything. For a piece of sausage. Then it was his turn to show me everything, but he wouldn't. He said, 'I can't, because you would see my knife and no one is allowed to see my knife.' "

That Monday was the kind of fall day anyone would want to spend sitting at a sidewalk café. The street was very quiet. Just like on the morning after a holiday. We had arranged to meet at Rosie's place because her mother had insisted on meeting the boy with whom her daughter proposed going on a trip. They lived near Maasstraat, on the other side of Beatrix Park.

We sat on the sofa and drank tea, and her mother said that she had studied Dutch at college and that the living room was bare because, as I could see, she was about to paint it, and I looked at Rosie, and I thought, I must mind my p's and q's. We had some more tea and her mother said she found it just a tiny bit hair-raising, two fifteen-year-old children going abroad on their own. I said that at fifteen you were no longer a child and that all mothers would find it a little hair-raising, because mothers were made like that. I could tell I was making a very good impression, since I was saying exactly what she wanted to hear. I would have said a lot more but Rosie wanted to get away. When we were in the streetcar, she said that her mother was scared she might come back pregnant, because her grandma had come by the day before and given her a sermon about teenage mothers.

In Antwerp we changed our money and then started looking for a hotel. It was raining, so we went into a snack bar and had waffles with whipped cream. Later we ate french fries out of a brown cardboard box that we bought from a Jew with a long beard. By then we had been to three hotels. The first was full, in the second the receptionist insisted that she had just two single rooms, and in the third they told us to go to a youth hostel. We were soaked to the skin; it was getting late and I was afraid we might have to sleep at the station. The gel had washed out of my hair and I noticed that it was beginning to curl, but Rosie said it didn't look too bad, that nothing was too bad now. We went to a fourth hotel.

We were given a room. The only thing was, it was incredibly expensive, much more expensive than we'd expected.

On one side of the room there was a bed, on the other side there was another one, and between them was a table with a vase of flowers. There was a small window overlooking a courtyard full of garbage cans and howling cats. The cats were either fighting or fucking, you couldn't tell which, because it was dark by then and pouring rain. She sat on the windowsill and lit a cigarette. I did the same, since by then I had started to smoke, just like her. Because I didn't inhale I smoked menthol cigarettes so as to get at least some taste in my mouth. "Old ladies' cigarettes," Rosie called them, though she smoked St. Moritz menthols from time to time herself.

"We've done it," she said, and I kissed her briefly on her hair, which tasted of rain and smoke and the shampoo she had last used. We stayed sitting like that for a long time. Finally she said, "We have to go and get something to eat."

I extracted another hundred guilders from my breast pocket, money I had been given for my trip to Israel. I changed it at a bureau de change, and I thought it was just as well that I hadn't gotten my hopes up too high for this trip of ours.

. . .

Every ten minutes we lit another cigarette in the pizza parlor where we'd been sitting for the past three hours. Rosie thought it stank of rat poison. We were drinking large mugs of beer and all I wanted was to think of nothing—not Amsterdam, not my mother, not Mrs. Haaseveld, not Mrs. De Wilde, not any of the subjects I would have to take in school very shortly, for there were no subjects in existence that I wanted to take. I had said as much to Mrs. Haaseveld.

Rosie said, "Maybe they used this pizza as an ashtray." That summer we had seen a movie in which someone had done just that. We ordered another round and decided that our pizza would definitely have to be classified as a species of garbage can. We swore never to touch another pizza.

Then she said, "Ash in beer can kill you."

After that we went for a walk around Antwerp because we didn't want to go back to our hotel right away. Everything was closed. Maybe we were just walking through the wrong district. Suddenly she said, "I want to go to a live show. It's about time we went to a live show. I've never seen a live show." I thought she must be joking, but she was in deadly earnest. We went to a phone booth and looked under L for live show. We found nothing. She pounded the telephone so hard that people stopped to look.

Our room was stuffy and damp. I opened the window. The courtyard was lit by a couple of spotlights, the people from the kitchen were emptying buckets of food into the garbage cans, and the cats were still howling. They were probably fighting for the food. Then Rosie started to move the beds. That took some doing because the room was tiny. First the table had to be moved out of the way. She shoved it against the door. The vase fell over, but luckily there was no water inside. The flowers were plastic. Then she tried to push the beds together. That was all but impossible because they were really heavy beds made of oak or God knows what kind of wood. She pulled the mattresses off, which made things a bit easier. I was sitting on the windowsill and I asked if all that was really necessary, all that moving of furniture. She said, "I haven't slept in a single bed since I was thirteen." I didn't believe a word. She often made up things like that and I still don't know why she did. Everyone thought she was beautiful, she could talk about almost anything, and even people who had never seen her before offered to buy her drinks. In the ice cream parlor they had wanted to keep her on for the rest of the year, but she had left them, too, because most things got on her nerves in the end.

The noise made by the legs of the beds as they were dragged across the floor was so loud that I thought they'd throw us out any moment. She said they wouldn't be able to because of the table in front of the door. No one could get in or out.

We had a shower in the room, the kind that's built into the closet. The shower curtain wasn't very new and we had already noticed that the whole room got wet when you showered, and where the beds stood now they were bound to get drenched. So we decided not to take showers until the next morning. Once we were in bed she couldn't make up her mind which side to lie on. She changed sides every five minutes until she finally decided on the side nearer the shower, so that she could be first to use it in the morning. In the middle of our bed there was a deep valley. If you fell into it you'd break a rib, at the very least. We might have been better off leaving the beds as they were, but I didn't say that. I could hear people walking up and down the corridor but no one could get in. Our door was locked, the table was shoved against it, and next to that was the bed.

Finally she came over to my side. She said, "I'm taking my T-shirt off."

"Right," I said. The spotlights from the courtyard shone through the window curtains. Those weren't all that new either and people had stubbed their cigarettes out on them, leaving a lot of holes. Her breasts were small and round, and her nipples so dark that they looked almost purple, like the small circles around them. I looked at them while I pretended to be asleep. I knew she didn't wear a bra. She hated bras, but I thought women who didn't wear them were pretty butch. She had undone her ponytail, and now she had long hair that came halfway down her back. It still smelled the same as it had in the afternoon, with some french fries thrown in.

I wound her hair into curls. Whenever I'm nervous I curl things. She told me to be careful because having your hair curled can hurt. Later I kissed her little breasts, exactly the way I had seen it done on TV and in the movies. I kept *Tender Is the Night* in mind the whole time and that worked very well. We said things to each other that must be at least ten thousand years old but that I was sure we had invented ourselves, the first and only people ever to say them. She said, "You can keep your underpants on if you like. It can be done with underpants on too." I said that in that case both of us would have to keep our underpants on. After a while she asked if it had hurt, but of course it hadn't. I looked at the hairs in her armpits, which were so short I couldn't curl them.

Her skin was much darker than mine, but then I have about the lightest skin you can imagine, which was particularly obvious under the blue glare of the spotlights. She wanted us to go to sleep together like that. It didn't take me long to realize that you can fall asleep much more easily on your own than together. After about an hour or so I dropped off, but in the middle of the night I ended up in the deep hole between the two beds. I crawled over to what had been her side.

As a result I was the first in the shower the next morning. It was almost full daylight, and only then could we see what a shambles we had made of the room; one leg of the bed was nearly broken in two. I took off my T-shirt. I stood in front of the shower curtain, because you couldn't get undressed any further inside the shower. It was too small. So I lit a cigarette, which I finished smoking in front of the shower curtain. Rosie was still in bed. She looked at me and said, "You look just like Koot. You know the scene I mean, don't you?"

I didn't know it and went on smoking peacefully. She burst out laughing. "The way you're standing there now," she said, "with your cigarette, you look exactly like Koot when he's all thumbs."

"I am not all thumbs, I'm just having a cigarette before I take a shower," I said.

"I'm going to shower first," she cried. Then the cigarette slipped from my fingers, and she stubbed it out on the sheet.

"I felt sorry for that sheet," she said. "There are holes in the curtains, there are holes in the shower curtain, there are holes in the carpet—why should the sheet be the only one with no holes?" Then I was naked and she was looking at me in a way that didn't show she was looking. I watched her on that bed, her arms under her head, while she looked me over with a slightly mocking expression. Just the way my sister used to look at me from her bed early in the morning, when she'd been frightening me with a little monkey that you could put your hand into and that had lost one eye in the washing machine.

We spent the whole day riding around on streetcars. We rode from one end of the city to the other. At first we had planned to go to a museum to get out of the rain, but Rosie said that she had been to so many museums in the past few years that she knew all the museums in the world by heart. I could sympathize with that, because at Vossius they would drag you to museums at the drop of a hat. Later we ducked into a video arcade. It had some game with a steering wheel that you have to drive through mountains. She insisted on trying it. "Let's smash ourselves to smithereens on that," she said. So we smashed ourselves to smithereens.

Then we bought cigars and a girlie magazine and ate mussels in a fancy restaurant. And we drank to Antwerp and to ourselves and to at least ten thousand other things.

We went for another walk around Antwerp. This time we were in a district full of cafés, but we didn't have much money left. In the end we shared a beer and watched all the other people knocking back one beer after another. She started going on again about a live show, how she wanted to see a live show before she lay down to rot in some garbage can. When she was in that sort of mood there was very little you could do with her. That's why we went back to the hotel.

Lying on the bed we looked at photographs of Henry Miller's girlfriend and read her letters in the girlie magazine. Rosie wanted to push the beds together again. I suggested that we leave well enough alone, but she said that in that case she'd rather not sleep at all or else go and lie down in the corridor in front of the door. So the mattresses and the blankets came off again. I was afraid that we wouldn't just break the legs on the beds but sink right through the floor. Everything in the hotel seemed made of cardboard, even the breakfast. The blue light was there again, of course, because the spotlights were left on day and night, and the cats were still howling and I went on smoking my St. Moritz cigarettes.

That night, too, I was allowed to keep my underpants on, and she took her T-shirt off again, but after a few minutes I said, "Could you please get off me for a little while?" She got off and lit a cigarette. She blew puffs of smoke—she could do that to perfection, blow puffs of smoke. I kept wondering why I'd said that to her, why I'd come out with such a thing all of a sudden. I remembered that the next evening I would be back in Amsterdam, that it would be Friday night and the candles would be lit, as they were every Friday night. But I didn't say anything to her and she didn't say anything either. What I wanted to say was, "I didn't really want you to get off me. I meant to say something else, something quite different." But I didn't know exactly how to say it, or else I realized that it was as pointless saying that sort of thing as thinking it, or maybe I was distracted by the cats.

After a while I lay down on her side of the bed and everything was exactly as it had been the night before. We listened to what the people in the corridor were saying. And the little hairs that stuck out from her panties were too short for me to wind into curls. Afterwards we ate a whole lot of licorice. She asked me if I had a subscription to *Donald Duck* magazine.

"Yes," I said, "I've had one for three years."

We were lying there with the paper bag full of licorice between us.

She said, "When we live together, one subscription will do for the two of us."

Then she asked if I knew that the man who delivered *Donald Duck* had murdered two boys in Beatrix Park. I did know that—my mother had told me often enough. I'd thought she only said that to stop me from subscribing. We spent the whole evening talking about the man, and later we discussed what the nicest thing in the world was, and of course she wanted us to sleep together in one bed again. It didn't work, because we kept kicking each other awake. Or else she would suddenly start talking again. Then she exclaimed, "Tomorrow I'm taking a shower first, just so you know."

Next morning I was first in the shower again, and because we wouldn't be coming back to the room we didn't worry at all about getting the wallpaper wet. Even the painting of the two people in a cornfield got soaked, along with the ceiling and the door. We sat on the windowsill for a long time after that, not because of the wonderful view but because we had paid for the room until twelve o'clock and wanted to get our money's worth.

The train ride home was like all train rides home, which is why we didn't say very much. We also felt a little sick from the waffles and the french fries. All she said was, "Next time I'll be the first in the shower, you'll see." We examined Henry Miller's girlfriend in minute detail again. I think that girlie magazine is the only thing I have left from that trip.

UNDER THE PINE TREE

*D*uring the next few weeks Rosie and I usually met in the Lusthof, a café where they didn't serve Dubonnet. "Try a brandy instead," said the bartender. "After a while everything tastes the same." We had no money for hotels, not even for restaurants; in fact, we had no money for anything. I hadn't yet realized that curiosity is all that gets left of desire, and that there is no name at all for whatever gets left of curiosity.

She asked if she could meet my parents. I said they were extremely busy, and I went back to talking about wanting to become an actor. This was something I had already told just about everybody. It meant there was a whole bunch of school subjects that would be a complete waste of time for me, so I dropped them. At eleven o'clock I would report sick with a splitting headache, then I would go off to the Wildschut and try to make a cappuccino last for two hours. Then it would be time to go home.

That went on for two weeks, until Mrs. Haaseveld said she

had to talk to me urgently. Or rather she whispered, "Come and see me in my classroom later." We had just been issued more copies of *Deep Sea*, the so-called "literary journal for young people," and we were answering questions on the hundred thousandth short story by Jan Donkers. I had absolutely no time to go and see her because I had a date with Rosie. So I went to the bathroom and never came back. That afternoon Rosie and I went to Brinkman's to sell our textbooks. The worst of them first: *Number and Space* and *Theoretical and Practical Chemistry*.

We used the money to get something to eat. She said she wasn't sure if I was allowed to kiss her, because she was eating pork. I told her that I only ate kosher food when my mother was watching and that my father was exactly the same. Whenever he had the chance he would slip into a Hema store for sausages and some wine. After we'd eaten we looked for a doorway. Doorways aren't ideal, because people keep coming and going through them, and once we were even chased away by a furious man who said we were keeping his children awake.

A few days later I was in the middle of a Greek class when Mrs. Haaseveld came in and took me to her classroom. She said she understood everything. She kept on repeating it. "I understand everything, I understand you very well." I didn't know what she understood or what I was meant to do about it. I had never asked anybody to understand everything, Mrs. Haaseveld least of all. "Do your parents realize that your Christmas report is going to be disastrous?" she asked.

My father had just left for two weeks in Israel. My mother had taken advantage of the opportunity to start repainting our kitchen.

"They do have their suspicions," I said.

"All is not yet lost," said Mrs. Haaseveld.

"I want to be an actor."

"That's a matter for later on," she said. "First you have to finish school." She started searching through her pile of papers and handed me back a composition.

"I hope you will put your talent to good use. Later on!" That's what it said. The "Later on!" must have been underlined at least twenty times. I distrusted people who went on about "later on." I still distrust them, because I know they're trying to bribe you with their "later on"s. When they know practically nothing about it. As little as I do in fact. There is absolutely no time to wait for later on. I said something along those lines to Mrs. Haaseveld. I didn't dare say that they could keep their good intentions and their understanding and she could keep what she scrawled on my paper. I went back to the Greek class and sat down next to Martinimartin. He was fast asleep. That was nothing unusual. Since summer vacation he'd slept through almost every class. At first they said something about it, but all he ever answered was, "I'm so tired." It was quiet in class. If anyone said anything, a piece of chalk would come flying through the air. I looked for my textbook, but then I remembered that Rosie and I had sold our Greek books the day before, so I tried to go to sleep too. Sleeping was allowed; talking wasn't. All they did was throw you out if you snored. The teacher said, "Anyone who snores has to go sleep in the corridor." Sometimes, if he was in a good mood, he would say, "You wait. Another few years and you'll all be sons of bitches just like me."

I couldn't fall asleep, so I wrote a note to Rosie. I told her she had to come over to my house that afternoon, because my mother was going to see my grandmother. She wasn't my real grandmother; she was an adopted one. We had adopted just about everything, so why not a grandmother too? We used to visit her every Saturday, when we would eat cake followed by soup and she would drink cherry brandy.

I thought of all the things we could do in our empty house. It was hardly ever empty, because they didn't trust me there alone.

I remembered all the books I had sold, saying I had lost them. Or that's what I told them at school. At home I said that the books were in my locker at school. There aren't many things as habit-forming as concocting lies. I told lots of lies, even to Rosie; after all, I had to tell her something. I thought of a boy I'd gone to elementary school and later to Vossius with. His name was Michael, and during recess we used to go to the nearest Albert Heijn store and steal plums. One evening when the store owners in Beethovenstraat put Christmas trees outside their places, we walked off with four trees, which we tried to sell but couldn't and finally left on the school playground. Since Rosie, I had completely lost touch with him. I hardly saw Eric anymore either. We always used to sit next to each other. He wanted to look like James Dean. He started to shave when he was only fifteen. Because he was convinced he was the reincarnation of James Dean. He used to go to a very expensive barber on Beethovenstraat, who cut his hair just like James Dean's. If you ask me, every boy in my class could have belonged in an institution the way he looked, especially me. Even though I didn't feel compelled to go to the most expensive barbershop in Amsterdam. One day I said all this to Eric, and also that I really didn't relish being told every recess how he swallowed his sperm.

He stopped talking to me after that. It didn't matter to me, because I was quite sure that I wanted to be an actor and that everything else was unimportant. Just as I'd be quite sure that I wanted to be a publisher. For a time I was also quite sure that I wanted to marry Rosie and have a baby. And that I wanted to live in Berlin. There was even a time when I was quite sure that I wanted to be dead, but I know now that what hurts is not so much that they don't like you but the fact that you don't have it in you to like them, or not enough anyway, not the way you'd want to or ought to. You could write a hundred letters and ask in each one why everything always ends in a nauseating state of collapse, but you won't get a single answer. I still thought that things might turn out differently and that those letters would be enough to tie someone to you. Perhaps you can't do much more than dream up names for what isn't there, to make it easier to talk about it or at least to try talking about it. The stupid thing, though, was that I thought it really was there. When I dreamed up all those names, I thought it was on its way and that it would soon be here. Perhaps that isn't important either, and the man was right to point out that life taught him that we can't afford to pick and choose. Maybe I was that man, or maybe I heard some- body say that once and thought, I wanted to say that myself be- cause that's exactly how it is.

When Rosie arrived, my mother had not yet left. I said, "Go around the back, climb over the little fence, and wait in the garden under the trees until I let you in."

It was a long time before I could finally let her in. She was numb with cold by then, swearing away, and she tried to explain to me how it had been no picnic standing for an hour under the trees in a completely strange garden. She demanded hot choco- late, which needless to say we didn't have. "I'll never be warm again," she said, and made me take the pine needles out of her hair.

Then she said, "I nearly forgot. I brought you a little present." She took a pile of letters from her purse. She wrote me so many letters that I hardly read them anymore. It was only later that I got around to reading them. I stuffed them into my pants pocket. We went upstairs, to the room meant for my sister that she had never used. She had run away to Israel in 1982. We lay down on the floor, on the green carpet, and I asked if this time her jeans button could be opened. The last time I had nearly broken my hand.

"OK," she said, "but I don't want to break my hand either."

I looked at her, and now I could see everything in daylight

and smell the smell of her shirt. She asked me no questions, and I should have said then that we ought to run away, but I had no idea where to and she probably had no idea either. I should have said that the only sensible thing you can do in this world is to run away and that knowing the truth is just as deadly and dull as taking a tour of hell. The only time I ever tried to run away, I got no farther than Hoofddorp, I guess because I didn't really have the nerve to go on. And that afternoon I didn't have the nerve to say that to her either. Nor did I have the nerve to say something when she told me that she was beginning to get bored with everyone's always saying nice things to her. She didn't think they meant a single word of it.

I ought to have told her that I, too, said nice things so as to hear something sweet from her pretty little lips in return and that people probably thought she was too young and too good-looking to be burdened with the truth. Which was why she ought to put up with the lies people were bound to tell her and the lies she was bound to tell them. Until she was old and decrepit, since then nobody would bother to spare her the truth anymore. She ought not to hold those little lies against me or all the others. When you finally get close to someone, you want to forget what you've done with your life and what you are going to do with the rest of it.

I said nothing. I even lacked the courage not to feel ashamed, because that takes courage too, and I felt ashamed of most things. Actually I was afraid of her being so close to me. I've always had that feeling, and though after a time it certainly diminishes, people are never around long enough to see it vanish completely.

Finally she said, "Would you please come and lie on top of me? It's awfully drafty in here." Which was true. "Come on," she said. It felt as if I had pulled up my zipper too quickly after taking a leak. So we lay there quietly for a long time. She looked at the ceiling and I looked out the window because you could never tell when my mother might show up. Only then did it hit me what we were up to, and she said, "I think we're doing something stupid."

"Me too," I replied.

A little later I heard my mother's bicycle, so Rosie had to sneak through the garden again. We repeated this maneuver three more times. But one afternoon when I went to the door to let her in she wasn't standing under the trees. I looked all over the garden for her but it was empty. I called, "Rosie! Rosie!"

The lady next door asked, "Are you looking for your rabbit?"

"We don't have any pets," I called back. "You know my mother's allergic to pets. She's allergic to the whole world."

That evening my father waited in vain for the stock reports and my mother said, "Death is just as boring as life, but I don't want to die just yet, because I begrudge you both the pleasure. Besides, I have my doubts about paradise."

4,320 MINUTES

The next day Rosie told me she'd run away from the garden because she thought her feet were going to fall off and because she couldn't bear to stand there freezing under the pine trees any longer. I could understand that because actually I couldn't bear it any longer either. We sold a couple of dictionaries and then went for a walk through the city again, stopping several times to stand in doorways. It was really too cold now to stand around in doorways for long. In fact, it was too cold to stand around anywhere. I was still wearing the sneakers I had bought in Israel, and they had begun to let in water. I couldn't bring myself to wear the shoes my mother had bought me. As hard as I tried, I couldn't.

We walked down Apollolaan. They have nice deep doorways in Apollolaan, so we sat on the top step of one and ate a bag of marshmallows. We prepared ourselves mentally for pneumonia.

"I can't walk another step," she said.

"Me neither. Maybe we'll have to spend the night here. Maybe we'll have to become bums."

She didn't want to become a bum. She said that her brother was a kind of bum already and that one bum in the family was enough.

I said, "Let's drop the subject. It's too idiotic to think about anyway."

"You know what I think?"

"No."

"I think you can be a big bore sometimes," she said, "but it doesn't matter because I'm sure I'm a big bore a lot of the time myself. I think school is a bore. I think the whole world is a bore. And my brother, who's so sure he's the only one around who isn't a bore, is actually the most boring of them all."

"We are the most boring people in the world," I said. "Maybe we can make money appearing as bores at fairs."

"I used to think that serving ice cream would be fun. But actually it's nothing special. And getting drunk isn't anything special either. Last night I read some poems by Judith Herzberg, and I always used to think her poems were so great, but last night I suddenly found that they were nothing special either. My mother yelled at me to turn off the light and go to sleep. But she's a bore too. More boring than she used to be when my father was still around. Did you know that I was an accident? It doesn't bother me all that much, but it makes me extra boring, I think."

We still had our book bags with us because we hadn't been back home. She leafed through her homework planner.

"Let's make a date for fucking," she said.

"Right," I said.

"Saturday, November 22," she whispered.

"Saturday, November 22. OK."

We entered "fucking" under Saturday, November 22, in our planners. Apart from that there was nothing in them, because I had stopped using mine and it looked as if she didn't use hers either.

"Where?" I asked.

"We'll find a place."

Saturday, November 22, was five days away. We decided we'd better keep on walking because fucking would be better if we didn't have pneumonia.

I knew almost all the doorways in Apollolaan, and I could still point out the best ones today, although I don't really think anyone needs to know that anymore. I told her I didn't want to be touched if other people could see me. She thought that was strange but didn't object. Even when no one could see us I sometimes didn't want to be touched, and then I would say, "I just want to smell your hair." That was fine with her too. That's why she was sweet.

Then she had to take the streetcar home. "Saturday, November 22," she called out.

"Saturday, November 22," I shouted back. "Five more days."

I walked home. I thought of all those faces at school next day. The fact is I had torn a few pages out of the class register. So that no one would be able to tell that I'd hardly shown up the past few days. It was for their benefit as well, because getting too worked up never did anybody any good. I assumed that a couple of darling girls would report having seen me tearing up the class register. In the name of truth or whatever. I could just see those faces staring at me solemnly and not meaning for a single second a word of what they said.

Still, I never would have guessed they would get worked up enough to send me to the school psychologist. Just because of a few pages out of the class register! They were out of their depth. Or at least that's what they said. Why didn't they go to the school psychologist themselves if they were out of their depth? Because the school psychologist was out of his depth himself. He didn't actually say so, but he looked it. And the class register lay on his desk like a six-pound bag of heroin. I am not exaggerating. That's the way it lay on the desk. They used long silences to put pressure on me, but I just kept thinking of November 22 instead. Then they started again about the war. They'd never had much imagination. As if the class register had anything to do with the war. They thought it did. Something in their brains had seized up. A few pages out of the class register were missing and before you could say Jack Robinson we were talking about the war again.

"Where did you go?" they asked. "During all those classes. Where did you go?"

"I can't remember anymore, I swear I can't. I probably went for a walk downtown." That was the truth, but they didn't believe me.

"We really ought to write to your parents," they said.

"Why? They've been through enough as it is," I said. They didn't appreciate that line of argument at first, although they came around in the end. This would be the last time they wouldn't write to my parents, but if anything else ever happened they would probably send my parents a hundred letters. That was a promise they actually did keep. My parents never received as much mail as they did that time from Vossius. The teachers were probably bored out of their minds, and that's why they wrote so much. As for my parents, the letters nearly drove them mad.

I had to pick up leaves in the playground for two weeks. I didn't do it, of course, so then I had to pick up leaves for four weeks. Then they said, "We can't make you pick up leaves for the rest of your life." The school psychologist was out of his depth again.

"We feel sorry for you," he said. "You're such a talented young man and you're squandering your future."

Suits me, I thought. I'll squander some more of my future so you can all feel even sorrier. I didn't say that, of course. I pretended that I was full of remorse, that I felt awful because I had made them suffer so much. Four more days and it would be November 22.

. . .

Selling textbooks was a thing of the past. They had all been sold. Now we couldn't go anywhere to get something to eat or drink anymore. "They're cloacas," I said to her. "Mrs. Haaseveld is a cloaca, the school is a cloaca, Stadionweg is a cloaca, my house is a cloaca, the streetcar is a cloaca, the Lusthof is a cloaca, and we're cloacas."

The word *cloaca* had been up on the blackboard in the biology classroom for the past three weeks.

She had an idea. At recess, everyone always threw their book bags into the main hall. Maybe we could take a few books out of other people's bags and sell them. At first I thought it was a brilliant idea, but in the end I didn't have the nerve. I could already see twenty school psychologists sitting in a row. If need be, endless doctors would be unleashed on me. To drive me completely crazy.

During recess I escaped from school and went off to the Wildschut again. Sometimes I'd go to the Central Fish Traders first for a fish cake. I could live on one fish cake for a whole day. I'd taught myself to do that. She joined me later at the Wildschut.

"Three more days," I whispered in her ear. I liked doing that because it meant pushing back the hair that fell over her ears.

"Three more days," she said. I asked how long it would take before things got better. She thought it would take a long time, a few years even. In fact, it might take so long that it was almost too long to wait. I thought that three days would be enough to change things. A little, at any rate.

"How many minutes is three days?" she asked.

We worked it out on a coaster. The answer was 4,320 minutes.

She said, "I wish that each of those minutes was one day in my life I could have lived differently."

"What would you have done differently?"

"Most of the days I would probably have just stayed in bed. But a few of those days I'd have wanted to get up." We tried to think of those days. First in her life, then in mine, and then in the very short life the two of us had shared together.

"Where should we meet on Saturday?" I asked.

"Somewhere downtown," she said. "Somewhere we've never met before, and where we'll never meet again, not with other people, not with anyone."

I couldn't think of anywhere, because we had already met in so many places and done our best to get drunk in so many cafés. I remembered all those fruitless attempts and all the downtown alleyways we had walked through until it had seemed as if we could recognize every last cobblestone.

FUCKING

*O*n the morning of November 22 I went to synagogue, as I did every Saturday morning. My mother was weeping and wailing. I had washed my hair with some color rinse that Rosie had managed to get hold of in bulk. My mother thanked God her parents had not lived to witness such a day. I said that as far as I was concerned I didn't mind in the least not going to synagogue if it meant she wouldn't have to feel ashamed of me. But she would rather feel ashamed than have me stay away.

There was an old Hungarian man in the synagogue who invariably came up to me, pinched my cheek, and asked when I was going to get married. He'd been asking that ever since I was six. "You'd better get married before I drop dead," he said every Saturday. "I don't know, sir," I said. "I don't know. That is something we have no control over."

Then there was a group of women who wanted to become Jewish. They all looked as if they'd spent their youth being dragged through a hedge backwards. If you ask me, they probably had. They spent the whole time going on about how only Jews knew what real suffering was, but you could tell that what they really meant was that they were in the know as well. The world is full of ugly people, but I had never seen anyone as hideous as those women who wanted to become Jewish. If you ask me, they must have thought that once you're Jewish it doesn't matter if you're ugly. If I'd had an Uzi, I would have shot them all, out of pity. For aesthetic reasons, too, of course.

After the service there was always a kiddush. You got wine and cookies and I saw my mother again then, because during the service men and women sat in separate sections. Her eyes were red. She'd been crying all through the service. She was being propped up by two other women. They knew why she was crying. A son with dyed hair! They looked at me as if I were a Nazi. I'd never seen a red-haired Nazi, not even in a movie. If you ask me, Nazis like that didn't even exist. I don't think you would have gotten very far if you had had red hair in the Third Reich.

They asked me why I had done it. What I had meant by it. And if it was henna. I didn't answer, I pretended not to understand. I went and stood next to the man who always prayed at the back because no one wanted to talk to him. They said he was a little slow. He'd been in a mental institution. He spent the whole service rubbing his cock. I hadn't noticed at first, only after a couple of weeks. What I mean is, it wasn't all that obvious, but he did it all right. He was forty and still lived with his mother. There was a father, too, but he hadn't left his bed for twenty years.

He kept talking about Picasso. It was always Picasso with him. He also lived in the Gold Coast, or rather his mother did. He would get up at two in the afternoon, eat two slices of white bread with chocolate sprinkles, and then walk around Beatrix Park a few times.

"Is this your red period?" he asked. Wisecracks like that. For hours on end. And eating nothing but white bread with chocolate sprinkles. And stinking of bad breath. He probably thought you weren't allowed to brush your teeth on Saturday.

My mother had asked two of those phony Jewesses over for lunch. It was something I couldn't fathom, why people would want to become Jewish. After all, they could always just go hang themselves if they decided things were getting too tough for them.

My father had the radio on but turned it off quickly because you aren't actually allowed to listen to the radio on the holy Shabbat. He began to interrogate them. He had to know everything. The phony Jewesses were sitting on the sofa. They came from Krimpen-on-the-IJssel or somewhere like that.

I had to say the blessing over the bread. My father refused to do that sort of thing. He called himself an agnostic. I called myself an agnostic, too, but I was less successful than he was with my mother.

He cracked a few jokes with the phony Jewesses. He was very nearsighted. He couldn't see that their faces looked as if they'd been soaking in hydrochloric acid for the past few years. Why hadn't they gone to the Salvation Army? At least there they'd have been given a snazzy uniform.

"And what do you want to be when you grow up?" one of them asked me.

Then the one with the lank hair started in again about how only Jews really knew what suffering was. God, I couldn't bear to listen. She went on and on. She was trying to find the true essence of suffering, she said. Why didn't someone stub out a few cigarettes on her face? Then she'd know for the rest of her life what the true essence of suffering was, so she wouldn't have to keep going on about it. I'd have been glad to oblige for a hundred guilders.

Three hundred minutes to go. I lay in the bathtub. My father banged on the door. The phony Jewesses had left. Dishes were being smashed again. "Go look for another bathroom," I shouted.

Then my father went and sat in the garden. It was freezing out there; it was November 22. He sat on a chair with his winter coat on, under his precious pine trees.

My mother opened the door to the garden. The birds flew away, but he went on sitting in his chair. "Stark raving mad," she shouted, "nutty as a fruitcake." Then she closed the door again. Another 274 minutes. I added some more bubble bath. One of my mother's friends, Mrs. Weinbaum, rang the doorbell. She came every Saturday afternoon. Saturday really was the best day of the week.

All she ever talked about was disease, Mrs. Weinbaum. Or rather all she ever talked about was her own diseases. She had just about every disease there was except for AIDS. Her days were filled with visits to doctors and hospitals. Her days had been filled like that for the past twenty years. She had no intention of dying, that's for sure. Every week she looked younger and more sprightly. She had never married. My mother said, "She'll get married to the angel of death." I thought, She's right about that—people who die take revenge on life. Another 260 minutes.

My father's hair was hanging down in front of his eyes; he had put a Russian fur hat on. He was still out in the garden, picking dead pine needles from his trees. Mrs. Weinbaum and my mother shouted for him to come in, but he wouldn't budge and pretended not to hear. "You'll catch your death of cold," shouted Mrs. Weinbaum, "and me too." Then the doors were closed again. I got out of the tub; if I'd stayed in much longer my skin would have rubbed off. Mrs. Weinbaum had knocked back another three sherries in quick succession, and now she was really hitting her stride. I've never met anyone who could talk as much about bloodletting as she could. Even her blood was diseased. Every week she had to have it drawn. That's what she talked about every Saturday afternoon. How the needle went in and how one time she fainted. It gave you the creeps. Once she said, "I dreamed I was living in a hospital."

A few years later she presented herself to the doorman at the Academic Medical Center in Amsterdam and said, "I want to be admitted." She was standing there with three suitcases. She'd tried several times before but they had always sent her back home. This time they couldn't. She had gotten rid of everything—her furniture, her plants, her books, her apartment. So they admitted her, although they immediately sent her on to the psychiatric unit. She remains there to this day. All she has is a sister, who can't come to visit her because she's locked up in an institution herself. My mother stops by to see her from time to time.

"She looks better than ever," she reports, "but every five minutes she shouts, 'I want to be admitted—otherwise there'll be nobody with me when I die.' I tell her, 'You've been admitted already. Everything's all right,' but she says, 'My God, you call this being admitted?'"

All that happened much later. She still had her sherries to drink and her tales to tell about all the fresh blood she had been given in the hospital. And the experience of seeing her in a wig for the first time was yet to come.

I put on my best pants, which happened to be the ones I'd been wearing for the past two weeks. I'd also been wearing the same sweater for a week or two, but it was still the best one I had. All Rosie smelled of was deodorant. My father had come in from the garden because of course he wanted a drink too. I shaved, although there was absolutely no need.

Mrs. Weinbaum admired my red hair. She also dyed her hair, or at any rate that part of it that was still there to be dyed.

That day it was all about her kidneys. My father sat slumped in his chair. He, too, was being driven mad by Mrs. Weinbaum. That's why he drank as fast as she talked. Mrs. Weinbaum took a gulp, and now it was my mother's turn. My father opened a new bottle. Mrs. Weinbaum started to look for a handkerchief to wipe her hands. She wiped her hands all day long. In fact, everything she could get hold of she wiped with her handkerchiefs. If you ask me, someone like her shouldn't be allowed in a house, but my parents let her in every Saturday afternoon.

My mother said, "Now let *me* tell you something." My father gave a deep sigh. He refilled Mrs. Weinbaum's glass and his own to the brim.

"I wasn't always old and ugly," said my mother. "You should have seen me years ago. I used to be very pretty. I was so pretty that they all ran after me. The war was when it began. I remember how afraid I was because we had nothing for menstruation. I worried a lot about that. But I never had a period in Birkenau. Not once. So I'd worried for nothing. I gave them all the brush-off. The men. In the end I married someone much older. I was truly in love then. When I was in love I got awfully flushed. That made me frightened they might think I'd stolen something. My teeth came through the war very well. That's because I cleaned them every day with a rag. After the war they were ruined by a professor. He was in love with me. He said, 'I'll be your dentist.' And then he ruined every one of my teeth. I used to be very pretty. Everyone wanted to be my dentist or my something or other. I hardly ever got beaten, you know. They threw pieces of sausage to me because I was so pretty. Really big pieces."

At the Red Lion I sat at one of the small tables under glass outside so that I could watch the whole street. I was glad when some old guy came and sat next to me after a while, since I'd be able to listen to him and wouldn't have to think about anything else for the next few hours until Rosie was due to show up. The man said nothing, so then I thought about all those recorders they had bought me because it goes without saying they wanted me to have a musical education. The recorder teacher was just about the nicest of all the people I knew at the time, with his gray curls and those idiotic shoelaces he wore as a tie. Every lesson he would talk about his wife, whom he was divorcing because she'd turned into a religious fanatic. She spent the whole day praying. When the lesson was over, he'd say, "We didn't do any recorder playing again today," and then he would wink at me. Now and then we'd give a performance in the Bach Hall and then I had to sit way at the back of the orchestra and pretend I was playing. Sometimes I forgot and blew by mistake, and an excruciating sound would come out right in the middle of a piece by Handel. At the next performance I would have to sit even farther back and for safety's sake wouldn't be allowed to put my recorder anywhere near my mouth, and at the performance after that I more or less sat in the wings. That recorder teacher really did me a good turn, enough so that my mother would bring him a homemade cake every couple of weeks. But when I was fourteen she bought a very expensive tenor recorder for me, which must have set her back a thousand guilders at least. That made me feel guilty, horribly guilty. I think the recorder teacher felt guilty too. Then he got married. To his girlfriend. A few months later he retired from teaching.

Her hair was still wet from the shower and she wasn't wearing any of the clothes she'd had on for the past two weeks. She had put on a new dress, a summer dress. She must have been a little cold, but she said that it only looked that way. She had put on makeup, as sophisticated as could be. And I knew that everyone was looking at her.

"Have you eaten?" she asked.

"No. What about you?"

She shook her head, so we ordered soup.

She had bought the dress that afternoon. "Like it?" she asked. I nodded.

"What did *you* do today?"

"Didn't buy a new dress."

"Guess what happened? My mother's place was robbed this morning, which means that instead of going to her aunt's in Limburg she's staying at home to straighten up."

"Let's drink to November 22," I said.

We drank to it.

"We must make a date for November 22 every year, even if we aren't together anymore."

"Let's do that," I said.

She said that we'd surely find somewhere to go, that she had a hunch about it and her hunches never failed her. So we stayed at the Red Lion and she told me that she would probably be leaving school because it looked as if otherwise she was going to be held back a year. She had promised to turn over a new leaf, but even she didn't have much faith in that. She told me a whole lot more, but we'd already talked too much. We had always done nothing but talk, in many different places, talked about every conceivable thing. Now we could only repeat what we had told each other before. That's why we said nothing after a while. We just drank, because we'd been saving up for this evening. Finally she picked up my notebook and started to doodle. I added captions, turning the whole thing into a comic strip. A pretty unappetizing cartoon about Pete, who did it with little boys. She was very good at drawing dubious-looking characters and I was very good at obscene captions.

We worked on the comic strip the whole evening, and we hardly spoke a word until we were thrown out because they were closing. She wanted to go to a disco. I had always refused to go to a disco and she knew that, but tonight I didn't want to refuse her. In any case, I didn't know where else we could go. She danced and I hung about on the side. She said, "Dancing calms you down." I begged to differ and that's why we left. It had started to snow. Not real snow. Wet snow that melted immediately. It was only half past one and everything was still open. We still had nothing to say. We found a dark enough spot, sat down, and started kissing. We went on doing that for a while until we were prodded in the ribs and somebody said, "Go do your kissing and cuddling at home. This is a bar."

Because he looked just like any other customer we took no notice. We should have, though, because he was back five minutes later. He said, "Are you deaf or something?"

"No," she said, "I'm not deaf, so beat it."

"You don't know what my job is here, do you?"

"No," she said. "Fuck off."

"I've been making other people do that all evening," he said. "So beat it."

"If you didn't eat so many french fries you'd be able to suck yourself off."

That was the best thing I'd said all evening. Rosie thought so too. Even so, fifteen minutes later we were soaked to the skin and walking around outside. I was still shaking.

Finally we found an all-night café.

"How many minutes left?" I asked. It didn't make her laugh. She just shook her head and went to get us something to drink. We worked some more on our comic strip, smoking and talking about everything under the sun except that one thing. We ordered another cocktail, because we had to try every cocktail before we died.

She came and sat closer and started to tell me a long story. I didn't get all of it, though. The music was very loud and we had drunk an awful lot. What she was saying was pretty pathetic, in my opinion. She had moods that made her pretty pathetic. Actually, the whole café was pretty pathetic, even the music they were playing, and the people who were hanging around the place were pathetic, too, just like the graffiti they had scrawled on the walls of the rest room, and even the bartender drew beer in a pathetic sort of way. All in all I couldn't stand the place, and that's why I only half listened to her. By the time she stopped talking I had forgotten everything she'd said.

She asked, "Do I still have any lipstick on?" I said I couldn't see, that for the life of me I couldn't see, really I couldn't. She went to the rest room. When she came back we tore the comic strip out of my notebook. It didn't really fit in with this evening, no more than the two characters hanging around the pinball machine did, or the people propping up the bar, or the bartender. None of them fit in with this evening, but we couldn't say so.

"I didn't have any lipstick on."

"No? Should we have a cocktail?"

"I'd like a grilled sandwich."

"I don't think they do that here."

"They don't do shit in this place. I want a grilled sandwich," she bawled. "Over here, a grilled sandwich!"

The bartender came over. We had learned that his name was Dov.

"What's the young lady's pleasure?"

"A grilled ham-and-cheese sandwich and a grilled cheese."

"Who is the grilled cheese for?"

"For me," I said.

"You know, I'll have to pick out the ham, and I don't much feel like doing that."

"Leave it as it is then," I said.

"Do you want a grilled cheese sandwich or don't you?"

"What I mean is, you don't have to take the ham off, just leave it as it is."

"It's no big deal picking the ham out, I've done it often enough before. We get these grilled sandwiches delivered ready-made, you see, straight from the factory."

She said, "We're going home now. Thanks for your trouble anyway."

To get to her house we had to go all the way across town, which meant another hour's walk, and the cocktails had left their mark. She was more used to it than I was; she was the kind of person who stuck around at parties until they started mopping the floor. Now and then I whispered in her ear what I thought you should whisper in your girl's ear when you're walking across town with her at night. I had never done that before. Walking a girl across town really late at night. Afterwards I would do it pretty often, and I always whispered something. Mostly things I could have said in my sleep without having to try very hard.

What I said got on her nerves, though. Because it isn't true that there are some things you can't hear often enough. So after that I kept my mouth shut, but that was no good either and I had a feeling she was about to have one of her black moods. By the last half mile we were staggering and had to stop every couple of minutes to recover. Maintenance trucks were parked on the streets. We had a terrific urge to bury ourselves in the beds of salt in the backs of them, but we didn't even have the strength to climb in. We couldn't figure out how to get in them anyway.

Then we were outside her house. It was an old building. We had to be very quiet, she said. I understood. I could hardly stand up from the walking and the cocktails and everything. She lived on the fourth floor. We took off our shoes, and I took off my socks as well. The stairs creaked all the same. I had a fit of giggles because the slower I walked the more the stairs creaked. It was pitch-dark, and I had to hold on to her because I didn't know the house. I couldn't keep up with her, though, so I whispered, "Not so fast, not so fast!" She whispered back, "I have to pee. Let go of me. I'll come back for you."

I said, "If you leave me alone here I'm going to scream my head off." I sat on the stairs and grabbed her leg and clung to it for all I was worth. I sat there like that for a while. Eventually she said, "I've peed in my pants."

Fortunately she had to laugh, and so did I. Fit to bust. I don't think I've ever laughed so hard. We had to stifle the laughter, though, which made me feel I'd choke any minute.

"Now you have to pee in your pants too," she said. "Otherwise it's unfair."

"What's it feel like?" I asked.

"Warm."

She sat on a step. It creaked. Everything creaked. What was worse, the stairs were really slippery; they must have been polished that afternoon. I wasn't able to pee because I'd done so four times in the street already.

"I can't go any farther, Rosie," I said. "I really can't. I'm going to lie down right here and go to sleep. I can't take another step."

"I can't either," she said. "But we have to go on. It's only one more floor. I don't want the neighbors to find me like this."

"Then leave me," I said. "Leave me here alone. I can't go any farther." I felt like a mountaineer giving up in the middle of a climb, the way they do in the movies, except there was no dramatic music.

Stuff kept on coming up into my mouth, like a sort of belch. I kept on swallowing it down, but it kept coming back, and finally I spat it out on the stairs.

It didn't bother me, but she absolutely refused to lie down on the stairs. So up we went, taking at least fifteen minutes to get to her floor because we had to go on all fours just to be on the safe side.

When we finally made it to her apartment, we had to climb another staircase and sneak past her mother's bedroom. I don't remember now how we did that.

She shut her door and right away took off all her clothes to get dry. We sat on the floor and drank water from a toothbrush cup.

"Cheers," I said.

"Cheers," she replied. "To November 22."

It was the first time I had been in her room, and the only light there came from the street lamp. I recognized all the things she had described in the summer, though. I was so tired that I wanted just to go to sleep with her and not wake up until everything had changed. Until everything was completely different. Us, the world, the clothing stores, the sun. That wasn't going to happen, of course, so we started kissing instead. I thought of the cashier at the drugstore who had exactly the same hairstyle as our family doctor. Which was why I went up to another cash register. But the girl there turned me off too. I wasn't afraid to tell old men to drop dead, I had no problem making Mrs. De Wilde shout herself hoarse, and I could frighten old ladies out walking their dogs so badly they didn't dare show their faces in Beatrix Park for days. I didn't find it difficult to buy gin and steal plums. Of all the appointments I had made in the course of my life, I had kept only a few. I had always had to make things up because I was afraid of what people might say if I told them the truth. I would have given a lot to know just one person I could talk to about exactly why I behaved the way I did, but of course all the biggest sons of bitches would have liked that too. In any case, I didn't know exactly why.

I told her that all the vending machines had been out of order or empty.

"Asshole," she said.

I said, "Yes." We were sitting on the floor, and I looked at the empty beer bottles on the table and the books scattered all around us and a concealer stick without a top in a wineglass and her hair hanging dripping over her eyes.

At first she swore a little, then she gradually stopped and I looked at her naked body, which had never before looked less naked to me.

"Let's have a fight," she said.

"No," I said, because that stuff was still coming up into my mouth. She grabbed my head and shoved it against the floor. I could see her foot and the veins that looked like my own and her toenails that had once been painted red. I was too tired and too drunk to do anything back.

"You're a jerk," she said. "Do you know what that is?"

Without waiting for a reply she kicked me in the chest a few times. She stood in front of me, her small body trembling, and asked, "Why won't you do anything back?"

I looked at the wobbling feet, the concealer stick in the wine-glass, the toothbrush cups, and the bottles. "I'm going home," I said.

"You do that," she said. "Your mommy wants you."

She had a beauty mark on her chin that I had always thought she put on with a pencil. From that night on I knew it was the real thing. My head was bursting with all the things people say if they want to hurt each other. That's usually pretty easy to do, even though the words are at least as old as the three patriarchs, in my opinion.

"You slut, you slutty little slut," I said. And "You could be Lucinda's sister." Hardly anyone knew Lucinda, but I knew Lucinda and she knew Lucinda and, believe me, she would a thousand times rather have been a slut than like Lucinda.

Then I picked up one of the cigarettes that were lying around, and I suddenly remembered that I always used to pee into a little orange pail with a white handle because I didn't dare go to the bathroom at night. I told her that and she said that we couldn't go to the bathroom there either, because her mother could hear everything. So we hunted around for a small pail. We didn't find one, but we did find a plastic box full of dolls. She tossed them out and then the two of us peed into the box.

After we had fucked she went and douched with salt water. I stood by the window and looked out over the square outside.

We were able to sleep for two hours. At eight o'clock I had to leave because that was when her mother got up. She had fallen asleep beside me. I smelled all the smells mixed up together and I looked at everything I could see in the light of that stupid street lamp because I wanted to remember as much as I possibly could.

If only I had done something really bad in my life, I thought, if only I had really beat someone's brains in instead of always just imagining what it would feel like to beat someone's brains in. Then everything would at least have been really ruined. Now everything was just half ruined.

WATCHING *SHOAH*

That Sunday morning was dull and overcast, and cars were driving with their lights on. Some people were already waiting at the streetcar stop, three young men who had been out partying all night. You could tell that's what they'd been doing by their faces and by what they were saying to one another. There was also a woman with a suitcase. She asked me if she was on the right side for Central Station. "Yes," I said.

We got onto the streetcar. It was almost empty. I sat behind the woman with the suitcase. She was wearing a very strong perfume. I took little sniffs, sampling it.

My mother had been sure I was dead. She asked why I treated my parents this way. I saw no point in having a discussion. For the past few years I'd stopped seeing any point in having discussions. She looked small in her red bathrobe, even smaller than me. They were both smaller than me and I was anything but tall. The bathrobe was a good twenty years old. That's because she refused to buy new clothes. She wouldn't have anything new. "Who would I buy new clothes for?" she said. "No one looks at me anymore." Shoes were the only things she still bought occasionally. Her life was over, she said, her life had been over for forty years. That's why I had to cut her hair. A hairdresser was another waste of money. I used to cut her hair while she sat in front of the TV. I thought it was nice cutting her hair. My father thought it was awful. "He's making you look terrible," he cried. "You look like a plucked chicken."

That was the morning I promised myself never to cut my mother's hair again, and I never did either.

I thought of Rosie, and of the woman I'd seen on the streetcar, and of how nice it had been lying next to Rosie and stroking her hair, hair that was stiff from the stuff she rubbed into it every day. It might easily be a few hundred years before I got the chance to lie next to her again. Stroking the hair of every woman who was willing to lie next to you was probably a good idea since it didn't really matter what they said to you and what you said to them, and it probably didn't even matter why they'd come to lie next to you.

My father came stumbling out of his room. I quickly locked the bathroom door. "I have to take a leak," he shouted.

"There's another bathroom downstairs," I shouted back. "Unbelievable," I heard him mutter, "unbelievable."

I looked in the mirror. It was November 23. Everything had changed. I walked into town. Everywhere was deserted. I took the streetcar to the Amstel train station, because that was the first streetcar to come along. I had no money for the snack bar, so I went and sat in the waiting room. A couple of other men were sitting there too. You could tell they weren't waiting for trains either. I had told them at home that I was going somewhere to work on my school project. I always said "somewhere." If you told them where, they might come looking for you and find out that you hadn't gone where you'd said you were going.

My father's birthday was in a few days. I would ask him, "How old are you now?" and he would answer, "Eighteen. We're celebrating my eighteenth birthday today, my boy." He gave the same answer every year. To mark the occasion, my mother would bring out our only tablecloth from the sideboard, and we would sit down at the table, and my father would drink all afternoon and all evening until the last of the guests had left. Then he would call out, "Hannelore, Hannelore, have all the visitors gone?"

"Yes," my mother would say, "they've all gone."

"Then bring in the food," he would say.

On his birthday we always had tongue.

"Actually, if I think about this tongue's having been in the mouth of a cow, I feel like throwing up," he said. "But I generally don't think about it, which is why I don't feel like throwing up."

"Seriously, how old are you?" I asked.

"Don't ask stupid questions," said my father, "your mother asks quite enough of those."

She came in with the tongue. "Why do you say you want to be a cowboy? Aren't you a little old for that sort of thing?" she asked me.

"A gunslinger, actually."

"Listen," said my father, "you'll never make a cowboy. I didn't make a cowboy either."

My mother said, "My ear, nose, and throat man has been run over by a streetcar."

"What?"

"My ear, nose, and throat man, Dr. Samuels, has been run over by a streetcar."

"Was he Jewish?" asked my father. "That's all we need. See? Death never gives us a break."

"You still have a slice of tongue on your plate," said my mother.

My father got up and stood by the back door.

"Look," he said, pointing to a footprint on the ground, "that was the foot of God. God was here. It's a pity I was out."

"What's he saying?" asked my mother. "Is your father starting on the foot of God again? Why do you fill the boy's head with such nonsense?"

"He always comes when we're out. That's God for you."

"I want to be the king of the Amsterdam underworld. Then someday I'll ask a girl, 'Would you like to be the queen of the Amsterdam underworld?' Then we'll give a huge party, and for you, dearest father, there'll be vodkas and loads of pretzels," I said.

"We don't have any kings of the underworld in our family," he said. "Emperors of the sewer and street princesses, maybe, and aunts who went crazy and started dealing in rags, and newspaper vendors who burned with their newspapers, and other street princesses who sold their bodies to save their lives and saved everything but that, and bakers who had no flour to bake bread but still managed to bake bread, and bald men who distilled vodka at the back of their houses, and grave diggers who dug graves for entire villages but not for themselves, and innkeepers who liked vodka as much as they liked the Torah, and, of course, your father, the emperor of the sewer."

"What happened to all the street princesses?"

"God plays marbles with them," he said, "because he's lonely."

We sat there like that until it was time to go to bed.

On the afternoon of December 10 Rosie and I went to a café called The Corner, where the same men sat around all the time and there are tablecloths on the tables.

Rosie said, "I think you're so sweet. I think you're so sweet."

I looked at her face and at the tablecloth, and I smelled the smell of her brown hair, which she had dyed red and which I would never smell again.

If there is some sort of God, then every love affair you miss out on has to be an insult to him, and every love affair you miss out on because you're scared has to be the worst insult of all to him. I wanted to say something along those lines to her because at the time I still believed it.

"You'll be sure to come to my birthday party, won't you?" she said.

"Yes," I said, "of course I'll come."

I asked for a Coke. The men invited me to come and sit at the bar and have a few beers with them. They asked my name and where I was from.

I said, "Listen, I'll talk to you about anything so long as it isn't about recorder lessons. The fact is, I was the only one left at the end. So the teacher said, 'There's really no point teaching just one boy,' and started to talk about his marriage. God, what an awful marriage. Once we were in the Bach Hall giving a performance and a girl was sitting next to me. After the performance she took me to the girls' rest room and started to spit in my face. Honestly. Started to spit as hard as she could in my face. Putting someone up against a wall and spitting at him for twenty minutes, that can't be normal. I was fed up with all those performances in the Bach Hall anyway. I was fed up with that whole music school.

"You know what I did the next performance? I punched her really hard. In the middle of the Bach Hall. She was sitting right in front. What a show-off that girl was. God, what a show-off. Just like her parents. They were show-offs too. Incidentally, my tennis club was called the NGBF, Not Glory But Fun."

That evening I went back to The Corner. Two days later she had a new boyfriend. Because his parents were away a lot, they were able to fuck each other silly. And that's what they did.

. . .

The Monday morning after that we were going to have to watch
Shoah again, which was the history teacher's bright idea. Watching *Shoah*. He summoned me to his room and said, "If you want,
you may be excused while we watch *Shoah*." Just before that they
had suspended me for a day for playing hooky again. They suspended me at the slightest provocation. So I deliberately got up
early the next day. They were all sitting there watching that drag
of a movie. At the end, one silly cow even started to blubber. I
swear. She started to blubber. Next time I'd make sure I was
excused. I suspected the teacher of blubbering himself while the
final credits were being shown. He was quite capable of it. That's
the kind of man he was. Toward the end of the year I ran across
him again.

He said, "I never see you in my class anymore."

I said, "You know, that's right. I thought you were all still
busy watching *Shoah*."

In the meantime my father had come back from Israel, and the
first thing he did was to send my mother to a psychiatrist. By then
the rumor had filtered through even to them that my report card
would have only one "satisfactory," and my mother had embarked
on a kind of roundup of my missing textbooks. She was sure they
had been stolen. She had a hunch that our cleaning lady had
made off with them. I was sorry for the cleaning lady. I tried to
convince my mother that the cleaning lady couldn't have had
anything to do with my textbooks, but she refused to believe me.
"They're dirty crooks all of them," she shouted, "and she's no
better than the rest." Luckily the cleaning lady had known my
mother for fifteen years, so she wasn't too upset at being called a
crook.

The day my report card arrived my father rushed off immediately to the nearest Hema store and my mother asked to see the psychiatrist, preferably that same day. When she came back she said, "He's senile, that doctor, and what's more he wants to see you too." My father worked himself up into a rage. He wrote a letter to the psychiatrist: "For the past fifteen years I have never gone anywhere with my wife, and I'm certainly not going to a psychiatrist with her now."

Mrs. Haaseveld came to see me at home one Wednesday afternoon. I had just been to the school psychologist. My mother plied her with cake and my father with all kinds of aperitifs. It was during the period when from about four o'clock on he would only speak very, very slowly. By half past five she still hadn't left. From about six o'clock he would start speaking in German, but by then she was back with her husband and child and her darling cats, so she didn't have to suffer that.

That evening at dinner my father kept nodding off to sleep and my mother would hit him on the head with her spoon. "There's a curse on this family," he said after she had hit him awake once again. My mother lives in a world where there is neither day nor night and where there are no people left, my father waits for stock reports that I'm sure haven't been broadcast for the past twenty years, and my sister is married to a man who says prayers three times a day—in the morning, the afternoon, and the evening—and works for an insurance company in his spare time.

My mother wanted to know what on earth I did in cafés all day long. It turns out that Mrs. Haaseveld told her about that. I didn't really know myself. You had to go somewhere, after all. You couldn't run around town all day like a lunatic, could you? She didn't think much of an answer like that. So I said that I did it because of the girls.

"Let's drink to the girls," said my father suddenly.

"To the girls," I said.

"There were a lot of girls in Mauthausen too," said my mother, "but I was the prettiest of them all. Even without my hair I was pretty. The SS thought so anyway. I was the belle of the ball in that place."

In May they kicked me out of school a few days after I'd started trying to sell an alternative school magazine. I'd done pretty well too. Even the teachers all bought one. A day later I was summoned to see the principal. The magazine was full of obscenities. Of course it was full of them. I was suspended again, the only thing they could do.

A few days later I learned that I would never have to go back again. Mrs. Haaseveld was standing in the downstairs hall. I held out my hand to her but she hissed, "All the trouble I took, and • for nothing." And she called after me, "My God, what I didn't do for you, young man. If you only knew!"

I felt like telling her that she really ought to be very pleased with me, since I had managed to survive her charity and the charity of a bunch of psychologists and all the rest. Which is just about the most difficult thing in the whole world to survive. I didn't say it, though. I didn't think that anything I could still say to her was of any importance.

That's why I also didn't tell her that Rosie had been just about the only girl I'd ever been in love with without constantly worrying. What I mean is, without having to remember the whole time that I had to act like a man and that I had to kiss like someone who had kissed at least twenty thousand girls already, like someone who had begun kissing girls more or less before he could walk.

I walked home. I thought of Rosie, and of all the things we had done and particularly all the things we hadn't done, and of my father, who studied stock quotations as if they were mystical runes that would reveal why we had smashed the dinner plates, whose destruction had been as futile as that of everything else. I hoped I wouldn't meet too many people on the way, because I had drunk an awful lot of gin and that makes me go all to pieces. I didn't feel like sitting under a tree in Beatrix Park. Luckily I was wearing a coat.

There's a song by Bob Dylan: "I was so much older then. I'm younger than that now."

Part Three

WALK LIKE AN EGYPTIAN

She said, 'Cut it out. There's no point,' " said the man next to me. I watched my father out of the corner of my eye. He was sitting at the table behind us, an almost untouched glass of beer in front of him. In the old days he would knock them back, but I could drink five now in the time he took to drink one.

"I buried him in the yard," said the woman on the other side of me. If she hadn't been sitting next to me, I would have called her a drunken slut. A drunken Beethovenstraat slut, because drunken sluts come in all shapes and sizes too.

"Who?" asked the man.

"My cat," she said. "He'd just turned twenty-two."

"That's old," I said.

"He was my first husband's," she went on, "but him I'd buried already. And his sister too. I mean the cat's. She's down at the end of the yard also. They're lying side by side now."

" 'Do I get a kiss?' she asked," said the man. Then my father fell out of his chair. I slid off my stool. "Give me a hand, some-body," I said. The drunken slut was already standing next to me. In her state there could be no question of her giving me a hand. A waiter came over to us. "Problem?" he asked.

"We have to help my father," I said.

The waiter picked my father up and put him back in his chair.

My father's long, almost yellow hair had fallen across his eyes and mouth, which shows how long it was. His upper dentures didn't look right either, but then, they never had. I could do something about his hair but not about his teeth. I took the hairbrush from the plastic bag that was always slung over his chair when I took him for a walk.

"So what happened this time?" I asked my father.

"An earthquake," he said.

"What's he saying?" the drunken slut wanted to know.

"An earthquake."

She began to giggle. She was pretty far gone.

I ordered another beer.

"Come on," I said to my father, "drink up."

My father sat in front of his beer, looking at it as if it were pure poison. He sat in front of all food and drink that way. I picked up the glass and put it to his lips. Most of the beer dribbled down his chin onto his pants, but his pants were all stained any-way. I wiped his chin with my handkerchief, which was hard to do now that he'd stopped shaving himself. We did have a home aide. His name was Roy and he came around every day to shave my father. He did it with an electric razor, keeping one eye on his newspaper. Before him, I had shaved my father every morning, but it used to make me late to the office, so my mother decided to call in Roy. It wasn't easy to shave my father. When I was still doing it, I had to get up a good half an hour early. I would prop his head up against a pile of pillows, place the electric razor against his cheek, and move it up and down a little at a time. The radio would generally be on because my father had gotten hooked on it after all those years, so that for me *Going to Work on a Song* and his useless bellowing are lastingly associated. While my father shouted that I was torturing him I would sing along with "The Sun Always Shines on TV" or whatever else they were playing that morning, tapping out the rhythm on the edge of his bed with my free hand. My father lay behind railings that prevented him from falling out of bed.

There were days when he didn't try to make things difficult for me, but those were few and far between. Most of the time he would bawl, "Let me shave myself, you morons!" Or, "I want a wet shave!" Sundays were the only day we would give him a wet shave, because by the time we finished my mother had to mop up the entire room. His stubble was white, and whatever else in his body had slowed down, his beard certainly had not.

Roy lived in Almere and drove a gigantic Mercedes. He had a long black beard, and when he had been with us for three weeks he invited us to the Catholic version of the bat mitzvahs of his two daughters. That day I looked after my father so that my mother could go. We sat in the garden and both of us took a nap. At six o'clock my mother came back and told us that the pastries had been delicious, if a bit on the skimpy side, and that his daughters were darling little black girls in white dresses. Their father may have earned a little extra by shaving my father every morning, but I really couldn't believe that one small shaving job paid for the enormous Mercedes he parked outside our door each time. Since I worked in an office I knew that a Mercedes like his was an automobile to lust after, which was surprising, because Brother Roy did not strike me as being the type who would lust after automobiles.

I ought to have taken my father for a walk in Beatrix Park. Then he would have had a little fresh air in his lungs while my mother had a few hours to herself. We hardly ever ended up in the park, though, and instead would find ourselves in one of the cafés on Beethovenstraat. We'd hang around there until it was time for supper and we were expected back home. Or until my father had made a mess in his pants and begun to stink.

"Come on, drink up," I said again. My mother was pleased when he drank anything, whether it was water, beer, or orange juice.

"Where's the shit house?" asked my father.

Ever since he'd fallen ill, he'd started asking for the shit house all the time. Before then he'd never used that kind of language. The doctor mumbled something about a personality change, but I hadn't paid attention to the doctor's mumbles for months.

"We'll go to the shit house in a moment," I said quietly. "But first I'll have another beer, and you'd better drink yours up now or we'll get an earful from Mama."

I sat down at the bar again between the drunken slut and the man.

"My daughter's left home with her boyfriend," she said. "They'd been living with us for a while. They were good company."

Another whisky on the rocks and she would start telling me the story of her life, unabridged, and I would never get away. That's what those drunken Beethovenstraat sluts were like. And by next week she would have forgotten all about it and would start telling me the whole thing all over again.

I looked outside and watched the couples strolling past the store windows, holding each other's hands as if they'd been doing it since at least World War I, in their oversized windbreakers and the jeans they'd pressed that very morning. I had watched this scene at least five hundred times, since I figured that was the number of Sundays I'd been coming here instead of taking my father for a walk in the park to fill his lungs with good fresh air.

"Where can someone my age still find a nice woman?" asked the man. "Not the kind with all sorts of little things wrong with her either."

"Where's the shit house?"

I went over to him. My father had to watch his mouth in a place like this.

"Are you all right?" I asked. "Is everything all right?"

"Where's Mama?"

"Mama's at home," I said. "Don't forget to tell her we went to Beatrix Park and had a nice long walk, a damned nice long walk."

I poured a little more beer into his mouth. "Just swallow it," I said. "Swallow it, then it'll be over and done with." He swallowed and I stroked his head, over the bald patch. I ordered one last beer.

"You shouldn't force him to drink," said the waiter, putting the beer down in front of me. "It's not right."

"It's right for him," I said. "He has to be forced."

I emptied my glass in one gulp. That helped. Not much, but a little. One of the couples came in, knife-edge creases in their jeans. They sat at a table by the window and said nothing. I looked at the girl's ass and got an erection. The worst kind of horniness is when you're just tipsy. Not when you're really drunk, because then nothing much gets through to you. But if you're a little tipsy, anything at all can get you going. A too-large ass in blue jeans. A bra under a white blouse, or an odd voice, or badly painted fingernails, or blackheads, or running mascara, or even varicose veins, but that was something I hadn't yet tried. I ordered another beer.

"Get me another too," I heard the drunken slut whisper. She had opened her purse and was busy applying lipstick. Couldn't she have done that in the rest room? The whole time, she kept glancing down at her breasts. If there's anything that turns me off it's women who keep looking to see if their breasts are still there. I feel like shouting at them, "Hey, take a look at something else. There's nothing worth looking at down there."

"Where's my beer?"

I turned around. Fortunately my father was still in his chair.

"It's right in front of you," I said. "There, right in front of your nose. For heaven's sake, drink up, because I'm beginning to not feel too good."

He laid his head on the table. I leaped across to the chair to make sure I'd put the brakes on. I'd forgotten to once, and it was something I didn't feel like going through again.

"Are you taking a nap?" I asked.

He said nothing. His eyes were open. The left one was turned up a little, but that had been happening lately whenever he laid his head on the table.

"Isn't it time you took him home?" asked the waiter.

"We'll be going in a minute," I said. "He just has to finish his drink."

I still had a hard-on and I didn't want to walk home like that.

"Sunday is actually the only day I'm on my own," said the man on my left. "It's actually the only day I ever think to myself, 'Golly, if only I had a wife.' "

"Cheers," I said.

"Your health," said the man.

"*Lechaim*," said the drunken slut. "My first husband's cats are all dead now. He was crazy about those cats and they were crazy about him."

On the way to the men's room I walked past my father. "Everything all right still?" I asked.

"I want to go to bed," he whispered.

I ignored the urinal, walked straight into the toilet stall, and opened my fly. The place smelled strongly, as if someone had recently been using eau de cologne. I thought of all the Sundays I had jerked off in here, and of all the women I had thought of, and of the fact that I would never think of most of them again because I had forgotten their faces and names. I thought of the girls who always hung around in the little smoking room at Vossius and would occasionally stretch out a leg as I walked past, and I thought that tradition gives a person something to hang on to.

Even if my father died I would still walk down Beethovenstraat on Sundays and jerk off in the men's room of this café. In memory of his life, of which I knew next to nothing and of which I would never get to know anything now, and of my own life, too, and of the Sundays we had spent here together, just like all the days of these last few months of his life. With a lot of beer, bad music, and ugly women and with the hope, above all, that supper would not turn out as awful as it had the night before, that it was still a long way off, and that Brother Roy and his Mercedes and that unctuous voice of his, which sounded as if he had come to hear confession—that all that was still a long way off, too, and that we ought to drink our way through quite a few more beers before we had to walk back home, for then nothing would matter so much anymore.

The drunken slut walked in.

"This is the men's room," I said.

"I never do learn, do I?"

"It's all right."

"*Motek*, sweetheart," she whispered and stroked my cheek. Then she shut the door behind her.

Rosie and I had eaten salmon trout one evening in this café. A few days before we went to Antwerp. It annoyed me that I couldn't remember what we had talked about that evening. As if it mattered.

I released the brakes on his wheelchair.

"Come on, we're going," I said.

He didn't lift his head from the table.

"We're not going to get home like that."

"I am the emperor."

He was off again. Before his illness he had been the emperor only occasionally, whenever he was drinking more than usual. He'd been a moderate though steady drinker. Except on birthdays, Jewish holidays, and evenings when visitors came around, when he could easily drink three times his normal quota.

"I'm a bon vivant," he had frequently said of himself. Though in precisely what way was never entirely clear to me.

I was just about to push him back into his chair when I heard the drunken slut say, "I've ordered you another one." Another one it was then. I put my father's head back on the table, whispered, "Sleep well," and went to sit at the bar.

"Your father's a little tired, isn't he?" she said.

"Yes," I said, "he's a little tired." I looked at that face of hers, a face that may well have been beautiful once upon a time and that might have been beautiful still if she had drunk a little less.

"My parents live in a community home in north Amsterdam." That was the man again. Why didn't the two of them go get it on in the rest room? Then they wouldn't have to rattle on at me.

I extracted some money from my father's inside pocket and paid. We'd run up quite a check for that sort of afternoon, for that sort of Sunday afternoon.

"Come on, we're going," I said to him, "we're really going this time." I lifted his head from the table and tried to sit him up straight.

"If you don't sit up, we'll never get home," I hissed. For that, too, had happened before.

Finally he did straighten up. His head had recently been inclining to the left, just like my cock, although that wasn't recent. I patted his hair down flat on his head, where it belonged, wiped his mouth, and pushed the chair toward the door. "Bye," I called just before I negotiated the doorstep.

The sky had cleared. Babes in ski jackets were out doing their Sunday rounds on the arms of their boyfriends. Old men were doing the same with wives at least as old as they were. My father wasn't the only one who felt worn out; I did too. So we skipped the AKO this time and went straight home. Normally we would have gone on from the café to the AKO, at the corner of Gerrit van der Veenstraat, the newsstand where I had bought my first sex book when I was fourteen. I had placed it between *The Cas-*

tafiore Emerald and *Red Rackham's Treasure*. Apparently my mother felt she had to dust even between the Tintin books, and one night when I came home from the movies, she said, "I've found something awful."

My mother was always finding awful things. She said, "You'll ruin your whole sex life for later on." I wanted to ruin everything, so why not my sex life as well?

"Can you take my teeth out?"

"Soon," I said.

"No, now," said my father.

I walked on. Luckily I had a good grip on his wheelchair.

"Don't forget: we were in Beatrix Park."

"I'm saying nothing," said my father. "First my teeth have to come out."

While I was waiting to cross Stadionweg, I ran into Mrs. Weinbaum. It was too late to avoid her. I might have managed if I'd been alone, but I was stuck with the wheelchair.

"How are things with him?" she asked. "Is he getting any better? Is there any improvement at all?"

I felt like a mother pushing a baby carriage.

"He's getting better," I said.

Mrs. Weinbaum bent over the wheelchair.

"How are you today? Are you feeling any better?"

"Take my teeth out," said my father.

Mrs. Weinbaum gave me a worried look. "He wants his teeth out."

"Yes," I said. "We're on our way home."

I had scratched a scab open just behind my ear. There was blood on my fingers.

"Maybe he needs a new set," offered Mrs. Weinbaum.

"I'll talk it over with my mother. Thanks for the suggestion."

Then the light changed and I raced across Stadionweg with my father. Mrs. Weinbaum shouted something after me. It could have been, "Say hello to your mother."

"Right. We were in Beatrix Park," I said. "Remember, or else Mama will get mad again."

"She is mad," said my father.

Now we were walking along the quiet part of Beethovenstraat. We had to cross the bridge, which loomed like the steepest mountain. Tomorrow was Monday, when I would have to be in the office at a quarter after nine again. I was working part-time for a publisher of directories. At first it had been from nine to two, but because I always showed up fifteen minutes late it was changed to nine-fifteen to two-fifteen. Not that that helped, since most of the time now I turned up at nine-thirty, but it was the thought that counted. It wasn't their own money, after all, and that's why they'd stopped mentioning it. I had been working there for a year. "You can stay for as long as you like," the manager had said, "but maybe it's time you did something with your life."

Do something with your life. That's what you were told by people who had invariably done nothing with their own. People who started in on you the moment they'd had one drink too many, with, "What did I do with my life? What in God's name did I do with it?" What did that mean anyway, "doing something with your life"? Could someone tell me exactly how you do that? You get kicked out of school, go and work in an office when you know nothing about it and have no business there anyway—was that doing something with your life? And what was it that the doctor always said? Ninety percent of people don't survive radical changes in their lives for more than two years, but that was irrelevant in this case. We were standing on the bridge now. I was hot.

"I have to pee," said my father.

"I have to take a leak too."

I looked down at eight ducklings and a mother duck. Of those eight, about three would survive. The rest would be eaten by rats. I had known Beatrix Park since I was four.

"What do you say I let your chair roll down the bridge?" I asked.

"Don't fool around."

"You'd be home sooner that way."

"If you fool around, I'll yell."

Perhaps that was doing something with your life, too, letting your father's wheelchair roll down the bridge. I was nineteen now, a good age to do something with my life if ever there was one.

It was from this point on the bridge that I would always fling into the canal the rice wafers my mother made me take to school. Later on I took just an apple, and I didn't throw that into the canal. I gave it away or sold it. I didn't take anything to the office. They always sent out at lunchtime for sandwiches from Pasteuning's delicatessen. I was the one who generally went to pick them up. I would take a good hour and a half doing that every day because I'd slip into the Café De Gruter, where I'd have a cup of coffee and read the newspaper. For food, I generally had a cheese on rye. From half past nine on I looked forward to that cheese on rye, just like all the rest of my colleagues who had ended up in the directory world.

The best days at the office were when I was sent to the Bijenkorf department store to buy panty hose for the manager. He had hired me one Monday morning in March. Ten months before that I had been kicked out of school. I told the manager that I was a poet but that in spite of that I needed money. The manager told me he, too, was a poet, and then he said, "You've got the job." I ended up in the telephone department on the second floor. I sat by the window and looked out over the stretch of gardens along Willemsparkweg.

After a few weeks the manager, Mr. Neustadt, called me into his office. He told me that as far as he was concerned *stone* rhymed with *alone* and *red* with *dead* and *love* with *dove*, and that was his limit. He looked at me and I didn't know what to say. "When I was your age," he said, "I would spend all day in the woods testing my literary and poetic skills, trying to put all the shades of green into words. It was beyond me. That's why I didn't pursue a career in that field and why I threw myself into the world of directories."

He took a sip of the espresso I always had to make for him.

"But one day a book written by me will be published," he whispered, and laid a hand on my shoulder. "The small book of the great rejection, or the great book of the small rejection. I haven't made up my mind which yet."

Whenever he said that, I knew I'd be sent to the Bijenkorf that day for panty hose, perfume, or champagne.

Neither of us works in that office anymore. Every three months we go out for a pizza together at the Scala della Pasta. He's a little grayer now and runs laps around Vondel Park to do something about his stomach. I have long since ceased thinking that he talks crudely about women, that he talks crudely about anything at all. He speaks of his beloved wife and we exchange private addresses and advice about where they don't wash you and about our other experiences in that area. In short, they are quite enjoyable evenings.

Last time I saw him he said, "Harnoncourt or some other conductor said in an interview, 'We artists don't write telephone books, we write poems.' That gave me quite a start. I've been producing telephone books all my life, and yet I'm a something of an oddball."

"Where's your father?" shouted my mother.

"I've left him in the front yard."

"Why haven't you brought him in?"

"Because I'm taking a pee."

"He'll catch cold."

"He won't catch cold."

Now came the hardest part. To get him up the foot and a half to the door, my father had to be pushed up two wooden planks. First I had to strap him into his wheelchair with a piece of rope we had bought especially for the purpose. He had fallen out once or twice during earlier attempts. We could, of course, lift him up bodily, but for that we needed Brother Roy and he only came in the mornings.

"Here we go," I said.

I took a running start. Without a running start you could forget the whole thing.

"I have to go to the bathroom now!" shouted my father. "And then to bed."

The first time it didn't work. The wheelchair slipped off the planks. We were back on the grass. The jolt of our landing made my father's head loll over the side of the wheelchair. I straightened it. Took a second running start, this time a little longer.

"And the riders are about to begin the steepest ascent of this stage," I shouted.

"Cut it out," said my father.

I ran up the garden path. My father's head wobbled from side to side but the rest of him stayed firmly strapped down.

I raced up the planks with the chair. At the highest point we nearly slipped back again, but with a sort of butt of my head in the direction of the front door I pushed him into the hallway and straight through into the living room. A ridiculously large hospital bed had been standing there for the past few months where his little wine cart used to be. The bed had an air mattress that pumped itself up every five minutes. The pumping was accompanied by quite a lot of noise, so that the living room sometimes sounded like an airplane. On top of which it didn't do him the slightest bit of good. There were countless bedsores on his back, and in some places the flesh had become infected and had formed little yellow blisters.

"And once again the stage has been won by Arnon and his regular co-rider. He's still the holder of the yellow jersey even after this exceptionally difficult stage. There he is once again, standing on the rostrum, receiving flowers and being kissed twice on each cheek."

"I have to pee," shouted my father.

My mother was standing in the kitchen cracking walnuts. She was making a purée full of vitamins and other things that she claimed would make him better. Most of the time I had to feed the purée to him while my mother saw to the rest of the supper. Upstairs in the bathroom I swallowed two and a half aspirin.

"Give your father his purée," yelled my mother.

The purée was kept in a round orange Tupperware container. My mother was a great one for tradition. Previously, he had been fed the purée in the hospital. Or rather I had had to take it to him in the hospital, where I would feed it to him at about four o'clock. My mother would come to relieve me at six. We spent the whole day feeding him. My mother honestly thought that the food the hospital provided was not enough for him. That he would die of starvation. In the end, of course, he did not starve to death but choked. Drowned in food, as it were. That's what the doctor said anyway: "You might say he died by drowning."

"Brute, monster, give your father his purée!"

Another aspirin. The critical dose was nine a day, so I still had some way to go. They were badly needed, because the way I felt now I could not have given anyone purée, least of all my father. My mother used to keep grated apple in the little orange container for me, because when I was little I apparently had diarrhea for months on end. It was so bad that my circumcision had to be postponed. That's why I wasn't circumcised a week after birth, as I ought to have been, but months later.

I came downstairs, picked up the Tupperware container, and walked into the room, crowing, "Here comes the crown prince with your purée. We're going to eat some yummy purée."

He turned his head away. I used to squeeze his cheeks just long enough for him to open his mouth so I could quickly shove the spoon in.

"I don't feel too well today," I said.

He said nothing.

I stuck the spoon into his mouth one more time. At least I didn't have to pinch his cheeks anymore.

"It's for your own good," I whispered.

Which one was I taking after? In God's name, which one was it?

I realized that I had forgotten to untie him. I undid the rope and threw it onto the floor. I always had to tie up both the upper part of his body and his legs, because otherwise his bad leg might catch on something when we climbed the wooden planks.

"What's your view on doing something with your life?" I asked when we had managed to force down half the food.

"No more purée," said my father, "I want to go to bed now."

Quite an enlightening answer, I thought.

My mother came in with the insulin. For the past few weeks she'd been giving him the injections herself so the district nurse no longer had to come to the house to do it.

"Did the two of you have a nice little walk in the park?" she asked.

"Great," I said, and brought the spoon back up to my father's mouth.

"No," he said.

"Yes," I said.

Then my mother pinched his cheeks with her free hand just long enough for him to be forced to open his mouth, and I quickly chucked in some more purée.

"Take my teeth out," said my father.

"No," said my mother. "First we're going to eat a nice piece of steak." Then the doorbell rang.

"That's all I need," she said. "They either turn up too soon or they turn up too late."

We couldn't lift my father back into his bed by ourselves, which was why the ladies of the district nursing service had to come. In the morning Brother Roy did it.

I went to the door. It seemed to me that it was about time for something stronger than beer. A big black woman was standing outside.

"Is this the Grunberg residence?" she asked.

"Yes," I said, "it is." I remembered that my father still had a bottle of whisky in the garage.

"They told me I'm supposed to lift somebody into bed."

"Yes," I said, "that's right, that's why you were called."

"And clean him up and wash him. I was supposed to do that too."

"Right again. Take off your coat and come in."

I wondered how much more aspirin I would have to take before it started to work.

The black woman followed me in. My mother said that she was just cooking a piece of steak and that she would like her to pay special attention to my father's bedsores. Then she closed the kitchen door.

The black woman shook my father's hand. "I'm Marga. I'm going to put you to bed."

"Hullo," said my father. "Please take my teeth out."

"First I'll wash you real good," said Marga.

"Fine," said my father, "but I have to go to the bathroom."

"Can't be done, Papa," I said. Then I spotted yesterday's open wine bottle and poured myself a glass.

"Are you the son?" asked Marga.

I nodded.

"That's the crown prince," cried my father.

Marga was busy with his shoes now. "What did you say, Mr. Grunberg?"

"Sexy little piglet," said my father.

I took a big swig and turned the radio on.

"Are you at college?" Marga asked.

"No," I said, "I work in an office. Part-time."

"I thought you must be at college." She took his shirt off. His hair was hanging in front of his eyes again. "Now then, we're going to have to stand up for a moment, Mr. Grunberg, so we can take your pants off."

"He can't do that," I said. "He can't stand up by himself." I refilled my glass. Wine was something we weren't short of at home.

"Could you give me a hand?"

I nodded. Rosie had sat at this table, I remembered, but what had happened during the three and a half years after that was something I really couldn't remember anymore. I pulled my father up out of his chair. He stood on one leg, but chiefly he leaned against me. His paralyzed arm hung limply around my neck. I began to feel the beer and the wine taking effect. "We're dancing cheek to cheek," I whispered in his ear. He started to laugh. He laughed out of one side of his mouth because the other side didn't work anymore. It was funny seeing him laugh like that. The spit dribbling onto my T-shirt struck me as less funny. "Stop fooling around," he said. There was no question of fooling around. I had the feeling I might hit the floor any moment. I could barely keep my own weight upright, let alone my father's weight too.

"Right. Put him back in his chair," said Marga.

I did. Now my father was naked.

I sat down again, drank some more wine. Marga washed his legs. They were thin, white, and bony. On the radio they were playing "Walk like an Egyptian," and I remembered dancing to it once upon a time. Back when I used to go dancing, that is.

"You mustn't do that, Mr. Grunberg, I don't think that's nice at all," I heard Marga say suddenly. She stood up and said, "He pinched my breast."

"Oh dear, how annoying," I said. And to my father, "Don't do that again." I took a good look at her breasts. Each one of them would have filled a large pail. My father had obviously stopped being choosy when it came to breasts.

"Do you like this song?" I asked her eventually, in order to clear the air a little.

"Are you talking to me?"

I couldn't answer because I was trying to suppress a fit of coughing. I knew for sure that if I was to have a full-scale coughing fit just at that moment it would turn into the kind of coughing fit that ended in spitting and maybe much worse, and that was the last thing I needed right then.

"No, all I asked was if you liked 'Walk like an Egyptian.' "

"No," said Marga, "it doesn't do anything for me."

"Me neither," said my father.

"Now I'm going to give you some nice new underpants."

"Sexy little piglet," said my father.

"Did you hear that?" cried Marga from under the table. "Did you hear that?"

"What," I said, "what's the matter?" It had suddenly struck me that black people don't have red pimples but black ones. They reminded me of little Easter eggs. With difficulty, Marga straightened up. She looked at me as if I had insulted her.

"I have to go to the bathroom," said my father. "Quickly. Where's the shit house?"

"Did you hear what he said?"

" 'Where's the shit house?' " I said.

"No, before that."

"I was listening to the radio."

"He said, 'Sexy little piglet,' " cried Marga.

"Sexy little piglet," said my father.

"I don't have to put up with that. I absolutely do not have to put up with that."

It looked as if she really wasn't going to put up with it. That didn't seem all that clever to me, though, since my father would have liked nothing better.

The wine bottle was empty again. "Don't say that!" I shouted at my father. "This isn't a sexy little piglet; this is Marga. She's a nice lady. She's come to help us put you to bed."

"I can't work like this," said Marga.

I wondered if all those aspirins I had taken were ever going to work, though I wouldn't have been at all surprised if I was beyond aspirin. I might have to try my mother's sleeping pills next. I was feeling pretty lousy, which was why I said, "Listen, I'm only his son, you understand." I spat as inconspicuously as possible into an empty glass on the table.

"I'll put him to bed then."

"Great," I said.

She pulled him up and rubbed ointment into the bedsores on his back with her free hand. A pretty strong woman, I thought.

"I want to go to the bathroom."

"You can't go to the bathroom," I said. "Just let Marga put your underpants on."

My father wore underpants that functioned as diapers.

"Sexy little piglet."

"You take hold of him," said Marga.

"He's sick," I said. "You ought to take that into consideration in your judgment of him." I enunciated this sentence with some difficulty.

I took over from her again. My father leaned naked against me and I leaned against the sideboard so as to have something to rest against. "We're dancing cheek to cheek again," I said. The fact is, I had come to appreciate that you might as well make the most of the rare moments of good cheer that life offers. Much as I had also come to appreciate that you should turn those few moments in your life that are filled with living, breathing naked women into a party. And who knew whether that didn't go for naked fathers as well.

"I'm going to have to talk to your mother," she said.

She had obviously stopped talking to my father.

I made another stab. "The doctor said he's suffered a change of personality."

"Change of personality, my ass. I'll take it up with your mother."

"Is that Coby?" asked my father.

Coby was another district nurse. I suddenly had an irrepressible urge to sing "If I knew Coby like you knew Coby."

"No, it's Marga. You ought to behave yourself a little better when she's around."

"He keeps pawing me," said Marga. Then she yelled into his ear, "You're a dirty old man, Mr. Grunberg."

My father laughed out of the side of his mouth with an air of innocence, and something was trickling down my neck again.

"Look, he's half paralyzed. Half-paralyzed people aren't able to paw all that easily. It's his reflexes. Like phantom limb pains, you know?"

"I'll take it up with your mother."

"You do that," I said. "You do what you think best. My mother is in the kitchen."

This was a Sunday to make you die laughing, I could tell.

"I have to go to the bathroom," said my father.

"Soon," I said. "Was all that really necessary? Did you really have to make trouble again?"

"I have to go to the shit house," he said. "Right now."

"The shit house comes to you these days, all by itself," I said.

Then my mother walked in, followed by the nurse.

"What did he say?" my mother asked me.

Before I could open my mouth, Marga answered, " 'Sexy little piglet.' Not just once but ten times at least. I can't go on working like that, Mrs. Grunberg."

"You wretch!" shouted my mother. "You never said that to me. Not ever. You've ruined my whole life. You'd never go to the doctor, so you only have yourself to blame."

"That's not the problem," yelled Marga, who could also yell fairly well. "The problem is that I'm done now and I'm not coming back to this place. I can do without being called a sexy little piglet."

"Somebody help me," I cried, "I can't hold him up any longer." My head was being hammered into the parquet floor by a pile driver.

"I have to go to the shit house," shouted my father. "I have to take a shit."

"You should teach your husband better manners!" yelled Marga. "I can't work like that. And let me tell you that none of my colleagues will put up with it either. If your husband goes on calling us sexy little piglets you'll be without home nurses for good."

"And let me tell you that I never want to see you in this house again," my mother shouted back. "Even if you beg on bended knee to be allowed to put my husband to bed, I won't let you back in, you or anyone to do with you, ever again."

"If you think you can insult me, you're mistaken, because we all know that you're bad news."

"I have to go to the shit house!" roared my father.

"I can't hold him up any longer!" I roared just as loudly.

They weren't listening, because they were too busy calling each other names. Then my father took his shit, like a horse. On the Persian rug and on my shoes and a little on my pants too. It lasted just a minute or two, maybe even less, but in my memory he took a shit for a good three hours.

I was reminded of the time after Charlie Chaplin died and my father took me to the Tuschinski. *Modern Times* was showing. It was the winter of 1977 or 1978. When the movie ended I couldn't get the scene out of my head with the goose in the restaurant and the people dancing, and the goose being held over their heads, and the man waiting for his goose, but there were too many dancers and the waiter couldn't get through with the goose, and finally the goose wound up hanging from a chandelier. After the movie we went to a café. I think it was the Café Schiller. We sat at the back and my father talked to a lady and they drank wine. After *Modern Times* I saw lots more movies and went to the Tuschinski 1 quite often, but I've never again known such certainty as I felt that afternoon, when I wanted to do what Charlie Chaplin did in that movie. That was the same afternoon my father talked to a lady he later told me was the one who tore your tickets in the movie theater, and I had ice coffee, which I stirred until the ice had melted and then drank through a straw. Later my father took me to see Jacques Tati and Buster Keaton, and then I wanted to be like Tati, and after that like Buster Keaton, but preferably Tati because I never saw anyone play tennis the way he played tennis. The school doctor told my mother to watch out because I was evidently having trouble telling fact from fantasy. While we were there the doctor told me to get dressed. I didn't know how to because my mother had always dressed and undressed me. That's why I only put on my scarf and my shoes. I came out of the stall like that. The school doctor said nothing, but she began to write like one possessed and my mother grabbed hold of me and dressed me. That Wednesday I went as usual with my father to see Buster Keaton or Tati or the Marx Brothers, or maybe, if there was absolutely nothing else, Louis de Funès.

When my father had finally finished, I said, "I'll have to put you down on the floor now because I honestly can't hold you up any longer."

"Don't put me down on the floor."

"I have to," I said, "otherwise you'll fall, and that'll be a lot worse."

"It's a shit house in here, you know that?"

"Yes," I said, "I know," and laid him carefully on the floor. That wasn't easy, because I didn't want to put him down in the shit. It wasn't until then that the black woman and my mother saw him, but I had to get upstairs. I leaned over the toilet bowl for a good twenty minutes. Nothing came up, though, but little drops of yellow acid. I rinsed my mouth with water and went downstairs.

"The emperor is in bed," called my father when he saw me.

"Where's the black woman?"

"Your mother sent her away."

A large yellow stain on the rug and on my polished shoes was the only reminder of what had happened half an hour ago. I brushed the hair from in front of his eyes. "I'm going now," I said. "Take it easy."

"I want my teeth out."

"No," I said. "You still have to eat."

I kissed him. He smelled of talcum powder.

"Aren't you staying for supper?" asked my mother.

"No, I have to go out," I said.

"I lifted him into bed myself. I'm ruining my back, but what do I care? I'm past caring."

My mother put my father's steak through the grinder because that was the only way he could eat it.

"Please help me give him his food," she said, but I walked away. I would keep walking through town until I thought supper was over.

I remembered one of my father's friends whom he used to meet in cafés when the two of us were still traveling together. His name was Nicola, and when my father stopped traveling, Nicola looked him up at home. They sat at the big table and didn't say very much. My father had had cards printed that read: "The Grunberg family wishes you a pleasant stay." He handed them out whenever we had visitors.

Nicola's face could have been made of old leather, and his nose was like a skinned beefsteak tomato. He explained that he had driven into a tree one day and gone up in flames. At first I could hardly bear to look at him, but later I got used to it.

One afternoon I was sitting at the table alone with him because my father had gone to the Hema for wine. Nicola called me Li'l Lantern. His chest and his stomach seemed made of the same leather as his face, except that they were covered with small blisters. He wore shorts, and his legs were normal, just like ordinary people's legs.

He said, "How would you like it if I made us some pancakes with sour cream?"

I said it was too hot for that. He drank tea with rum because he always had a cold, and he said, "I was born in Budapest and I used to work in a barbershop there, but actually I'm a cook. I was in the army, and let me tell you, every soldier who ever tasted my food longs to have me back. 'Our mothers could learn a few things from you,' they'd say. At the end of every afternoon I was told who I wouldn't need to cook for anymore. I thought to myself, They'll be digesting my food in paradise, anyway. Best not to spend the whole day looking forward to a nice chop, thinking of how your mouth would water at the very thought of a drumstick, just before they blew you to kingdom come. I could teach them a thing or two about cooking even in paradise, I can tell you."

He said, "This time I'll have it without the tea." Then he went on, "You're not the only one I've called Li'l Lantern. The first woman I ever had a crush on I too called Li'l Lantern, because it happened to be her name. She worked in the kitchen just like me. I guess stories like this must bore you."

"No," I said.

He scratched one of his little blisters. "It itches," he said. "It doesn't hurt, it just itches. It itches like hell. Excuse me."

He took a big gulp and I did too. That was the way to drink rum, he'd taught me.

"Me and Li'l Lantern always went along to look after the day's casualties," he said. "Some might have lost their hands. Or they still had their hands but they couldn't use them anymore. We had to feed those. We could see that a little soup was unlikely to do them much good anymore and that we'd do better saving the soup for those it could still do some good for. But how can you refuse a little soup to a dying man? So Li'l Lantern would pour the soup down their throats. Each time she'd say, 'He's fallen for me, the fool.' She meant me. Next thing I knew she was transferred. With love it's just like with soup. I knew some who had to make do with their mother's love. They died without ever having touched a girl. There were orphans among them, too, and Li'l Lantern was probably the only woman who ever kissed them. Other ones were married, even had children, but still called for their mothers when they were brought in to us. There were some who whispered a message in my ear for their girl, but I couldn't make out all the dialects they spoke. And often they were so far gone they had no idea who I was. There were also some who were carrying photographs of maybe five different women, and others who walked around with a letter from their sister. They all ate my soup and my pancakes. If they couldn't hold a pen anymore, I'd often write something for them. When all is said and done, most letters are as alike as your right breast is to your left, whether it was for their sister or their wife or their old mother. Later I met women from the city who said, 'Give me a couple of pounds of flour.' I'd give them the flour because that much flour wouldn't be missed, and then I'd make love to them. Sometimes for less than fifteen minutes, sometimes for a whole night. Sometimes in the open air or in a derelict house, sometimes in a house where there was still sugar on the table and cups of tea, but I never knew whether it was the woman's own sugar. I made love to women who had given birth to thirteen children, but I also made love to girls who could have been my daughters. I've loved brunettes and women with gray hair. I've held redheads in my arms, I've shared a bed with women who hadn't been able to wash for weeks, but even unwashed women are still women. I've made love to women who were so ugly that I would never have dreamed I could ever make love to them. There were some who showed me photographs of their children and others who showed me photographs of their husband. And they'd ask if I hadn't maybe run into him somewhere and they'd describe him down to the last detail, but I had seen so many people. Some of the men said to me, don't you think it's too bad they give themselves to *us* for nothing? 'Ah well,' I said, 'I'd sooner have them for nothing too.' I'd also sooner have had this rum for nothing, and I can tell you that my mother, who bought these leather shoes for me, would just as soon not have paid for them either. I lived at a time when love got cheaper all the time. When Li'l Lantern left us, half a pound of flour was the going rate, and sometimes a little soup.

There were some men with us who scared even me, who would as soon poke your eyes out as shoot a rabbit. But even human scum stop being scum when they're about to die. Not because they feel any remorse but because they can't help themselves. So we poured soup down those men's throats as well. They changed, much as beautiful women don't look like beautiful women any-more after they've stepped on a mine.

"There was one who had been the most beautiful of all. I only knew that from what the men said who brought her in. The most beautiful of them all, they said, they swore it to me, the most beautiful woman in the village, a beauty out of this world, due to be married in a month. I said, 'Which one of you is the bride-groom?' A man stepped forward. I said, 'You can have some soup, but not the rest, or we won't have enough for the wounded.' I only got to know that beauty who was out of this world after she was a mess, and she wasn't even in that state for more than two hours, because then she died. She still had a little of my soup. The boy stayed with her all night. His wails and screams were so dreadful and so loud that none of us could get any sleep. We were due to move on the next day. So that's why we laid the bride outside in a place out of earshot early in the morning and that's where she was buried the next day."

Then my father came back from the Hema and Nicola said, "Sometimes I think it would be nice to be lying in some little grave somewhere, but death doesn't need a helping hand in this world of ours so I wait my turn in patience."

When I returned at eleven o'clock, supper was still going on. And my father was still looking at it as if it were poison.

Part Four

THE GIRLS

CARPENTER'S GLUE

*H*e ordered a coffee in the bar of the Okura Hotel and I had a vodka. We were trying to figure out whether the girl with the Japanese man was a bar girl. We couldn't really picture a bar girl in a kilt. But then, what did we know? There were probably hundreds of bar girls walking around in kilts.

"So I became a driver," he said, stirring his coffee. "A driver for my girlfriend."

He drove an old Opel Kadet to Poland and back three times a month, transporting carpenter's glue, which his girlfriend then sold in Poland, supporting him out of the profits. He would be leaving again in half an hour. The last time this month.

The Japanese man and the girl in the kilt got up.

"She'll be waiting at the border with the papers at eleven o'clock," he said. "I'll probably take a nap somewhere in Germany, just an hour or so in some parking lot."

I ordered another vodka.

"Go easy on that," he said. "For the price of two vodkas in this place you can buy a whole bottle at Gall and Gall's."

The Japanese man gave his room number. The girl had already put on her coat.

"No," I said, "no way she's a bar girl. If she's a bar girl, then so's my mother."

"What do you know about bar girls," he said, "let alone the kind of bar girls Japanese men go for?"

"That guy's has been talking to her for a whole hour. Why would he bother talking to a bar girl for a whole hour?"

He waved dismissively. It was clear he didn't feel like discussing the matter any further.

"They play Mozart in the men's room here," I said, for something to say.

"I would never have thought I'd become a driver," he said. "A hauler of carpenter's glue."

He ordered another coffee, and when the bartender put it down in front of him he said, "Sir, I'm a hauler of carpenter's glue," but the bartender ignored him.

A man and a woman came in, both wearing black shirts with a pattern of brown violins. They sat at the other end of the bar. They were drinking beer.

"I'm a loner," he said.

"No, you're not. Otherwise you wouldn't be sitting here."

"I'm sitting here because I'm off in a moment to Poland with a load of carpenter's glue. She'll be waiting at the border with the papers at eleven o'clock. That's why I'm sitting here. Because I have to take a load of carpenter's glue to Poland. For my girlfriend."

"Are you in love with her?"

"Don't ask complicated questions. Please. I have to be on the road all night."

I ordered another vodka.

"That makes one and a half bottles at Gall and Gall's," he said under his breath.

"If you mention Gall and Gall's once more . . ."

"Well, what?"

"Nothing."

"I hope it isn't going to freeze."

"What's the forecast?"

"Black ice. I bought a side-view mirror from a wrecker's yard this afternoon for nineteen and a half guilders, because the last one broke off when I was trying to park in Poland."

He asked for a Pils. "You mustn't drink anything but Pils in the Okura," he said.

The people with the brown violins on their shirts were kissing now. "A bar girl?" I asked softly.

He slapped his forehead. "What do you know about bar girls?" he said, and emptied his glass. "A side-view mirror for nineteen and a half guilders is a bargain, one hell of a bargain, let me tell you. Normally those things can set you back two hundred guilders or more, but I can't see a thing through that carpenter's glue. The car's packed to the roof with that damn carpenter's glue. Another Pils?"

A couple more Japanese men came in.

"Maybe you should start a trucking business. You might have a big success with it."

He just looked at me.

"Is that a new deodorant or have you just polished your shoes?"

"Come on," I said. "I've just polished my shoes."

"My girlfriend in Poland is absolutely crazy about perfume, French perfume. She really lets herself go with Coco or whatever it's called. I always take her some perfume to keep her sweet."

"Another vodka."

The bartender came over to fill my glass. He no longer asked if I wanted it on the rocks, which was a good sign.

"That makes two bottles from Gall and Gall's," he said under his breath, tapping on the bar along with the music.

"Let's go to Gall and Gall's then," I said. He was driving me mad.

He asked the bartender the time and reset his watch.

"I just hope that glue isn't going to shift around."

He put on his coat.

"I'll be back Tuesday night. I'll come here for a Pils then. And Thursday night I'll be off again because they're crazy about that carpenter's glue in Poland. On the way back I always eat sauerkraut and sausage somewhere near Hannover. I'm a great one for tradition, you see. I'm a great one for tradition."

I nodded to show that I saw. He wanted to pay for me. I said there was no need, but he insisted.

"It's on my girlfriend. I'm going to keep her sweet with half a gallon of perfume. There are people who expect much more than that." He laughed.

"Is it going to freeze tonight?" he asked the bartender.

"I haven't a clue, sir." The bartender was wearing a pink bow tie. He started to turn away.

"Listen, I asked if it was going to freeze tonight. It's a perfectly normal question. Is it going to freeze tonight or not? How long have you been working here?"

"Three years, sir."

"And you mean to say that in all those three years no one's ever asked you if it's going to freeze? Or maybe it never did freeze in all those three years? As far as you know."

"As far as I know, it must be freezing in your head, sir."

He came back and sat down next to me again.

"I use diesel. That makes a big difference. You save over 50 percent. And the engine's less noisy. It's smoother, you know. It goes toof, toof, toof, almost like music. Would you like a lift?"

"No, I'll hang around here for a while longer," I said.

He walked outside but five minutes later he was back.

He pointed to a girl who had sat down at the other end of the bar.

"A bar girl," he said. "Thirty bottles at Gall and Gall's."

He picked up a bowl of nuts from the bar, emptied it into his coat pocket, and walked off.

TINA

*I*t was four o'clock, and although I knew that by now my
mother wouldn't have eaten ordinary bread for hours and that
I shouldn't really be eating ordinary bread either, I was hungry.
And I knew that I'd be going around to see her that evening and
we'd tell the story again about how we'd been slaves in Egypt,
and we'd mention the ten plagues, and we'd recite the piece about
why this night was different from all other nights. God, it made
me feel sick just thinking about it. That's why I ordered another
beer. I was sitting next to the Pole, and tonight my mother and
I would be on our own again, because no other guests would be
coming. She'd invited a whole lot of people but no one had
wanted to come, and in the end she'd called me.

"You wouldn't leave me by myself on seder evening, would
you?"

"No," I said, "I wouldn't leave you by yourself."

"What's the soup of the day?" I heard a woman ask.

"There's no soup of the day. We only have a soup of the year."

Leo turned around and said, "The only thing they have in this café is a soup of the century."

"The soup of the century is gas chamber soup," I said. "Does this café have any gas chamber soup?"

I'd been doing nothing all day, which is when I come out with that kind of thing. Anyway, no one listens to me—that's why I come here every day. To be among people who have one mouth and two ears. According to the Pole there were fewer and fewer of those around, people with one mouth and two ears. "You hardly see them anymore," he said. "Only at fairgrounds."

Finally I rode my bike over to my mother's. She was sick. That was all I needed. She was coughing and spluttering. Now and then she'd yell, "I can't get my breath!" She'd been yelling that for as long as I'd known her.

We sat at the table. She pointed to the black swivel chair. "Two years ago your father was still sitting there," she said. I hated that sort of sob stuff. So I said, "He didn't sit—he slumped. And his food dribbled out of his mouth the whole time. In fact, his whole body dribbled out of every orifice you care to mention."

"Don't be so cynical," she said. "I don't like it."

I wasn't being cynical, I was being truthful. It's too bad the truth can end up sounding cynical, which is why you're often better off lying. If you want people to like you, that is.

We did everything we were supposed to do that evening. We dipped radishes in salt water, we mixed *maror* with *charoset*, we referred to the bread of affliction that our ancestors ate, and we sang the song about the sea that fled and the mountains that skipped like rams, the hills like lambs. And about the earth that trembled in the presence of the God of Jacob, who turned the rock into a pool and the flint rock into a fountain. And then we sang about being in Jerusalem next year. We also drank the obligatory four cups of wine, only my mother wasn't allowed alcohol— she was back on sleeping pills. So I drank her share. That wasn't too difficult.

At about twelve o'clock I went home. I kissed her and wished her good health and happiness. "How do I get those?" she asked, but I didn't have an answer to that.

The next morning I had to be up early because I was going to lug books around again for forty guilders or so. I got paid for doing reader's reports now and then, too, but because my head had been feeling as if people were dancing on a stone floor inside it I hadn't read anything for a while, so I had no choice but to go do some lugging. I'd beg money from my mother occasionally, too, but to be honest, I preferred lugging things till I was practically dead.

When all the books had been stacked in the warehouse, I ate a piece of cake and bought *De Telegraaf*. It took me a good half hour to read all the personal ads. There were a lot of them. To start with, I had no idea which sort to go for. In the end, I opted for the kind, good-looking woman who received clients privately. Kind, good-looking, and private—that suited me perfectly. I dialed her number. Sometimes when I'm on the telephone I say, "Sorry, my hearing's not too good anymore. Would you mind speaking up?" I do that to sound older. I did it this time too. It worked. I asked what she charged. A hundred guilders an hour. That was a lucky break. I'd thought it would be a lot more. I had three hundred guilders in the bank, all there was left. I asked if I could still make an appointment for that afternoon. I could. At five o'clock, because she stopped work at six. I hung up but I'd forgotten to ask her address. I nearly died of embarrassment calling her back. It was on Brederodestraat. I didn't even know where that was so I had to go to my newspaper man to buy a map of Amsterdam. Fortunately, it was on the other side of Vondel Park, not very far away. I took a shower, brushed my teeth carefully, and put on clean socks and a new pair of underpants. You had to make an effort to look decent and avoid bad breath. It was the least you could do. I drank another couple of glasses of wine but then I really had to go.

First I walked through Vondel Park. That part was fine. But I came out at the wrong end of Brederodestraat. Gradually, though, I came to her number. What I really wanted to do was walk straight past, just like everybody else on Brederodestraat. I said to myself, "Be a man." I'd never said that to myself before, so that was a new experience for me as well.

I rang the doorbell. A black cloth had been hung across the windows instead of curtains, but the place looked like an ordinary house otherwise. She opened the door, and I couldn't tell if she was kind—it was too soon for that—but I did know for sure that she wasn't good-looking. Far from it. My parents used to have a cleaning lady named Mrs. Kanon. She used to pull my hair a lot, and then she'd say, "What lovely curls you have. I wish I had curls like that, boy." She always called me "boy," and she was so old then that she's in an old age home now.

We went into a sort of doctor's waiting room. At least that's what it looked like. It was an entrance hall with a telephone and even a small computer. I headed for the first door I saw. "Whoa, whoa," she said. "I'm the one who knows where we're going."

"Right. Of course," I said. "Sorry, ma'am."

She showed me into a room where everything was blue. Blue light, blue sheets on the bed, blue basin, blue lace curtains, everything blue except a black sofa and a green plant, but that was probably made of plastic.

"My name's Tina," she said.

I introduced myself and she asked what I wanted to drink. She didn't have wine. Just mineral water, Coke, or tea. "Then let's have tea," I said.

"We work in pairs here," said Tina. "The other girl will be here to introduce herself in a moment and then you can choose which one of us you want to go with."

She left me alone sitting on the sofa. There was a photograph on the wall, but the light was too blue to make it out. There were two blue bathrobes hanging from a hook, and music was coming out of a cassette player. It was the kind of music they play in cafés when there are too few customers and the ones who are there are so old that they're too deaf to pay any attention.

Then the other girl came in. She was, if possible, even uglier than Tina, and it seemed to me that it would be only a matter of months before she'd be entitled to travel on a senior citizen's ticket. I got to my feet and held out my hand. "Arnon Grunberg, ma'am," I said. "How do you do?"

"Never give your last name," she hissed at me as if I'd made an indecent proposal. "I beg your pardon," I said. Then she went away again.

It was incredibly hot in the room. I couldn't help it—I had to take off my jacket. Then I sat on it. I thought, Before you know where you are they'll steal it. Business is business.

Tina came back. "I'll go with you," I said, since at least with her I could keep my last name, and that was worth quite a bit to me.

She came and sat down next to me on the sofa. We both drank a cup of tea. I started to feel quite at home.

"Have you ever been in a house like this before?" she asked.

"Long ago," I said. "Abroad. So long ago that I've forgotten the rules."

"Don't worry about the rules. You'll get to know them as you go along."

She drew closer. I remembered the line from that poem by Gottfried Benn: "What a wonderful thought, to be lying between the legs of a girl." Suddenly I couldn't understand why I'd ever thought the line was so great.

"Do you do this every day?" I asked her eventually, when she was sitting so close to me that her leg was touching mine. "Tell me if my questions bother you, ma'am."

"No, it's all right," she said. "Yes, I do this every day, although I'm really just the telephone girl, hostess, and bouncer, but after five o'clock one of the girls knocks off and then I fill in for an hour or so."

"I see," I said.

"And what sort of work do you do?"

"I'm a correspondent for the *Berliner Morgenpost*," I said.

"Oh, that sort of work."

"Too bad there's no Jacques Brel music, ma'am, isn't it?"

"Jacques Brel's more for listening to in private," she said. "And please don't keep calling me 'ma'am.' We're going to have intercourse in a minute or two and it'll be a lot easier if you call me Tina. Incidentally, are you Jewish, if you don't mind my asking?"

"I don't mind at all. I expect you could tell by my big nose."

"No, it's more the way you act. Actually, I'm Jewish too. An eighth Jewish, anyway. And take a look at *my* nose!"

She showed it to me. A hook nose if ever there was one. I swallowed the last of my tea.

"My grandfather was Jewish," she said.

"Oh," I said. "How nice."

"It's Passover. Did you know?"

"Yes," I said, "I know it's Passover."

I looked at the photograph on the wall but still couldn't make it out, and then I looked at the bed, where a towel was lying, just as blue as the sheet.

"Usually we get down to the financial details at this point."

"Of course," I said. I fished the hundred guilders out of the inside pocket of my jacket.

"We, too, have to eat," she said. It sounded like an apology.

"Of course you have to eat, ma'am. I have to eat, we all have to eat."

"Tina," she said. "You must call me Tina." Then she went out of the room to put the money away and I tried but failed to remember what Rosie had looked like when I'd seen her naked that first time.

She was back. "Did you come by car?" she asked.

"I don't have a car. I walked through Vondel Park."

We sat down again next to each other on the sofa. I could

smell her perfume now because she was sitting very close. She ran her hand over my leg. "Shall I get the ball rolling, then?"

"Yes," I said, "you get the ball rolling."

"What do you like best?" she asked.

"Well," I said, and wiped my nose with the back of my hand.

"Well?"

"I don't want to sound impolite, ma'am, but I really would appreciate it if you'd go down on me."

"You say exactly what you'd like," said Tina. "You really want me to go down on you? You don't want to have intercourse?"

"No," I said, "I'd rather not have intercourse today."

In fact I didn't want her to go down on me either. I didn't want anything at all. I just wanted to go on sitting on that sofa and talking about this and that until the hour was up, but I was too scared to say so.

"Let's get undressed then."

"Right, let's do that."

She took her clothes off very quickly, but I was pretty quick too. I was surprised to find that I didn't feel embarrassed in the slightest, which I generally do if I get undressed in front of other people. We stood there at the foot of the bed and for a little while there was silence, and eventually I asked, "Do you have any pets?"

"We'll go and wash now," she said.

I looked at her wrinkled belly and at her breasts, which drooped like wilting flowers, and I followed her to the washbasin. She washed herself with the blue washcloth, first her pussy, then her ass. That didn't seem all that promising. I was about to pick up the other washcloth to wash myself but she said, "No, let me do it."

I put the cloth down again. "That's nice," I said. "I haven't been washed since I was seven."

"But you've been under the shower since then, I hope."

"Of course. What I meant was that I've washed *myself* since then."

She washed me very thoroughly, just the way my mother used to.

"Now a quick wash of your hands too," she said, seizing my left hand and squirting liquid soap into it, while the music went on twanging away.

"Go lie down," she said.

I lay down on the bed, my head on the blue pillow, and I couldn't help wondering how many heads had lain on that very spot.

"Don't you want to take your glasses off?" she asked.

"I think I'll keep them on."

"You want to see everything, is that it?"

"Yes," I said, "I want to see everything." But to myself I thought, If I take them off I can kiss them good-bye.

"Try not to knock them off my face," I urged.

"What funny ideas you have about us," said Tina, running her hand over my stomach. I was reminded of our family doctor, who also used to feel my stomach and whose hands were just as cold as Tina's. "People think we hate men, but I honestly don't."

I believed her, that she didn't hate men. No more than I did, anyway.

Then she flicked her index finger against my prick, as if trying to knock some dust off it. I lay with my arms under my head, talking a blue streak while I stared at the ceiling as if the angel were about to appear and call out, "Drop the knife, Abraham!"

"Does it tickle?" she asked.

"Yes," I said, "just a little."

"My grandfather never came back," she said.

She had set to work on my member. She was kneading it and kneading my balls too.

I said, "I'm sorry. How terrible," and I thought that this was all much easier than I had expected. You lay down, you made some small talk the way you would with anybody, you looked at the ceiling for a while in just the same way as you looked at the ceiling anywhere else.

"Turn over onto your stomach," she said, because I still didn't have an erection. I wasn't embarrassed about it, but it was a little disappointing.

"I'll give you a nice massage. Would you like that?"

"Fine, great."

So I turned over onto my stomach and she sat on top of me, or that's what it felt like, and massaged me with some body lotion that smelled like Dreft. While she busied herself with my shoulders my face was being pushed into the blue pillow and I could smell yet more nameless smells.

"So are you still observant?"

"Well, not really. What about you?"

"I used to be, but not anymore. For a while I was very committed."

She was now massaging my neck, and asked if I liked it. It wasn't such a big deal.

"Very nice," I said.

"Do you think the Palestinians are entitled to a state of their own?"

"Give them thirty-five states if they want them," I said. "I don't know anything about it. I'm not all that interested in politics."

She told me to turn over onto my back again. She kissed my face. That was something I hadn't expected, that she'd kiss my face too. Then she started sucking my nipples. I went on staring up at the ceiling and at the photograph, and I noticed that the towel had been moved so that I was now lying on the sheet, where they had all lain, of course, and I wondered how often she changed the sheet. She was still working on my nipples.

"Do you like that?" she asked. I didn't dare say no, because I'd already answered "No" or "I'd rather you didn't" a couple of times to the same sort of question.

"Great," I said, and I could hear that weirdo Jackson singing "Heal the World," and I suddenly remembered the man in the café, because he'd thought that song was fantastic.

"Randy Newman, he's all right," I said.

"Yes," she said, "Randy Newman's all right. But stop talking all the time. You don't have to go on about everything."

"I'm not much use unless I can talk."

"Relax," she said, "relax." It was an order, but you can't relax to order. Not me, anyway.

Then she started to play with my prick, just until it got stiff. She did it very professionally because I'd been convinced she'd never manage to give me an erection this side of the millennium, and then, presto, she'd got a condom over it. After that she pretended to suck me off, but because I was wearing my glasses I could see everything. All she did was jerk me off a bit.

Luckily there was a good song on that tape of hers, and I told her so, but she said, "Take it easy, take it easy. You're talking a lot less already."

I could smell my own armpit because I was lying with my arms under my head on the blue pillow.

You wouldn't have called Tina ugly, at least not if she'd been working in a diner. Things would have been different then. As it was she was just plain unappetizing, and no doubt she found me unappetizing as well. She'd been trying to jerk me off for fifteen minutes by that time. Nothing was happening. I had stopped thinking about anything anymore except perhaps, just in passing, about Randy Newman, since one of his songs was stuck in my head.

Finally she looked at me. "Have you ever been with a woman?"

"Yes," I said.

"How many before me?" she asked, laughing.

I said, "Exactly twenty-one."

She was the second, and I tried to remember what it had been like with the first but failed again. I thought that Tina really should have been the twenty-second, or the last, or the ninety-eighth. Not the second. She asked if perhaps we should have intercourse. That was fine by me.

"That's nice," she said.

Why did she have to say something like that when no one asked her to?

"You do what you want," I said.

"No, it's you," she said, "it's what you want that counts."

"That's just what I don't know."

She sat on top of me and guided me inside, but there wasn't much difference between inside and out.

"Did you lose a lot of your family during the war too?" she asked.

"No one," I said. "I was born after the war."

"My grandfather was the only one I lost."

Then she started to move up and down, and I watched those breasts of hers flapping about in all directions like flowers in an autumn gale, and her belly with its twelve double chins was pressed close to my stomach like meat on a butcher's slab.

Pretty soon she stopped again, and then she just stayed there sitting still on top of me.

"You'd better come and lie on me now."

So I did. But if she'd said that I'd better go and hang in the closet, I would have done that too. Because it had become clear to me by then that I had to be careful not to make an issue out of anything around there.

She grabbed my prick and pushed it inside her again. She felt warm and a little damp. In fact the whole room felt like that.

I looked at her face and I could smell her perfume now even more strongly than before.

"Go on!" she suddenly shouted. "Oh, go on, go on, go on!"

I would have liked to say, "Please shut up. I can do without the noise," but I didn't dare to because it couldn't have been a joke for her to have to shout "Go on, go on" all the time, and certainly not when you remembered that she must have been shouting it since ten that morning. I could see by the clock next to the sofa that it was five after six already, and I suddenly had the sneaking feeling that she wouldn't let me go until I'd come.

It was probably a matter of honor with her. Even if she had to go on till seven o'clock. So I looked at the wall, grabbed hold of her head, her curls, or rather her half-grown-out perm, stuck my nails in her head, and pressed it against my chest, and I could smell twenty beauty parlors all at once. I looked at the wall, but no angel appeared. I thought of Rosie, I kept thinking of Rosie, and then I shut my eyes tight and went on thinking of Rosie. After that I came. Then she stopped shouting "Go on, go on."

"You know which is my favorite Randy Newman?" I said. " 'Everybody knows my name, but it's just a crazy game. It's lonely at the top.' "

"You'd better get off me now," she said. "Otherwise you'll get too heavy."

I lay down beside her. "You can say a lot of things about me, that I have hair like a poodle or a big nose, but you can't say I'm too heavy."

She laughed. I wanted to get dressed but she said, "No, don't. Wait a moment, I still have to wash you. I can't let you go all dirty."

"What service!"

She took off my condom and washed me for the second time. I just hoped she was using the good washcloth. I could see that the towel had slipped off the bed, but luckily the light was so blue that the sheet was almost invisible.

I got dressed.

"Do you mind if I don't get dressed again, and just keep my bathrobe on?" she asked.

I nodded. She sat beside me in her blue robe and I put on my sweater.

"I don't like Randy Newman one bit," she said.

"Really? But you told me you liked him a lot."

"That was then."

I looked at her face again and discovered that it put me off much less than it had when I first walked in.

"Do I have time to put my shoes on in here or would you rather I did it outside on the stoop?"

"What a low opinion you have of us!"

"Not just you, the whole world. Incidentally, it's incredibly hot in here, did you know that?"

"That's probably because of me."

I thought she was joking, but her face told me that she meant it. Or that she wanted me to think she meant it. So I said, "Yes, Tina, it's because of you."

And I put my hand on her leg, but I could see that she didn't like my hand on her leg anymore. So I took it away quickly.

"Do you happen to have a piece of cloth for my glasses?" She did.

"What service," I said again. "The Hilton can't touch you." I promised to bring around a bunch of flowers for her later that week. Then we both stood up. I looked at the plant, the bed, and the wall.

"Where are you going to eat tonight?" I asked.

"At my mother's. Endive. And you?"

"I'll be celebrating seder. At my mother's too. And then I have to go see a family with four daughters."

Tina said, "Well, you're bound to have a much more relaxed seder now."

"Yes," I said. "Much more relaxed."

I kissed her hand. We walked to the door and I looked for the other girl but she had probably gone home.

"So long," I said, and lifted my hand to my head, the way soldiers do.

"You're really a bit of a nut," she said.

I kissed her hand again. Now that she wasn't wearing heels she was shorter than I was, and I said, "Goodbye, Tina. It was a great pleasure to meet you."

"You were born in the wrong century," she said. "You ought to be wearing a top hat."

"We were all born in the wrong century," I said.

"Will you be coming by again?" she asked.

"Yes," I said. "With the greatest of pleasure. *Blayb mir gezunt bis hundertzwantzig*, a *gutn yontif*, and a *kosheren Pesach*."

Then I was out in the street again, with my mouth tasting of soap. I felt like asking all the women I came across, "And what's your price these days?" Pretty hokey, but it's what I felt like saying. I didn't go back home, although I wanted to take a shower. I went to the café and ordered three light beers. Needless to say, the Pole was back again, and beside him a man with a beer belly was holding forth. The Pole was pretending not to listen and I despised him for that. The girl was back again, too, the one who the Pole always said looked like Renée Soutendijk, although I didn't think she looked like anybody.

"Have you been sticking your head down the toilet?" asked the Pole.

"No," I said.

"So what have you been doing?"

I felt like asking the girl what her price was, too, although the urge to ask the question was less pressing than it had been ten minutes before, and it would be less pressing still ten minutes from now. I felt like telling her that Tina was a whole lot cheaper than a meal in the Oyster Bar, though not cheaper than the caviar in this place. And that it was Passover. And that on Passover you weren't allowed to drink beer. I didn't dare say any of it, although I couldn't recall ever having wanted to talk to someone as badly as I wanted to talk to her. I knew I'd be able to say that sort of thing much more easily to Tina, because she didn't give a damn and because she wouldn't run off before the hour was up.

"You don't have much to say for yourself, do you, pal?" said the drunk to the Pole.

"Don't you 'pal' me!"

"You don't have much to say for yourself, sir, do you? You

want me to bug off, is that it? Do all of you in here want me to bug off?"

"Listen," I said, "when I was in elementary school there was a song they always used to play. I've forgotten the tune; all I remember is the words. They went like this: 'What shall we drink in the week to come, what shall we drink for our thirst? There's plenty and more for everyone, so let's drink together in the week to come, yes, let's drink together—we're not on our own.' Can you sing that for me, that song?"

"No," said the Pole. "I know it, of course, but I can't sing. I don't have a voice."

"No one in here can sing," said the drunk.

My mouth now tasted less of soap and more of lemon and stale beer. The second seder was due to begin in an hour and a half and I still had to take a shower.

I thought Tina probably didn't have a Jewish grandfather. She was just very kind, that was all. If it had been an American with her, naturally she would have said that her husband had been killed in Vietnam, and she would have told a Dutchman that her grandpa had fallen on the Grebbeberg, and for a German it would have been Stalingrad. Probably it wasn't even true that she thought I ought to have lived in a different century. She had simply said what she thought I wanted to hear, since that was what all the Tinas in the world were like. I ordered another light beer to wash the last remnants of that soapy taste out of my mouth.

The fact that I had thought of Rosie was just one of those things. All the men who had lain on that blue pillow had thought of their Rosies as well, of course. They had all kidded themselves, like me, that they were different from the others. That they were much more polite, that they hadn't treated Tina like a whore. Some had even promised her flowers and kissed her hand, believing that Tina talked to them as she did to no other client. Just like me, they had all pissed in Vondel Park and had then gone into a café thinking they were unique, exactly as I had thought, quite different from all the other whoremongers. Well, sitting in this café, I wondered how polite you could really be to someone who would get you off for a hundred guilders.

Now that I had been with Tina I was afraid of almost nothing. All you had to do was down a couple of drinks and say to yourself, "Be a man!" That was all there was to it. It probably wouldn't be all that difficult to shoot someone either. Or to hack someone to pieces, or to jump off the Okura. It would only be a question of a couple of drinks and saying to yourself, "Be a man."

I bought flowers for my mother, and we did again exactly what we had done the night before. After we finished the meal I had to go visit the family with the four daughters. The oldest, Deborah, had been in my class at Vossius, a long time ago. I had been in love with her, and her parents used to play me that Randy Newman record. This evening I asked if I could hear it again, but they couldn't find it.

They had finished their supper when I arrived. I had to sit next to one of Deborah's sisters. She had two sisters there, Zotka and Nitka. Those weren't their real names, though. It's what I called them to myself. I was sitting next to Zotka. She kept looking at me but I didn't look back at her.

After a while I said I was awfully tired and would it be all right if I lay down on the sofa? I pretended to sleep, and I could hear them wondering in whispers whether I really enjoyed the seder. Oh, I enjoyed it very much. I enjoyed it immensely.

I thought of Rosie. That everything was all right. Even though she had never written to me again and I would never see her again. Everything was all right, and I also knew that I would never call her again, because I had nothing to say to her.

Wherever we might meet, I would always see her in a blue bathrobe. And whatever she said to me, all I'd hear her say would be, "Shall I get the ball rolling, then?" And I would answer, "Yes, you get the ball rolling."

A PRAYER FOR MARCELLA
(PRONOUNCED MARSHALLA)

I took the seven o'clock train to Zandvoort. I had a thermos of wine with me, but it wasn't properly cold anymore because I'd been lugging it around with me half the night. It was the first really warm night of the spring and my bathtub was stopped up.

I'd been visiting my Polish friend but had overlooked the fact that it was past three in the morning when I rang his doorbell. He hadn't been able to sleep either, and we played chess. He warmed up some soup, to stop us from getting drunk, he said, but the soup didn't help. At five o'clock he decided to crawl back into bed.

I knew that a plumber would set me back two hundred guilders, which was why I decided to go to the beach at Zandvoort. I rode my bike home and filled the thermos. I tried emptying the tub with a pail, but more water kept running back in. It was starting to stink.

Then I walked to the station. No trains were running yet. Some people were standing about at the entrance, but I didn't feel like company. I could see that face again, and it occurred to me that I'd probably be seeing it for quite a while. There are some faces that lose their beauty slowly, there are others that have had all the beauty battered out of them, and there are still others that will have all the beauty battered out of them one day. The nice thing about poorly lit cafés is that not only can you have a drink in them but you can turn a blind eye to lots of things there too. If you ask me, it would be a very good thing if not just cafés but the rest of the world were a little more poorly lit.

I walked along the islands to the west of the station. It's a beautiful part of town, especially early in the mornings, when there's nobody around. On Prinseneiland I opened my thermos for the first time, but the wine was already lukewarm.

The beach was still empty when I arrived. I rented a deckchair. The Queen's Birthday had been splendid, I read in the paper. That was all I read because then I fell asleep. By the time I woke up, the beach was full of people. That made me thirsty, so I opened my thermos again. It had been a present from my mother. I thought of my mother and of the Queen's Birthday and tried to remember why I had wanted to become a publisher once upon a time. I had made up a whole lot of different stories about it and could no longer recall which of them was true. Probably I had simply forgotten the reason, much as I had forgotten why I had written that girl all those letters, or why I had pulled the curtains down in Mrs. De Wilde's classroom, or why I had made that appointment with Tina one Tuesday in April. There were some things that you just did, leaving the thinking about it for later. Of course the psychologists who had treated me had been full of wonderful explanations for my behavior. They were so wonderful that the tears came to your eyes every time you heard them.

All right then, I had pulled down those curtains, I had been kicked out of school, and I had had to work in an office. After they had kicked me out of there, too, I had turned to publishing books, and not long after that I had gone broke.

I could no longer remember why I'd ever wanted to do any of those things. A few weeks before I had received a letter from a printer. I left it lying around for a few days. Some letters I open only when it seems that things may be looking up a little. One evening I read it: "Dear Sir, You say you have no means of settling your debt. I must tell you that anyone on welfare and with a little goodwill can find three hundred and fifty-five guilders (four hundred and fifty, including fees). You are nothing but a fraud. We will shortly be paying you a visit to collect in person. If I were you, I'd make sure to be at home, and with the money in hand, for experience has shown that the costs can otherwise mount up considerably. Regards, Lou."

There were quite a few other printers I owed money to, but none had ever threatened to come around to collect in person.

The next day I went to my mother and said that I needed three hundred and fifty-five guilders urgently, or else my windows would be smashed in.

I hid the money in the bottom drawer of my desk. I was due to go back to my friend's that evening for wine and some of the garlic sausage he brought back from Poland every time he delivered his carpenter's glue.

I had tried to read all day, but it was no good. In the evening I didn't have any luck either. That's why I looked at the ads again. I didn't think about calling at first; I just wanted to read them. I was drinking Sicilian wine, which was going down quite nicely. After a while I made a call anyway, because the money was sitting there in the bottom drawer of my desk.

The lady asked what I wanted.

"What can you offer?" I asked.

"No," she said, "what do you want?"

"Something European."

That was the most noncommittal thing I could think of.

"What do you mean?"

"A blond."

But I was only saying that for the sake of something to say.

"I'll try to get one on the beeper. I'll call you back in a moment."

"Fine," I said, and went on drinking the Sicilian wine.

She called back in five minutes.

"Mr. Greenberg?" she said. "Did you just call us?"

"Yes," I said. "It's me. Hello."

"Right," she said. "We've been very busy because of the Queen's Birthday."

"I'm not surprised."

"All the blond girls are out working or due to start shortly. But I have a gorgeous little girl for you. Mixed. She really is the most beautiful girl we have."

"A gorgeous little mixed girl." I took another drink. "Suits me fine," I said.

"Would you like a brief description of her?"

"No, no," I said. "I'll see for myself." I thought of Tina, and of much more.

"Then I'll send her around to you now. Have a good evening and enjoy yourself, Mr. Greenberg."

"Many thanks. You too."

I sprayed my armpits with deodorant, looked in the mirror, and squeezed a pimple. Then I jerked off over the wastebasket. I do that quite often. Over the wastebasket. With my head leaning against the wall, and then I look at everything that's in the wastebasket. When I finished I went back to my desk and read the printer's letter again. Then I tore it up.

The woman had said the girl would be coming over at eleven, and when she wasn't there by eleven I told myself that she wouldn't be coming at all. Which wouldn't have surprised me. Far from it.

At five after eleven the doorbell rang. A boy and a girl were standing outside the door. I took her for eighteen or nineteen. As for the boy, I felt sure I'd seen him before. I couldn't remember where.

"Come in," I said.

"Let's settle up," said the boy when we were standing in the hallway.

"Yes, of course."

I went to my desk. Then I remembered where I'd met the boy. In the fall, when my mother had gone to the Black Forest for a cure, I had ordered out for pizzas regularly.

"See you in an hour, Rick," said the girl.

"See you," he said and shut the door. Now I was alone with her.

"Come in," I said.

"Let's introduce ourselves."

"Yes," I said. "Let's do that. I'm Arnon."

Only now could I see her clearly, since it had been too dark in the hallway.

"I'm Marshalla," she said, and held out her hand.

We sat down at the table and I asked her what she wanted to drink.

"What have you got?"

"Wine, water, beer."

"Water, please," she said.

I gave her a glass of water. She produced a pack of cigarettes from her shoulder bag. Dunhill Reds.

"Do you have a light?" she asked.

I passed her a box of matches and poured myself some more Sicilian wine, of which I had bought a whole case.

She could have been twenty-four or sixteen for all I knew. And she really was fantastically beautiful.

"Marcella," I said.

"Marshalla," she said. "Wait, I'll write it down for you."

She picked up my pen and wrote.

"Oh, Marcella," I said.

"Marshalla. God, you've got a lot of books."

"Yes," I said. "Do you mind if I ask how old you are?"

"Didn't they tell you I'm eighteen?"

"No," I said. "They didn't tell me, but then I didn't ask. In any case, they always say that, don't they?"

"And you?"

"Twenty-two."

"That's young," she said. "That's awfully young."

She was wearing a white blouse knotted around her midriff, and a short black skirt, pantyhose, and long knee-high boots with buckles all the way up. I had never seen boots with so many buckles.

"What do you do?"

"I'm a journalist," I said. "What about you? How long have you been doing this sort of thing? You'll say if I'm boring you, won't you?"

"You're not boring me. It's just that they *always* ask the same questions. You're the fourth I've ever been with."

"Were the others OK?"

"The first one was. He was thirty-five. We hit it off all right. But there was another one who wanted me to pee in his mouth. There are limits, right?"

"Yes," I said, "there are limits."

Then both of us were at a loss for words, and I poured myself some more wine.

"Do you need the money? Do you owe people?"

"Well, nothing out of the ordinary," she said. "That's how it goes. My mother was on coke . . ."

"And your father abused you."

"How did you know?"

"It sounds familiar, like I'd heard it a thousand times before. Really, don't you want any wine?"

"No," she said.

So I poured some more for myself because the wine was going down quite nicely.

"Did you have a nice Queen's Birthday?" I asked.

"Very nice. Walked around a lot. How about you?"

"Nice as well."

Silence again.

"What should we do?" I asked.

"Sit here and talk," she said.

"Yes, that's fine too."

She nodded.

"I think I'd like to go to bed with you."

"Do you?" she said.

I had drunk too much wine to be able to tell good lies. When we were out in the hallway, she said, "Do you want to hear something funny? I used to live in a foster home right on this street, and now here I am back again."

"That *is* funny," I said, "very funny."

We went up the stairs, and under her breath she said, "A thing done from compassion finds favor with God."

"Excuse me?" I said.

"That's from the Bible. Didn't you know that? Don't you have a Bible?"

"No, not here."

"You have so many books, and you don't even have a Bible? Don't you believe in God?"

"No," I said, "not in the God you believe in. I have more belief in a little bird fallen out of its nest."

"It's cold in here," she said when we were upstairs.

"My bathtub's not working at the moment, and the heat isn't either."

We sat on the sofa and she took off her boots.

"I can't concentrate too well anymore," she said.

"Sure," I said. Maybe I had misunderstood.

I touched her hair, her beautiful brown hair, which smelled

of the same scent as the whole place had ever since she came in.

"I can't do it," she said suddenly. "Wouldn't you rather have another girl?"

"What's the matter?"

"We did so much talking. When that happens I can't do it. When I talk so much with someone. You can get another girl. Really. I just can't do it. You understand? We did so much talking. Ask for another girl. Send me away."

"Come on, we didn't really talk all that much," I said.

It was a good thing I'd remembered to bring the bottle of wine upstairs with me.

I took a long drink and thought of what that man had told me, that hookers told you nothing but lies. So I said, "No, Marcella, it's you I want. Don't be scared. God is looking after us. God is love. You know that, don't you? Please get undressed."

She stood in front of me and took off her clothes. I sat on the sofa and drank Sicilian wine. She kicked her clothes all over the room. I don't know if all of them do that, kick their clothes all over the room, or if she was the only one to get undressed like that.

I was drinking the wine out of the bottle now. She was naked except for her panties. She stood like that in front of the window, and I thought maybe I ought to have drawn the curtains but I didn't feel like doing that just then.

I went up to her. I put the bottle on the floor.

I held her close. I put my hands on her panties, I moved her a little to one side, and I felt her little hairs that felt no different from the little hairs of other women. I thought of nothing. Just of her, and of her skin that was so light, so light, light brown and smooth and without a single blemish. I smelled the smell of her body, and I felt how warm she was, because every living person is warm when you hold them close.

"Am I making you do this?"

"No, I'm making myself do it. But you take your clothes off now too."

We sat on the sofa again and she said that it was really cold in the room. I got undressed slowly.

"I don't mind anymore," she said, "I honestly don't. Do you know why?"

"No," I said, "but I don't want to know either. In any case, you're the most beautiful girl I've ever met."

"You shouldn't say that."

"You didn't expect me to say something like that, did you?"

She shook her head.

"I didn't either. I swear I didn't either," I said.

"It's been said to me a little too often, you know what I mean?"

I did. I got up from the sofa, kicking over the bottle, which spilled on the carpet. I didn't pick it up. I remember telling myself that all I wanted was to get just a little bit tipsy, just pleasantly loose, and how I had accidentally got slightly drunk instead, and how my slight drunkenness had turned into full-blown drunkenness. As inevitably as night turns to day and day turns to night and night back to day. I started wondering who it was who had written that not every night ends with the dawn.

We lay down on the floor and I stroked her hair and her face and we kissed. They had told me that hookers never kiss, but I tasted her mouth and she must have tasted mine. I remembered all those nights when I had walked home and had kissed somebody somewhere in the street, and how I could no longer remember who they were or even what sex they were. Sometimes you're so loaded it makes no difference. A tongue in your mouth is a tongue in your mouth then, whether it's a man's, a woman's, or a dog's. My gums had been giving me trouble lately, and when that happens just one tongue in your mouth is really too much. There were nights when I came home and thought, If I hang

myself now I'll leave a note: This isn't suicide, just sex by stran-
gulation.

Her hair tickled my chest and I could tell that she was looking
at me. I saw from her brown eyes that she was watching my face.
I liked that, being watched by her.

I took off her panties.

"Do you have a condom?" I asked.

"Do you need one already?"

"Yes," I said, "I need one already."

She opened her purse, and in a single rapid movement slid
the condom over my prick.

"Would you like me to go down on you?" she asked. "Do you
like that?"

"No," I said, "but thanks all the same."

Then I thought of everything she had said and of the way she
had come in and the way she had looked at me when she took
off her clothes, and I thought of her skin, and the small patch of
hair between her legs, and of her shoulder bag and her boots with
all those buckles and her white blouse, and of her tongue and the
grooves in her lips highlighted by her lipstick, and I thought of
her small nose with those tiny, almost invisible blackheads, and
of what it felt like when I entered her. I thought of all those
things, which is why it didn't last long.

This time I was allowed to remain lying beside her.

"Little Marshalla," I said.

"Little Arnon," she said.

I saw that she had a very, very slight moustache, although
you couldn't really call it that. You could only see it when you
were very close to her, and I wouldn't normally have been as
close as I was that night.

"Do you think I'm pretty?" she asked suddenly.

"Yes," I said.

"Don't you have a religion?"

"I'm Jewish. You don't hate Jews, by any chance, do you?"

"No. Why should I? I don't hate anybody. It's just that I haven't come across all that many."

"Then it's good that you met me. Because I'm a good Jew."

Both of us had to laugh. I had only asked because almost the first thing *she* had asked when she came in was whether I minded her being slightly brown. She had only asked that, of course, because she had heard that I had actually wanted a blond, and she had looked at me very seriously. That's why I told her I'd only said that because at the time I hadn't been able to think of anything else to say.

She stood up, picked up the bottle, and sat down on the sofa. I looked at her again. I would have loved her to stay a little longer, but I knew that I couldn't ask, because my money had run out.

"Don't forget to take that thing off," she said.

So I took it off, but I did it carelessly and a small amount dripped onto her skirt. We had made love on the carpet and her clothes had been left lying all around us more or less in a circle, like spectators.

She picked her skirt up.

"That's all I needed," she said. "Shit!"

"Sorry," I said.

"Shit," she said.

"We can easily get that off," I said.

"It's brand-new," she said.

We went to the bathroom, where it was pretty cold because we were both still naked, but I couldn't find a decent washcloth. So I went to the kitchen. All I could find there was an dishcloth and a dishwashing brush. I took them back with me. We went to work brushing the stain out of her skirt with the dishwashing brush, which did the job quite well.

Then we both put our clothes on, although I didn't put on my shoes.

"I don't have any lipstick left on, do I?"

"No," I said, and we went downstairs. She wanted some more

water and to smoke another cigarette, and I had to give her the matches again.

"Is Rick coming to get you soon?"

"He's waiting outside."

"Oh, I see."

"There are some agencies where they don't wait for you outside, but I'd sooner not work for one of those."

"Well, I can understand that. I can understand that very well."

She picked up one of the books from the table and leafed through it.

"I admire people who can write books like this. I think it's really clever."

"It's nothing," I said. "It's harder to live well for a single day than to write a book."

She smoked another cigarette. The pack of Dunhills was empty now and she placed it on the table. Next to the condom wrapper. Bene-Luxe, it said in green letters, and we could have used it until May 1997.

"Oh, shit," she said.

"What is it this time?" I asked.

"I should have called them," she said. "We have to call when we arrive and again when we leave. And that old cow's probably on duty tonight. There's an old cow working there who really has it in for me."

She looked for something in her purse but apparently couldn't find it quickly enough, because she said "Shit" a few more times. Then she found her notebook and went over to my telephone with it.

"Luckily it wasn't the old cow. Some of the girls working there are very nice. They all have a story to tell, you know."

"Girls from the escort service aren't the only ones with stories to tell."

"I know that," she said, and then she asked for a tiny drop of wine in her water. I said I couldn't believe that would taste like anything, but I gave it to her anyway.

"Do you have a boyfriend?" I asked.

"Two. One is nineteen, and he doesn't have a cent. The other one is twenty-four and loaded. He deals drugs. I live with him. But the one who's nineteen is my real boyfriend."

"I see."

I wondered why the one who was loaded couldn't let her have some money, too, but that was something else I wasn't going to spend sleepless nights over. Besides, the whole thing was probably nothing but lies.

"Is Rick nice?"

"Oh, yes. All our drivers are nice. None of them bother any of the girls. They're there to protect us."

"Didn't Rick used to deliver pizzas on a scooter?"

"That's something we don't talk about. That sort of thing."

She stood up and walked through the room, now and then picking up a book.

"How much did you actually pay for this? For me?"

"Two hundred and fifty," I said. "And how much do you get?"

"A hundred."

"The truth stinks."

"No," she said. "It doesn't."

"Leave it there," I said, when she tried to push her empty cigarette pack into her purse.

"Do you do more than one a night?"

"No, one is more than enough."

She stubbed out her cigarette, emptied her glass.

"I have to go now," she said. "It was an . . . *interesting* evening."

"Yes," I said. *"Interesting."*

I walked with her to the hallway.

"Give my regards to Rick."

"Will you pray for me?"

"What?"

"You can pray, can't you? Somehow or other."

"Yes."

"Then pray for me. Do it before you go to sleep. It helps when people pray for you."

"It's nice to know that," I said. I thought, I'll be thinking of this another time when I'm with another woman. Perhaps it really does help, even if you only think it does, but I didn't really want to think that sort of thing ever again.

Actually it annoyed me, all that praying of hers. It was just another lie, of course. I didn't think she was capable of telling me even a shred of truth. She'd fed me what she fed everyone. There were probably quite a few men walking around with the feeling that they ought to be praying for her. Thinking that made me feel much better. Thinking that was a big relief.

I kissed her and she kissed me.

"Hope everything works out all right," I said. I couldn't think of anything better to say.

"Don't forget your promise."

"I won't forget."

Then she said, "Oh, there he is now," and shut the door. I sat at the table and opened a new bottle of Sicilian wine and looked at the piece of paper she had written her name on. A made-up name but I didn't care.

I didn't go to bed, so I couldn't pray for her that night. Even if I had gone to bed, I wouldn't have known what prayer to say for her because I hadn't prayed for anything for a very long time.

The more the memory of my father dimmed, the more convinced my mother became that she had murdered him, she and I together. She had recounted the events of the night of November 24 so often now that no one could tell what had actually happened anymore. Sometimes she would call me in the middle of the day and say, "I murdered him. I think I'm going mad." Then she would hang up. My father was not the first man she had murdered. She had killed her own father in the Theresienstadt concentration camp in 1943. She had been reluctant to reveal the details of that to anybody, probably because she had simply forgotten them. My mother was a woman who no longer realized that she had secrets. She did say that the rest of her life was her punishment.

So now she had murdered my father as well. For the first few months after his death I kept trying to persuade her otherwise, presenting her with arguments to prove that he had died a natural death. But she had long since stopped listening to reason.

My father had choked on his food. One Sunday night. I had visited him a few hours earlier at the Academic Medical Center. My mother is convinced that that was when I became her accomplice. That night I did in fact feed him a few spoonfuls of the purée that my mother always made for him, but I stopped the moment I noticed that everything I shoved into his mouth was coming back out of his nose.

When I went around to my mother's for supper last month, she said, "You are all I have left. If you die now, too, I'll throw myself under a train."

One evening I heard her tell an acquaintance to whom she had not spoken for a couple of years, "My husband is dead, but my son is still alive. He's sitting beside me now, eating a steak I just cooked for him."

I stopped eating at that and went into the kitchen to whip some cream.

My mother said, "I was standing right next to him when he choked, but I didn't realize he was choking. I only realized when it had already happened. So I called 'Help!' But the doctor said, 'There's nothing more I can do for your husband.' "

That was true enough. That part of her story was quite correct. My mother was standing next to him, hitting him over the head with a spoon for refusing to eat and yelling, "Eat! Eat! You've ruined my entire life, so don't think you're going to die on me now. You're going to eat!"

That she hit him over the head with a spoon was nothing new. She'd been doing it for years. She used to hit me over the head too. The only difference was that my father had choked and I hadn't. My father was lucky, in a manner of speaking. For that piece of luck he had had to reach the age of seventy-eight, almost seventy-nine. I think that was too high a price for luck.

During the last moments of his life he was hit over the head with a spoon. Whatever else happens in my life, I definitely do not want to be hit over the head during my last few moments on earth, no matter what the circumstances.

My mother has been dreaming about my father a lot recently, although it's been a year and a half since he choked on her purée of strawberries, blueberries, and raspberries. After one such dream she called me and said, "He told me not to grieve for him."

"Good," I said. "Great. So now you've been told by somebody else."

My mother writes down her dreams. When I went over to see her, I found the latest dream on the back of an unopened Postbank envelope.

I opened the envelope, filed the bank statement, and threw the envelope in the wastebasket. I figure in her dreams too. It seems I used to call myself Arna. In her dreams I appear as Arna and I say, "Don't keep yelling at me." But my mother says, "If you can't stand people yelling at you, you die. That's why we yell at each other all the time."

They used to call me Arnon Yasha, for those are my names. I have a snapshot taken at the time. I am standing in our Dintelstraat garden, beside the green oil barrel that hadn't been used for a few years. I'm squinting because I'm looking into the sun. I'm in an orange-and-brown striped T-shirt and short blue pants. A key ring dangles from them; it has no keys on it, just a large metal A. My hair is lighter than it is today and has bigger curls. I have a deep tan; I don't tan like that anymore. There is nothing remarkable about the snapshot. It is not the photograph of a boy who is being yelled at all day. So my mother's dreams lie.

The back of the photograph says "Summer 1979" in her handwriting. I can't remember anything about that summer except that we went to Switzerland for four weeks, to Disentis, a little place southwest of Chur. That summer I saw year-round snow for the first time and I had to take part in a badminton competition.

My mother is convinced she'll end up murdering me too. "I don't look after you properly," she's said more than once. I doubt that she'll murder me. She's had enough chances and missed them all. There won't be that many more now.

Recently she's been leaving the same message over and over again on my answering machine: "Please don't drink yourself to death, I beg you." She can't drink herself to death, because she doesn't touch alcohol. I ignore all messages left on my answering machine. People ask me to call them back but I never do. I don't feel like it. All those messages do is irritate me. They're not the messages I am waiting for.

I happened to ride my bike past her house and saw her in the backyard. She was mowing the lawn. She had mowed that lawn three times that week already. I got off and said, "You don't have to do that."

She looked at me. "There you are," she said.

"Yes," I said. "Here I am."

I found my mother's dreams on the back of the day's mail again. I read them quickly, as I did the letter from Silver Cross Insurance. Her dreams are nothing out of the ordinary. They aren't frightening. I'm sure there's no need for her to feel either pleased or relieved when she wakes up from them. In any case, I no longer feel that they have anything to do with me. In fact, I no longer feel that I can influence other people's dreams at all. We populate one another's nightmares and have no idea what we're doing in them.

My mother believes that we are the dreams of the dead. I don't want to be a dead person's dream. That's why I listen to her as if I were reading letters addressed to somebody else.

It was one of the nights when I hadn't drunk enough to fall asleep. It often happens that I'm in bed by ten o'clock, because by then I find that the day has gone on long enough. So at eleven-thirty

I got up again. I dressed and went out to the café around the corner, where I ordered two tequilas. And then another two, with lemon and salt. There had been no mail that day. Not that I was expecting any, but you can never tell.

Actually, everything was quite simple. That's why I ordered another two.

"That's nice to drink at night, isn't it?"

"Yes," I said, "it's nice to drink at night." I poured salt onto my palm, bit into the lemon, and emptied my glass.

When I was fifteen I took a book out of the school library, Oek de Jong's *Massimo's Ascension*. I found most of the stories in the book unreadable, but one struck me as so beautiful that I had to have it. That's why I tore "Rita Koeling" out of the book and put toilet paper between the pages to fill the gap. Since the library had two copies of *Massimo's Ascension*, they both had to be the same thickness.

Then I took the book back to the Vossius library, which was run by a lot of bored mothers. Most of the mothers who worked at Vossius seemed bored, but the ones in the library were the worst.

Although it was seven years ago, I can still remember entire passages from "Rita Koeling." " 'Get out of here,' she said in a trembling voice, 'get out of here this moment or I'll scream.' It was a familiar phrase, but this time she said it without pressing her hands to her throat, without lifting her eyes anxiously to heaven; she meant it. And I left."

A few days later the toilet paper was discovered between the pages of *Massimo's Ascension*. That day a mother with reading glasses was in charge of the library. The moment I came in I realized that something had gone wrong. *Massimo's Ascension* and a whole pile of toilet paper were lying on her desk. I turned back toward the door but she had seen me and beckoned me over.

"Is this yours?" she asked, and pointed to the pile of toilet paper.

"Well, to be perfectly honest, it's my parents'."

Then she did something no one would have believed possible, something the principal refused to believe, anyway, and the other teachers too. We are talking about 1986 here, and it should be remembered that she was a *mother*. The women in the Vossius library answered to the name "library mothers." A nice name, but a student with any brains didn't need more than ten minutes to grasp that "library mother" signified nothing more than occupational therapy for mentally handicapped women. Vossius teemed with women like that. The mother with the reading glasses and the culottes stood up, pulled my ear, and said, "You hate books, don't you?" "Yes," I replied. What else could I say when my ear was in her hand and was being slowly mangled to a pulp? It was only when she had dragged me out of the library by the ear that she let go. While I was at Vossius, it was by no means unusual for pupils to be dragged from one classroom to another by the ear. She took me to the deputy principal, who came to inspect the library; she showed him what I had done with the book and burst into tears. Library mothers were the sort who blubbered about books and baby seals but left their own children to rot.

I was banned from the Vossius library for a year. On top of that I had to buy them a new copy of *Massimo's Ascension* out of my own money. The incident was discussed at a staff meeting, and the library mother who had dragged me by the ear got a round of applause for dealing with me so hard. As if I'd been bent on destroying the whole library and she'd only managed to stop me by throwing me out of the library by the ear. For a few weeks I nursed the idea of sending her anonymous threats. One afternoon I followed her when she was taking her dog out, since she lived practically right across from the school. That sure made her nervous. I also wrote a long poem, entitled "Library Mother with Reading Glasses," of which I can only remember the first line: "Your mouth is a pockmark of grease." The poem was rejected by the editorial board of the school magazine for unspecified reasons.

At the time I had long hair dangling in a mass of small woolly curls over my forehead and down the back of my neck. I never washed my hair, because washing made it frizzy. I didn't go to the barber either, because my hair hid areas of skin that needed to remain covered. I did brush my teeth, though, and I also squeezed a pimple every so often. I read *Football International* because I was interested in soccer, and now and then I took the train to Utrecht without knowing what I was going to Utrecht for. A few times I went on my own to see Ajax play. I stood in the stands close to the barrier, right near where Vanenburg took the corner kicks all the time. A bald man next to me kept shouting "Vanny, Vanny!" over and over again. After a while I started shouting it too. And now Vanenburg has gone to Japan.

I think it was Jerzy Kozinski who said, "If I have to, I think with my legs." I would have loved to think with my legs all day long, which is why I liked soccer.

In cafés and trains I smoked other people's cigarette butts without giving it a second thought.

I owned five sweaters, but I only ever wore one. My mother said it was beginning to stink, but I couldn't smell anything. One night she secretly washed it. I didn't bother to pack my book bag anymore, but then I didn't unpack it either. I always had the same books with me. I don't remember which ones they were.

On my way home there were always a couple of girls smoking on a bench in Bernard Zweerskade. One of them was so fat she could easily have made three of me. She went to my school. One or two grades ahead of me, I think.

One afternoon she was sitting there by herself and she called out, "Want a cigarette?"

I looked at her for a moment, then answered, "All right."

We smoked in silence and after about half an hour she said, "Let's buy a bottle of Kibowi."

Kibowi was the new kiwi liqueur made by Bols.

We bought a bottle. The liqueur looked like detergent and tasted like scented vomit. We took turns drinking out of the bottle, and I noticed that she was not only incredibly fat but ugly as sin too.

"Yesterday I snuck into the Ideal Home Exhibition, and you can get Kibowi there for nothing."

"Great," I said.

She was called Fleur, a name I didn't think suited her.

The Kibowi didn't make me feel particularly mellow, just like throwing up. That didn't surprise me, because things looked like I wouldn't be feeling mellow again for another hundred years.

We smoked another couple of cigarettes and then she said, "That's all," and kicked the pack away.

"Right," I said. "That's all." On the canal a man was busy painting his boat. He'd been doing it for the last two years.

"Your forehead looks like a turnip field, did you know that?"

"What?"

"Your forehead looks like a turnip field," she said emphatically. "Don't you know that song about the two rabbits?"

"Never heard of it," I answered.

I wanted to say something about her tits or her ass, but since I couldn't think of anything amusing I said nothing.

The Kibowi bottle was half empty by now. She pushed it into my hand. "Take it home with you," she said.

I did.

The next day she was sitting there again, this time with a girlfriend.

"You were drinking Kibowi together yesterday, weren't you?" said the girlfriend.

I nodded.

"Last year we were both held back a grade."

"Was that fun?" I asked.

"Yes," said Fleur. "A lot of fun."

She was drawing stick figures in the gravel with her boot.

"I've got some Kibowi at home too," said the girlfriend. She wasn't as fat as Fleur, but her tits were just as big.

We went to the girlfriend's house. At first I didn't want to go, but Fleur said, "Come on, we'll have a laugh." So I went along.

It was a large house near Olympiaplein. Before we went in, the girlfriend said to me, "I'm Danielle, by the way."

"I'm Arnon," I said.

"That's a funny name."

"Arnon stinks," said Fleur.

"Hey, come on," I said, "it could be a lot worse."

"Just take a whiff."

Danielle sniffed. First my neck, then near my arm, and finally near my stomach.

"Yeah," said Danielle when she'd finished sniffing, "you stink all right. You need a bath."

Then we went inside. The house smelled of cat piss.

"Where are your parents?" I asked.

We went upstairs. She opened the door to her room and as soon as we were inside she shut the door quickly and locked it. On the floor were magazines, two ashtrays that needed emptying, and three plants in the process of dying. About twenty pairs of nail clippers were lying on a bureau next to the window.

"I collect those," said Danielle.

"What?"

"Nail clippers. I collect them. You have to collect something, don't you?"

She took a bottle out of her closet. It was wrapped in a pair of jeans, and the contents weren't green this time but yellow. So it couldn't be Kibowi, even though the taste was just as disgusting. Still, the three of us drank from the bottle and ate potato chips to disguise the taste.

"Do you mind?" Danielle asked after a while.

"Mind what?"

"That you stink like that," Fleur explained. "We'd like to know if you mind."

"I don't stink. It's just my sweater that stinks. A little."

"Oh yes, you do," said Fleur. "You stink. Why don't you admit it?"

I was wearing the yellow sweater with the squares. It did stink a little, but only if you took a deep breath. Normal human beings didn't breathe as deeply as that.

Danielle wanted to know why I didn't buy a new sweater.

"Don't feel like it," I answered.

But Fleur said it wasn't just the sweater, it was actually all of me, particularly my hair, my socks, and my shoes—in fact, everything.

"We could wash him, of course," said Danielle, and drank some more of the yellow Kibowi. It could have been Kibowi that had gone bad.

"Let's wash him," said Fleur.

I stood up, because I had no desire to be washed, but Danielle pushed me back so hard that I stumbled over a plant and fell. Fleur kneeled on my upper arms. The two of them must have done this sort of thing before. There could be no other explanation, since the operation proceeded so smoothly. Fleur put her whole weight on my arms and Danielle began to hum.

"Does it hurt?" she asked.

I nodded. It felt as if my arms were being cut off.

"Then stop struggling," said Danielle.

"Open your mouth." That was Fleur.

She shifted her weight a little, which hurt even more. Then she started to rock her elephant's knees on my upper arms. I felt as if I'd never be able to get my breath again.

"Open your mouth, I said!"

I opened my mouth. I could have gone on keeping it shut, of course, but by that time I knew what it felt like to have your mouth pried open, which is why I preferred to open it myself. It wasn't even wide open before Fleur dropped a large gob of spit into it.

"Swallow it," she said.

I didn't swallow, I gargled and allowed all the spit in my

mouth to dribble out the sides. I was reminded of that girl recorder player who had taken such pleasure in spitting in my face. I must possess some mysterious powers of attraction that make people want nothing more than to spit in my face the moment they see me.

Danielle delivered a bored kick to my knee with her boot. You could see the black strap of her bra over her left shoulder.

"Well, Mister Greedy-Guts," she said, "you can have a gob from me now."

Her gob was far less accurately aimed. It landed not in my mouth but on my nose and ran down my cheek and my neck into my sweater.

"We're two witches," said Fleur.

"Oh, I see," I said. That explained a whole lot. There was a poster on the ceiling, and from his earring I recognized George Michael staring at me with a guitar in his hand.

"If you let me go," I suggested, "I'll buy you a bottle of Kibowi." This proposal only made them burst out laughing, and Fleur said, "I suppose you think almost anything goes here."

That was exactly what I did think, and Danielle said, "If he does, he's right. Anything does go. Except for sticking an umbrella up your ass and opening it."

They started to whisper. They had obviously had an idea because Danielle took some tampons out of the closet and tried to stuff them in my ears. The tampons were too large to go in easily. She had to twist them around a lot, and when I finally had a tampon in each ear, it was really painful. If tampons made your ears hurt like that, then what the hell did they feel like in women's genitals?

"Do you have those pathetic curls all over?" asked Danielle.

They poured some yellow Kibowi into my mouth and into my nose, then pulled my sweater up and colored my nipples red with lipstick. When they had almost finished doing that, there was a knock on the door and a woman's voice called, "I'm back."

"Coming," Danielle called.

The tampons were pulled out of my ears. Fleur got off my arms. I was ordered to stand up and leave the house.

"Next time we'll make mushroom soup out of your mushroom face," said Danielle.

It was such an unlikely thing to say that I began to laugh. Danielle was having absolutely none of that. Hissing, she said, "Off you go now, Mister Greedy-Guts. Or else I'll stick a pair of nail clippers in your dick."

I made for the door.

"So long," I said with as much dignity as I could muster.

"When you come next time, don't forget to wipe your ass," Fleur said, pinching my rear end in a way in which it has never been pinched since.

Downstairs her mother was standing in the hallway, a person in a raincoat. I had the immediate impression that I had seen her a thousand times before.

"Are you Danielle's new boyfriend?" she asked.

I wasn't sure what to say to that. I straightened my sweater, felt in my ear to make doubly sure, and said eventually, "Certainly not."

"Thank goodness for that," said Danielle's mother. She made for the kitchen but turned around and said, "What I mean is, our Danielle was held back last year, and the last thing she needs right now is a new boyfriend."

I nodded. She showed me the door.

"Bye," called Danielle's mother.

"Bye," I called back.

The next day I had to give a talk at school on Jan Wolkers's novel *Crew Cut*. I read it that evening but skipped all the passages that weren't about fucking, so I finished it in less than half an hour. During recess I went to the Vossius cafeteria, known as the Club, which was where I usually went during recess. You could buy Cokes and potato chips there, and the servers were girls who would only serve you if they liked you. The Club was in the Vossius basement, next to the bicycle room. It was dark and smelled of too many people and of french fries; they always played the same old music. The lighting was blue, except when there were parties, and then it was red. In the middle was a table for playing Foosball.

I leaned against the concrete wall, which felt damp as always, ate my lunch—a bag of chips—and waited for the end of recess. Next to me someone was talking about a Greek test, probably Eric. Eric ate his own sperm every day, but it didn't help him and I had told him more than once to share it with his younger brother.

Across the room, Fleur was deep in animated conversation with a boy who was cultivating a moustache. From moustaches to potbellies to tits, everything was *cultivated* at Vossius with a determination you usually come across only in sports stars. Then a place at the table opened up. I pressed the bag of chips into Eric's hand and played Foosball until the second bell. I would have liked nothing better than to play Foosball for the rest of my life in dark corners where you didn't have to see other people's faces or agonize about what you were going to do with the rest of your life or listen to all the b.s. dished out by people who thought there was something positive to discover even in shit.

I got a nine on my talk, just about the last decent mark I got at Vossius.

I motioned to the woman behind the bar.

"Can you make me a margarita?"

"No, I can't."

"Just for me?"

"It's not on the list but I'll make you one free."

I went into the rest room. A man was combing his hair. I

tried to remember what I had eaten that evening, but my mind was blank. I leaned against the cigarette machine. I wanted to lie down. I wanted desperately to lie down. The man put the comb back in his pocket and left.

I sat on the floor. It was wet but I didn't stand up again. Perhaps my pants had been wet even before I sat down. I couldn't remember, but then my memory didn't reach beyond about one-thirty that afternoon, when Deborah called me for the first time in months.

"How're you doing?" she asked.

"Fine," I said, "just fine."

She told me that she'd been to a cowboy party the night before.

"A what?" I asked.

"A cowboy party," she explained. "We all had to go dressed as cowboys. They're the latest thing, parties like that. At the end, I suggested to someone that we tie our shoelaces together and walk home that way. It took us three hours. And the guy thought I was after him, when all I wanted was for us to tie our shoelaces together and walk across town that way. That wasn't too much to ask, was it?"

"No," I said, "that wasn't too much to ask."

"Seen any good movies lately?"

I told her I hadn't been to the movies for a couple of months.

"I have to hang up now. I said I'd babysit tonight. I should have been there already."

"What did you call for, actually?"

She said she really had to hang up now—she was late as it was. I searched for my diary among all the junk on my desk but I didn't really know what I needed it for. "What a confusing conversation."

"Yeah," she said and hung up.

That's what my telephone calls are like—short, confusing, and obscure. Recently I've been getting the feeling that I'll wake up as soon as I put the phone down. I found my diary and between its pages a picture postcard with the slogan "Mascotte Cigarette Papers, 3X Better."

A man came in. He pissed right over me.

"It smells like shit in here," he said.

"Look," I said. "We're in the men's room. They always smell like shit."

He left without washing his hands. I wanted to drink some water but didn't have the strength to get up.

"You've been gone a long time."

I emptied my glass and paid. She winked at me and I winked back. She'd given me a tequila for the price of a lager. That was certainly worth a wink. Then I went home and lay down on the sofa.

I saw Fleur once again, on the Queen's Birthday. She was playing the violin under the Vondel Park bridge. I recognized her immediately and started to walk past but she saw me and called, "Hi!"

"You're looking well," I volunteered.

"You spotted that pretty fast."

Conversations with people you meet when you haven't seen them for a while tend to get shorter and shorter. There isn't that much you still have to say to each other, as the two of us discovered. I try not to be rude. You mustn't take up people's time unnecessarily. If someone says to me, "I used to work in an office, and you were expected to wear something different there every day," I don't ask, "What exactly do you mean?" I make do with what he's told me; I don't need to have things carved in stone. "Maybe we should be satisfied with what we can still talk about," I suggested. She agreed with that.

I hesitated for a moment, produced a two-and-a-half-guilder coin from my pants pocket, threw it into her violin case, and walked on.

I woke up at two o'clock. I went into the kitchen and poured a glass of cold tea with rum, more rum than tea. I felt like calling a girl, drank a few glasses more, and decided I'd better lie down first for an hour or so.

When I got up it was five o'clock. My tongue was like a stale sour ball in my mouth. I held my head under the faucet and opened a bottle of cognac.

"A pretty girl is what you'll get," I listened to the lady say five minutes later.

"Great," I said, "great."

"But it could be an hour."

I looked at my watch.

"Six o'clock, then?"

"Yes," she said.

I drew the curtains, shoved my cash cards and my passport into the drawer, opened the French doors, and sat on the wooden steps. It was a warm night. Another hour. I watched the sky lighten and went on drinking steadily.

At five to six the telephone rang. It was a man's voice, which I could barely make out. I told him I couldn't understand a thing he was saying.

"Sorry," said the man, "it's the car phone. Is it better now?"

He was a black man, that was the first thing I heard.

"Did you call for a girl?"

"Yes," I said.

"Listen," said the black man, "somebody stole my street guide."

I had a coughing fit and sat down. For the first time that night I felt very sick.

"What did you say?"

"My street guide was stolen from my car this afternoon."

"What a drag," I said, "a real drag."

"Yes," said the black man. "So can you just give me directions?"

I gave him directions. "I'll be there right away," he said, and the conversation was over. A glass of water and a glass of cognac stood on the table. If God had mercy on me he'd surely see to it that I didn't puke during the hour the girl spent with me. Puking was something I'd rather do on my own. I didn't need a girl for that, certainly not an expensive one.

At ten after six they were outside my door. I paid the black man and showed the girl in.

"So, here you are," I said. I could think of nothing better to say. She was wearing an odd red jacket, which seemed two sizes too small, a short skirt, and high heels, and for the rest, although they'd promised me a brunette I hadn't expected someone half Surinamese or half South American. She asked for wine, which I found surprising, but wine it was. I went to the kitchen to open a bottle. It looked as if I might get through the hour without puking. It seemed certain now that God was with me.

I put the glass down in front of the girl, who answered to the name of Natasha, and asked if she was a student at the university, because for a change I had called the student escort service.

"Me at the university? No." She laughed. "I'm going to pass this year, though."

I clinked glasses with her. "Let's drink to that," I said.

"There's a fruit fly in my glass."

There was indeed a fruit fly in her glass, so I poured her another.

I looked at her slight body and her little head with its little snub nose.

"I'm taking my university entrance exam next year, and then I'll go on to study law. Or maybe something else."

"Great. Have you been working all night tonight?"

"More or less. And you?"

"More or less."

It was full light now, a new day.

"You're eighteen, right?"

"Is that what they told you?" She laughed again, a sort of hollow laugh, a sort of old man's laugh. "I'm nineteen. What's that you're drinking?"

"Cognac. Should we start?"

She emptied her glass and nodded. Like all the others, she wore a small purse across her front in which she kept condoms, cigarettes, a lighter, a list of telephone numbers, lipstick. Whenever I see people in the street wearing a purse like that I think of escort services.

She undid the purse and followed me upstairs.

"Get undressed first," I said. "I enjoy watching that. There's nothing more seductive than a woman taking her clothes off." She laughed again. She drew the curtains even closer than I had.

Just in case, I had brought the cognac with me. I poured another glass and watched her take off her shoes. She was neither particularly pretty nor particularly ugly. Just the thing for an escort service. She looked like a girl leaning against the wall of a school playground in her new and already wrinkled clothes, having a smoke after a school party that had ended in disappointment. Except that her face expressed nothing, absolutely nothing. No surprise, no pleasure, no anger, no hatred. Nothing, nothing but emptiness. The look of one of those people who come shambling out of a video store late at night, a tape under their arm, looking like zombies. Perhaps I looked like a zombie too.

"Nice perfume," I said. "What is it?"

"It isn't perfume, it's baby powder."

"Baby powder." I touched her hair.

"I just went home to take a quick shower."

So that's why I had had to wait an hour, so that my lady could take a quick shower. She walked half naked over to the tapes I kept on the mantelpiece.

"Guns 'n Roses. Do you like them?" she asked.

"Once in a while."

"Can I put something on?"

I nodded. "Where do you live?"

"In a block of student apartments over in the Bijlmer."

She was wearing frilly red panties and a black bra. She was the first girl I'd ever had with red panties. "Don't you cry tonight, I still love you baby," came blaring through the room louder than I ever played it. I remembered that it was early Sunday morning, walked over to the tape deck, and turned it down. "If you don't mind," I said. I began to feel dizzy and slumped onto the sofa.

She sat down next to me. "It's your turn now."

"You're a very attractive woman," I whispered in her ear. "Did you know that?" I could still taste the last mouthful of cognac.

"I don't believe that anymore."

"You're right, you shouldn't believe that sort of thing." I was busy taking off my socks.

"I'm a little on the fat side."

"Oh, come on," I said, and pinched her stomach gently. "Plump maybe, but not fat."

"No, I'm fat."

That was that. No further discussion. I'd heard of women who thought of themselves as pigs and who even answered the telephone, "This is your pig speaking."

"Do you have a boyfriend?" I asked, taking off my sweater.

"No, it isn't possible. Not with this kind of work."

"Some of the girls have boyfriends."

I was naked now like her. There was no way I was going to be able to stand up, so she leaned over me and ran her hand over my stomach and my nipples and everything in between.

"Have you been with this agency long?"

"No, I only just started with them. Before that I worked at a club, but it nearly drove me crazy. You had to hang around the bar all night. Sitting up straight and smiling. And then you'd go upstairs with a couple of guys, and after that you were worn out. But you still had to go on sitting up straight and smiling. And the other girls spent the whole time staring at you. I got absolutely paranoid."

I had placed my hand on her breast but I was too weak to feel anything much.

"Cold hands," she said. "And the worst thing in that sort of club is that you're expected to make the advances—if you want to work, that is. And I'm absolutely no good at that. At making advances. If they give you the brush-off you feel pretty small. I never make advances to people."

"Me neither," I said.

My hand was still on her left tit, which I kept trying to kiss, but I couldn't manage to bend over far enough.

"Not even in discos. I just dance by myself. I don't like being snubbed in public."

"No. Nobody likes that. So the escort service must suit you better."

"Yes, it does. In a club like that you get absolutely paranoid."

She got down on the floor and took my cock in her mouth. She was the first to go down on me properly for money; the others had only pretended. It was early in the morning of July 4, 1993, and it's true she did it as if she were trying to polish off a too-hot croquette at the Febo automat, but that's a mere detail. This was a special day. To make doubly sure, I drank another cognac.

"How many do you go with in one night?"

She took it out of her mouth. "What did you say?"

"I asked how many you go with in a night."

"You're my sixth tonight. I've been to Weesp and to Nederhorst den Berg, and the rest were in Amsterdam."

"Mostly old men, or what?"

"Mostly old men. That can be a lot nicer, you know. Young guys tend to think they have to prove something."

"And the old ones are nice to you?"

"Usually. If they're not nice, then I can get nasty, too, which usually makes them nice pretty quick."

I poured another few drops.

"But flabby old bodies like that . . ."

"You don't think about that. All you think about is the hundred-guilder bill."

I leaned back. For a moment I thought I was having a nose-bleed, but it was just my nose running.

She took my prick out of her mouth again and shifted her weight.

"I get a hundred, the agency gets a hundred, and the driver gets fifty. And tonight I made myself six hundred guilders. That isn't bad, is it?"

"Not bad at all," I said. "So I'm your last tonight?"

"You can never be sure but I think you're probably the last, and that suits me fine."

"Do you ever remember your clients?"

She pulled my condom back up again. Then she looked at me. "Can I tell you something?" she said. "I don't even remember what the man before you looked like. The moment I shut the door I put them right out of my mind. Otherwise I couldn't go on. I have to be back at school as usual on Monday. I'm on vacation right now, you know."

"Don't you go away on vacation?" I asked.

"No, I work all the way through it. This is actually a vacation job. If you want to make a lot of money, you have to work hard."

"Yes," I said, "you're right."

I tugged a little at her still-damp hair while she continued with her work.

"Do you know any of the other girls at your agency? Like the one who calls herself Marcella?"

"No. I was introduced to a couple of them, but I don't want to make any friends in that crowd and start hanging out with them. I prefer to go my own way."

After five minutes she took my cock out of her mouth again, gave it a little squeeze, and examined it as if it were some strange insect.

"Is that spit or is it sperm?" she asked.

I thought, I'll play along with her, so I bent over my cock, stared at it as if I had never seen it before, and said after a few seconds, "It looks suspiciously like sperm."

"Well, that's that then," she said and pulled the condom off as if she were taking laundry off the line.

"I'll save that one," I said quickly.

"Oh." From the way she said "oh," I could tell that she'd seen things that were even stranger.

She lay down next to me. I smelled the baby powder again. Above her eyebrows I could see the light brown smear of concealer covering her pimples.

"With all this work, do you ever have time to go out?"

"Sure," she said, "I go to discos pretty often, but I don't dress like this. These are actually my work clothes. Sneakers and jeans is what I wear. Sometimes you see girls in discos wearing short skirts and high heels like these, and you think, What a tramp. They shouldn't do that. All they do is lead men on."

"Ah," I said. "Do you consider yourself a tramp?"

"No. You know, with most clients you think of absolutely nothing, you only think of the hundred guilders. But sometimes it occurs to you that, God, it's obvious this guy wouldn't stand a chance of picking up a girl in the street, and then you really feel you're doing it out of charity. But the girls who turn up in discos in short skirts like that . . . I really wouldn't do that. And I never go home with anyone, because you know the kind of night you're in for then. I want to get married one day."

"And have children?"

"Yes. Definitely. About four."

From the way she was plucking at the skin of my belly I could tell that she was tired, perhaps just as tired as I was. I poured myself another drink. There couldn't be much left in the bottle.

"How did you get started in all this?" I asked.

"I saw an ad for girls to do massage, and to begin with it really was just massage. But in the end it included everything. I got absolutely paranoid in that club, though. And at the beginning I ran away a few times too. I'd already have gone upstairs and then I'd run off, but you'd be sent back up again and finally you got used to it."

"Yes," I said, "that's what so great about life."

"Look," she said, "my sister has a child. She's on welfare."

"Oh."

"I have seven brothers and sisters. What do you do, anyway?"

"I'm a radio technician."

"With all these books, I thought some sort of professor."

"No. No sort of professor." I took her left nipple between my fingers.

"You could do this work, too, you know that?"

"What work?"

"There's an escort service for women as well. You could easily make five thousand a week. But we girls have it easy by comparison. You just try and get a hard-on with a woman of seventy. And with us there's always a condom in between, but if you have to go down on that sort of old bag . . . Well, you could always use a dental dam, of course."

A dental dam. I had read something somewhere about dental dams but I couldn't have told you exactly what they were. I suddenly felt completely drunk. "I'll think about it," I mumbled.

I lay on top of her and fumbled with her hole, which was as dry and as hard as the shells I used to collect from the age of eight until I was eleven, when one fine day I stomped them all to smithereens.

"You want another go?" she asked.

"Yes," I whispered.

She sat up. "But it's not allowed, is it? You already came."

I sat up myself—otherwise I would have slipped off the sofa. "What? That's a new one. I've never heard that before."

"Of course you have, you must have, you've called up for girls often enough before now."

She looked like a real bitch now, an unbelievable bitch. She was nodding her head up and down, right in front of my face.

"Listen," I said, "I've paid for an hour. There's never been any trouble before about how often I'm allowed to come. Christ Almighty!" I was getting hoarse.

"You knew all about it and you still tried your luck! You still tried your luck!"

She was wagging her index finger like an elementary school teacher putting a little boy in his place.

"I've never had any trouble about the number of times I was allowed to come. Never. Absolutely never. You're the first one ever to give me any trouble. Sometimes they even ask, 'Would you like to go again?' You know that? I've paid for an hour. The telephone girl said an hour costs 250 guilders. She didn't say a single orgasm costs 250 guilders."

I felt like falling asleep there and then and not waking up again until everything had disappeared—the girl, the burning sensation in my eyes, the taste in my mouth.

"You were trying it, weren't you? Come on, own up, admit that you were trying it."

"I was trying *nothing*." I was the last one, so of course she wanted to be rid of me, the bitch. I felt tired, the sort of tiredness that would never go away.

"All right," I said. "I don't feel like arguing about how many times I'm allowed to come. I just don't feel like it, OK?"

"You tried. You tried it. Admit it."

She was hassling me. She was just hassling me. I stroked her belly, which she thought was so fat, and her neck, which really was fat. Suddenly I felt like hitting her over the head with one of the empty bottles standing around in the room. I once saw a black man beat a drum for ten minutes straight. That's the way I wanted to beat her over the head. Not because I had anything against her or hated her or thought the life of a whore worth even less than that of a Jew or a black person. It was just that I was tired and wanted her out of my life that very minute. That's why I felt like grabbing an empty bottle and starting that drum solo. I could hear the tape running out, and I could see that the girl was just as exhausted as I was, and I saw the whole world as a collection of whores and johns and women who wanted to turn every woman into a hooker except themselves. I could see all the people I knew begging day in, day out, for a crumb of love that they would then fling at each other like a piece of bread to a mangy dog. I saw myself trudging from one to the next until I succumbed in the arms of someone who could no longer remember what the man she had made love to an hour before looked like and who in a few minutes wouldn't be able to remember what I had looked like and what I had said and what I had left unsaid and what we had done and what we had left undone. But I wouldn't be able to forget, and when I sat in some café late at night I would see their faces and remember the words with which the agencies had advertised their charms, and I would remember what they had said when they took off their clothes and what they said when they left again at the agreed time, and I would count my money to make sure I had enough. Then I would go up to them to smell their smells and to listen to what they had to say. It didn't matter to me that I had to share their smells and their words with all those others, because in the end not one of them would remember me, and that was all to the good. They, too, didn't want to be remembered, not as whores at any rate, though perhaps as something like little princesses.

So if I now found myself hitting her over the head with one

of those empty beer bottles, I wouldn't be at all surprised. That deed would in no way differ from what I had done with the rest of my life; it would be no better and no worse. It would be no more random or logical than the fact that she, instead of one of her colleagues, had been sent to me. Later I might easily listen to myself saying, "I had already put the money aside in my drawer the day before. But I only called that Sunday morning. I remember wondering what exactly a double D cup meant. Her name was Natasha. I was her sixth and last that night."

I didn't move, because I was scared of starting that drum solo on her head, after which she would *never* disappear from my life. For the rest of my life I would remember one evening, one night, and one morning, all of which I wanted to forget as soon as possible. That was the only reason I went on sitting where I was: I didn't want to grow old with the memory of a face I wanted to get straight out of my life. That's why I stroked her neck, her shoulder, and the tops of her breasts. When Natasha looked at me, she saw a hundred-guilder bill with two arms, two legs, and a prick, and all the others who looked at me saw the same thing, and one day I would look in the mirror and also see a hundred-guilder bill with two arms, two legs, and a prick. I really didn't want to wait for that day.

"Let's get dressed then."

"OK," I said.

Again I saw those odd frilly red panties. I remembered a school party; it was around the time Vanenburg left the country because they said you couldn't win the war with players like him. Or was it a year later? In any case, Deborah had had to borrow a dress because she'd squirted ketchup all over hers while preparing a salad. That's why Deborah was wearing a dress that was too small and had to pull it down all the time. That night we played backgammon and I lost. I still remember that perfectly. It so happened that the whole time during the game I could see Deborah's white panties, which had precisely the same brightness as my father's shirts. They shone out from the darkness of her legs and her dress like a burning cigarette at night. The next day I wasn't sure anymore whether I had been drunk or whether I really had seen them. The people who'd been sitting on the floor watching the game couldn't remember any white panties when I asked them. Yet I swear that I saw them and that a few days later Rosie started to write me letters, not all that long before Martinimartin downed two bottles on the beach and about eighteen months before I got kicked out of school. Martinimartin now claims that he took only a few sips, and others say so too. Yet I swear that it was two bottles, because later that evening we used the same bottles as a goal. It was when they said you couldn't win the war with players like Vanenburg. The evening I kept looking the whole time at Deborah's panties while we were playing backgammon, I went home at eleven o'clock but a few girls went on to a disco and the next day I received a letter from Rosie. Of course it isn't true that it all started that evening, with that too short dress of Deborah's. But a few months ago, in November, I wrote a couple of letters to Rosie asking if she could still remember Deborah's squirting ketchup all over her dress the night before she wrote her first letter to me, because Deborah couldn't remember anything about it at all. I added that the whole business was completely unimportant but that even so I was extremely anxious to get her reply because memories tend to disappear. Other memories come to take their place, and in the end you're left with nothing but the names of the people you used to know and maybe a funny story about them to tell at parties, even though it really happened to somebody else. I admit that in three letters I called her my little mouse and that I wrote that I wanted to marry her, but any imbecile would have understood that that was just a polite turn of phrase. A few years have passed since then and there have been quite a few women to whom I have said that I wanted to marry them. Why can't anyone remember those two bottles of Martini, and how is it that it's never become clear what actually happened that night, and why can no one remember those white panties when everyone must have seen them, and what did my getting a letter from Rosie the very next day mean? Rosie, who dared to do things that none of us dared to do, things I solemnly swore never to mention? That promise, too, is something I might just as well break now because no one is likely to remember—that's how I ended my letter. I never got an answer to it or to any of the four letters I wrote after that one, and in any case, none of them were intended to renew our friendship. I was only trying to shed some light on the events that summer when we rooted for Denmark to become the soccer champions of the world.

"What happens if you're not back after an hour?"

"Then the driver calls."

"Well, don't let's wait for that," I said.

We went downstairs. I took the empty bottle with me.

"You ought to think about it," she said.

"What?"

"Being a ladies' escort. Then you wouldn't need to work for the radio station anymore."

"I'll definitely think about it. I've been giving it some thought all along."

"You'd be good at it if you ask me."

"Thanks." I sat down because I couldn't stand up any longer.

"Great pants you're wearing," said Natasha.

"Brand-new. Put them on specially for you."

"That's nice. Thanks."

"Don't mention it."

"What time did I get here?"

"Six-fifteen."

It was seven o'clock now. "Would you like another glass of wine or do you want to go?"

She said nothing.

"Off you go then," I said. "Have the last fifteen minutes on me."

She hitched her purse up again over her stomach.

"Natasha is a lovely name."

"It's just a name. It's not even my own."

"I know that. It's a lovely name all the same."

"Well, I'll be going," she said.

"Good luck," I called. "Can you find your way out?"

"Yes. Good luck to you too," I heard, then I fell fast asleep on the carpet.

At nine-thirty I was woken by the doorbell.

I wondered if I had called the escort service again after Natasha had left. I couldn't remember, but it's something I could easily have done. Even though I had no money left. That's why I looked out the window first. My mother was standing there.

"We made a date for me to come here and clean, don't you remember?"

I told her I had forgotten.

She started to mop the bathroom. I sat on the floor and watched her mopping.

"Don't you realize that I live for this," she said, "that I live for you?"

"Yes," I said, "I know. That's why I let you in."

She left at eleven o'clock. I realized that I had run out of salt, so I walked to the café around the corner. I ordered tomato soup.

The waitress stopped abruptly. "Do you know what you just ordered?"

"No," I said.

"Tomato spit."

"Tomato spit?"

I started to giggle, to giggle alarmingly. It was embarrassing; tourists with huge cameras on their stomachs turned around to look.

"Make it vegetable spit instead," I said.

This time she laughed. Just as well. I remembered the time I'd cut open a mosquito bite on my arm with a small fruit knife because my mother had refused to lend me money, and how I'd threatened to go on cutting until she changed her mind.

After ten minutes the vegetable soup arrived. I picked up the salt shaker and turned it upside down over the soup.

I would rather have turned it upside down over my palm and slowly licked the salt up but I didn't dare, not in that café anyway.

Later that afternoon, when I had slept for three hours, I discovered a letter on the floor among all the other junk that Deborah had sent me in 1987.

"Please come . . . to Class V . . . unless you're going to play the fool again . . . ? My love, with all my heart & soul," she wrote.

I felt like answering that letter even now, July 4, 1993. I picked up the 3X Better Mascotte postcard. When the card was still blank after half an hour, I crumpled it up and used it as a stopper for the bottle of wine I had opened for Natasha. I couldn't find the cork anywhere, and if you leave wine open it gets full of fruit flies.

HAVE YOU COME FOR AN ANAL? NO, FOR ASTRID

I stood outside the all-day movie theater and realized that I had at least another fifteen minutes to wait. But even if I had had to wait an hour and a half I would have kept on standing there. It was Monday and it was raining softly, just as it had been raining softly all summer. I'd be going to my mother's for some herring salad at lunchtime.

The woman behind the glass was old and grouchy. There wasn't even the hint of a half smile when I asked, "Or have you sold out?" It can't be a joke, of course, sitting behind the ticket booth window all day knowing that you're so old you'll be sitting there for the rest of your life. That's why I said, "Keep the change." Even then she acted as if she hadn't heard.

I walked inside, into a kind of bar with no stools, only mirrors. A moment later I realized that they weren't mirrors but dark glass. You could see through the glass into the auditorium, and then I realized that meant they could keep an eye on the people inside the way the porter in some brothels sits with about twenty little TV screens in front of him. I asked the girl behind the bar what movie they were showing.

"*The Flodders in America,*" she said.

She didn't look healthy. She had a sort of mousy face, half hidden by lank dark hair. She was just what you would expect; anything better would have been transferred to the Tuschinski 1. Behind her I could see the back of the ticket seller's head because everything here was made of glass.

"Is it starting to fill up?" I asked.

"We have our regulars," she said. "Have you come to see the Flodders?"

I didn't know what else I might have come for, actually, but clearly that wasn't something that had crossed her mind. "I've come for the company," was about the most noncommittal answer I could think of in the end.

"That's what most people do," she said, "and in winter they stay all day until we close."

I could hear the ticket seller shouting something. The girl looked around and said, "Oh, it's him again."

"Who?"

"One of our regulars. He always tries to take his dog inside. But dogs aren't allowed. Bicycles aren't either, for that matter."

"Disabled people are allowed inside but they don't come." Only then did I notice the boy behind the bar. He was sitting in a corner reading a comic book.

"So that man turns up every morning with his dog, you see. And then he's told that his dog isn't allowed in. So then he goes back home and then he comes back without the dog, and for the rest of the day he doesn't give us any trouble."

"No one gives us any trouble," said the boy, without looking up. "Not in winter either, because then half of them are asleep."

"That's because it's warm," the girl explained, and I ordered an espresso.

. . .

A few hours earlier I had been making pancakes. I had been driven home by the friend of mine who transported carpenter's glue to Poland but who had just lost his job. We dined extremely well on his last paycheck, I have to admit. That had been early in the evening, and afterward we drank extremely well on it too. He had shouted, "So long, carpenter's glue!" and I had told him that he could do a lot worse than become a driver for an escort service and that he could mention my name.

"Then you'll have to buy me a car first," he said, "because I have to give this one back tomorrow."

I said I didn't have enough money for that so we'd better forget the whole idea, just like all our other ideas. It was two o'clock by the time I got home but I felt like having pancakes.

I had to borrow a frying pan and some flour from my fellow lodger, and I had eggs and I assumed that a whole pile of milk powder packets would do for the rest.

I stood in my fellow lodger's kitchen. It so happened he was away. Both his parents had just died abroad, one after the other. He certainly wouldn't mind my using his things, including his pot holders, because I didn't have any of my own.

I remember his saying to me in English, "My father is very sick." By that time his father had already been dead for three days. My fellow lodger is from Israel and was a boxing champion there. His name is Sergius, and he's the best-looking man I've ever known; anyway, that was the opinion of my women visitors when they caught a glimpse of him walking by carrying a couple of grocery bags or saw him lying asleep on the sofa. He once said to me, "I don't love anybody." I no longer remember in what connection he said that or if it was in any connection at all. What I do remember is that we had pita sandwiches that evening from the Yamit grill and that we hung our bare feet out the window so the rain would wash the sweat off. He dealt in fake diamonds

from Brazil and talked as little as possible. But when he was standing there downstairs in the hallway with his suitcase, holding out
his hand to me and saying in English, "My father is very sick. I'm
back in ten days," I was the one to say nothing.

The movie had already started. Inside it smelled the way some
subway stations smell in summer, of popcorn and hot human
flesh. There were three little boys about six and a few little old
men, an Indian woman, and a mother with a baby. I wondered
how many of them had been to see *The Flodders in America* yesterday too. We watched Ma Flodder stub out a cigar on the carpet
in a very expensive hotel but nobody laughed. The baby started
to scream, though. I watched the mother take a bottle from her
shopping bag and pop it in the baby's mouth.

I had eaten three pancakes with sugar. After that I had hung
around in the kitchen so long that the grease in the pan hardened.
Then I thought of Sergius and the night he told me that his father
had been a grocer and that one day a Mrs. Feingold had come to
live above his father's store. The first morning after Mrs. Feingold
moved in, she came into the store at seven o'clock and bought
two eggs. Ten minutes later she was back. She said the eggs were
too small for her and her husband, so Sergius's father changed
them for bigger ones. Then she said, "These eggs are dirty."

Again she was given two different eggs, which she scrutinized
as if she had laid them herself. "One is all right," she said, "but
the other is still a little on the small side."

Then Sergius's father said, "Look, Mrs. Feingold, the chickens
don't wipe their behinds before they lay eggs, nor do they plan
to stretch their assholes any more than they have to for a few
cents from you." After that Mrs. Feingold was never seen in the
store again, and even when they passed each other on the stairs,
she didn't greet him. Sergius told me, "The fewer customers he
had, the more they began to irritate him. We often had to eat
the cream cheese and the eggs ourselves before they went bad."

That's what Sergius told me three months ago. Since then I've heard nothing from him, but all his things are still in his closets, and the chairs and the table he picked up from the garbage dump are still in his room. And Jack London's book on the Mexican revolution still lies open on the windowsill.

When I used to come home late, he would generally be lying asleep in front of the TV or changing the channel with his toes. When he saw me he'd always ask, "How're you doing?"

He often spent whole nights in front of the TV. Once he volunteered to teach me boxing but I said, "Some other time." One night, when we were both staring at the test pattern and drinking beer and vodka, I asked him how many people he'd killed. He said he was very sorry but he honestly had no idea anymore. He said that all he remembered was the names of those friends whose funerals he had had to go to. For the rest of that night we said nothing, just looked at the test pattern and dozed. He tried to learn Dutch by reading *De Echo,* marking all the special offers at the liquor stores for me.

I put the frying pan to soak, pulled on my sweater, and went out. I knew a place in Amstelveenseweg that opened at six in the morning.

First I talked to the drivers who sat there every morning and then to a woman with a knapsack. The color of her face testified to the number of beaches she'd been lying on that summer. Her hair was brown, too, and so were her eyes. After a while she said, "You shouldn't drink so much beer. You'll get a potbelly." She pointed to the sort of belly she meant. Sure enough, it was enormous.

"Come home with me," I said. "Otherwise I'll have to go back to the whores."

We must have been having a good conversation up until then because she replied, "You're just like all the others."

I told her it was a good thing she'd noticed that so quickly, seeing as how it was dangerous to entertain too many illusions about each other or about the world and how the best thing to do was to chuck most of them out the window until you were left with just a couple you were sure you couldn't live without. Those you had to guard like a lioness guarding her cubs, because they were all the treasure you were going to get in this life.

She wasn't really listening. I could see from the narrow pencil lines drawn around her eyes that she'd been using a mirror just a few minutes ago. "You don't know what love is," she finally said.

I'd heard that often enough, from many different lips. This time, too, I agreed, but I added quickly that I was still young and that I would be happy to have her teach me.

I stood up. At the door I turned around. "Good-bye, thou loveliest of all roses," I called.

It wasn't she who answered but the owner of the place, whose parting words were, "Go on home now."

Only when I was outside did I remember that I had gone in for a cup of coffee. It was eight o'clock and people were going to work.

I waited for a number 6 streetcar and thought of the herring salad I was going to eat at my mother's for lunch. The recipe was my father's.

One lunchtime when I came home from school he said, "Radio Deutsche Welle broadcast a recipe for herring salad today, but you could hardly hear it because there was interference again from pirates." That night he wrote a letter to Deutsche Welle and asked them for the recipe, and he also started proceedings against the pirates. It took him four years to lose the case. He ordered a suit from his tailor in Hong Kong especially for the hearing.

He ordered suits for every special occasion in his life. The last one he ordered was a tropical suit, intended for a visit to my sister. He would have looked like a fool in it, and my mother and I said, "All you'll need now is a butterfly net." But he banged his fist on the table and said, "In that kind of heat I'll *need* a tropical suit." By the time the tropical suit finally arrived from Hong Kong he was in the hospital.

Every two years he would go to southern Germany for a cure and write us letters with detailed reports on the state of the weather, his hotel, the train ride, and the slow passage of time in one or other of the spas, where the people, according to him, could talk of nothing but their state of health and the food. What he liked best about these vacations was the train ride, which he whiled away in the dining car with a bottle of wine and German chocolate layer cake. To judge from his letters, he spent most of his vacation on the balcony of his hotel room listening to the radio.

He sent me postcards with messages like, "Everything here is sick, even the trees. So stop bemoaning the fate of the world."

A few months before he died he developed a dermatological condition that slowly transformed his skin into a lunar landscape. He was moved to another hospital, where they rubbed cream into him from top to bottom three times a day. Then his skin started to flake off.

I would often lock myself in the men's room at the hospital and say, "God, please make it stop. I beg of you, make it all stop. I'll live by your commandments if you make it all stop." I never told anyone about the God to whom I was praying then, not my mother, my sister, or anyone else. I didn't tell Marcella anything about it either. When she'd asked me if I ever prayed to God, all I'd said was, "God is love, as you know very well, so take off your clothes."

On his last night the hospital seemed almost deserted. The blond nurse took my hand and said, "It's a good thing you're here, because your mother's gone completely to pieces. Would you like some coffee?"

"Yes, I'll have some coffee," I said. "Or do you have anything else?"

"No," she said. "We don't have anything else, we're on duty."

We drank coffee and I looked at her. Another nurse came in and said, "Your mother's waking up all the patients with her shouting." Two nurses tried to approach my mother from behind, but they couldn't have been fully trained because they didn't manage to grab hold of her. The little blond stayed with me and said, "Would you like to go back in there?"

I didn't really know if I wanted to.

"Is it the thing to do?" I asked.

"Come on," she said.

I walked behind her. You could see her panties under all the white. We went into his room. The remains of his supper hadn't been cleared away yet. He had turned completely yellow. I looked at her because I couldn't look at that yellow.

"You're late," she said. "We couldn't reach you."

"I was in the bar," I said, and heard my mother's screams outside. I stood there for a little longer. It was freezing cold because they'd already turned the heat off.

She said, "Would you like to give him a last kiss?"

"Is it the thing to do?" I asked because I didn't want to do anything that wasn't the right thing.

She went over to stand by the window. She was wearing sneakers and rubbed one of them back and forth on the floor. She was smiling very sadly and I was getting horny, which was honestly something of a nuisance. Then she said, "Come on." I walked after her with my hands in my pockets. I didn't know where to look because, honestly, you could see everything.

Two boys came and sat down in front of me. Instead of watching the movie they talked to each other nonstop. The rest of the audience watched the acting of Huub Stapel, ate popcorn or potato chips, and blew pink bubbles of gum.

At first I didn't listen to the boys, but then I heard one say that he had a rash on his prick and the other one said that all men got that and it was nothing to be worried about. The first one said, "Fuck you, OK? Fuck you. I bet *you* don't have it."

I went into a secondhand bookstore on Kloveniersburgwal

and bought *The Dog with the Blue Tongue* for two guilders, walked toward Central Station, and went into the café where I had watched the Parma-Antwerp match a few weeks earlier. I sat in a corner near the men's room and remembered what Sergius had told me about the time when they were in the desert and sick to death of canned food. There'd been five of them sitting jammed in a small tank when two Mirages appeared overhead. "At first we thought they were ours," Sergius said, "but then we realized they weren't. I was sitting beside the driver. Yossi was sitting behind me. Yossi had only just joined us. He had taken the place of someone who had stepped on a mine. Yossi was extremely religious, and he asked me to stick my head out to see if the Mirages were coming back. That's just about the stupidest thing anyone can do, stick his head out a tank. From the moment you spot the Mirage until the rocket hits you takes exactly one and a half seconds, and in those one and a half seconds there's nothing you can do. Either they get you and that's the end of your problems or else they don't. But even if they miss you and you've stuck your head out, there's a good chance it'll get chopped off by all the stuff flying through the air after the bang. A few days later we sent Yossi back home. The trouble with fear is that it's infectious. There are some people, of course, who say that it isn't infectious because it never bothers them, but even they have to admit that it can get on your nerves."

He told me that the evening we watched that western with Jane Fonda and Gregory Peck. Halfway through I fell asleep, and I only woke up again when Gregory Peck had to die and said to Jane Fonda, "You won't remember anything about me, all you'll remember is that we fought, but you'll forget what we were fighting for," or something like that.

When Sergius was living with me he would sleep for whole days at a time. He was even too lazy to go out shopping. That's why he ate an entire apple pie my mother brought for me. Or he'd stand in front of the window and ask me if I knew who Bessie

Smith was. Then he'd make Turkish coffee and say that the best thing about being young was that you were slightly insane. You had to be, he said, otherwise you wouldn't go charging through the desert with a gun just to get your officers promoted. The other good thing was that you could talk endlessly about fucking and never really get bored with the subject. When you were forty, you could still talk about it, of course, you didn't have to be bored by it even then. But it wasn't something you honestly went out of your way to look for anymore.

A few days later he packed his bag and said that he'd be back in ten days.

The bartender gave me a beer. He pointed to a table where two men who had been busy playing snooker earlier were sitting. One of them slapped his hand on an empty chair. They asked me my name. "Stephen," I said. They asked if I was looking for work.

"All the time," I said.

They asked what I could do.

"Nothing," I said.

"Just like us," said the one wearing a short brown jacket with shiny patches on the back, and I thought of my mother, who always mopped the kitchen floor on Monday mornings.

"Listen to this," said the man who wasn't wearing a jacket but a white shirt with a fountain pen in the breast pocket. "A man goes to a whore and says, 'I want you to suck me off.' 'Right,' says the whore, 'that'll be five hundred guilders.' 'Five hundred guilders?' says the man. 'You must be completely out of your mind.' But the whore pulls the curtain to one side and says, 'Look outside. See that Cadillac? I earned that by sucking men off.' Well, the man thinks, she must be something special, and he pays her the five hundred. Next day he comes back to the whore and says, 'Look, I want to fuck your asshole.' 'That's all right with me,' says the whore. 'That'll be a thousand guilders.' 'A thousand guilders?' says the man. 'Forget it.' The whore opens the curtain again and says, 'You see that mansion over there? I built that and paid for it by having my asshole fucked.' Well, thinks the man, that must be something very special, so he pays her the thousand. Next day he comes back to the whore and says, 'This time I want it straight.' The whore takes him up to the window again and says, 'You see that street? I could own the whole street if only I had a cunt.' "

I spat the drink in my mouth back into the glass. Life, too, could be considered a gift from God, couldn't it?

"So you're looking for work," said the one in the brown jacket.

"All the time."

"Listen to this," said the other one. "A man walks into a brothel. There are two doors. One says fifty guilders and the other one says five hundred. He thinks to himself, Well, I'll try the fifty guilder one first. So he goes inside, comes into a small room, and there's a cow. All right, he's paid, so he fucks the cow. Next day he comes back because he's really curious about the other room. He pays five hundred guilders, goes inside, and there are a whole lot of people in the room standing in front of a small window. He pushes to the front, and through the window he sees a couple banging away. 'Is that what we've paid five hundred guilders for?' he asks. 'Oh well,' says one of the others, 'this is nothing. If you'd come yesterday, you would have seen a guy fucking a cow.' "

We had some more drinks and I said, "This happened when the Reds were fighting the Whites in Russia. One day the Reds captured the most-wanted White general. I've forgotten what his name was but he was notorious, he was known in the smallest village in the land. The Reds debated the best way to execute him. One of the soldiers suggested the Tartar method of torture, where they shove a pole up your ass until you croak. But the others thought that was too mild for the general, so someone suggested having him torn apart by four horses, but that was rejected too. Then Lyupka said, 'You know what? We let him drink all night, we let him drink as much as he wants, and then, next morning, we don't let him have another drop.' 'Oh, you're a cruel bastard, Lyupka,' said the leader, 'you're as cruel as they come.' "

They ordered another round and we listened to the Moody Blues singing that song about Dr. Livingstone. Finally I stood up because I was going to meet my mother. The one with the brown jacket stood up as well. For a moment I thought he was going to embrace me but he said, "Listen, if you're looking for work, you'd better come see us."

"Yes, we'll send him to see Dreese," the other one said with a grin.

I called my mother from a phone booth and said I'd be there any minute. Then I bought *De Telegraaf* and sat on a bench behind Central Station, where the ferries leave for the north. I looked at the girls who stand around there. One of them was some kind of Indian and had hardly any teeth left. There was a cigarette sticking out of her mouth all the same. Another had wrapped herself up as if it was winter. She looked pleasant enough but she certainly wasn't waiting to hitch a ride on a bicycle. When I walked past the second time, only the toothless Indian was left.

My mother was waiting for me with the herring salad. A week ago we had sat in her backyard. When the neighbor's children had finally stopped their shrieking, I'd said to her, "I won't give a damn when you kick the bucket. It really won't matter to me." I didn't even know at the time if it was true or why I had said it; all I knew was that, a few moments before, we had been talking about a pine tree that had been transplanted.

"You're a monster," my mother said.

"Yes," I said, "that's me."

Even when you were freezing to death, it felt as if you were on fire. At that moment I could think of nobody I felt really close to, nobody I felt I owed anything other than a stray thought. Maybe I cared about the whores I had been with, because I did think about them during the hours when I wasn't with them or when I wasn't on my way to them. But I wasn't too sure even about that. I had met many people, in cafés and at parties, who all wanted to make a lot of money and become celebrities or good soldiers or good mothers, but most of all they wanted to believe that they still loved those they had desired, whose framed photographs now stood on their bookcases. And they wanted me to believe that too.

"And what about your father?" she asked, and I could hear her swallowing her coffee. Farther up the street a mother was calling her children inside. I thought of the time he'd said, "We don't remember the dead as the living beings they once were but as corpses brought to life, as if they'd never had any other destiny than to be dead and haunting us."

I said that I hadn't really meant any of it, that I was sorry, and quickly finished my coffee.

Yesterday she called me and said that she hadn't been able to get what I'd said out of her head. Even though she'd tried she couldn't forget it. I said "Yes" when she asked, "Couldn't you say that you love me?"

You either love what you've got, which is something you shouldn't look at too closely, or you don't, and then you go off into the wild blue yonder where there is always some madman ready to take a shot at you.

When I walked past a third time, even the Indian woman had gone. I wondered who had taken her. There were just two boys, sitting on the ground, and they certainly weren't planning to go off with anybody. I thought of my mother and of her expression every night not so many years ago when she came to give me a good-night kiss in bed. She was like every other mother in the world, wanting me to be the handsomest and the best. She was just a little more fanatical.

Without too much effort I could hear my father shouting, "He's scratching them raw, right here at the table. I'm going to throw up!"

We were slouched over our plates and the candles were lit. My mother cried, "Stop it!" and my father yelled, "You're letting all that muck fall into your food. It's disgusting, it's enough to make anyone puke!"

"I can't help it," I said. "They bother me."

"They'll go away if you leave them alone," said my father.

"Pigs!" cried my mother.

The radio played, the candles flickered, we were still slouching over our plates, and my mother shouted at my father, "You belong in an old age home, you useless old geezer!" Then she said that she was beginning to feel like throwing up herself. She grabbed the hot towel she always kept handy, placed it over my face, and started to squeeze my pimples while the rest of the family went on with their soup. The rest of the family was my father, and it didn't take long before he was shouting, "That filth's all dropping into the soup! Go and do that upstairs, the two of you. It's the same every night here—my food gets ruined."

After I had brushed my teeth, my mother went to work on my back as well. She said that my back was the hardest part to do because I wouldn't sit still. She warned me that I'd get a crooked back if I kept looking at the ground all the time instead of walking straight and proud the way she did. I did look at the ground a lot. I had the feeling, although I knew it was crazy, that people wouldn't see you if you didn't see them. I said that I'd rather deal with my back myself but my mother explained that that wasn't a good idea, because I bit my nails. You needed nails to collect all the muck, she said.

This went on for a few months, until one evening I snatched

the hot towel out of my mother's hands and held it in the candle flames. My father sat stock-still in his black swivel chair and my mother tried to beat the burning towel out with her handkerchief. There was a news broadcast on the radio.

My mother didn't say a word but my father started banging his knife and fork on his plate, shouting, "Fire, fire! Do something, somebody! Do something!" while I stood there with the corner of the towel in my right hand.

There's still a black mark on the parquet floor under the rug, where the towel burned itself out.

After that we went back to our dinner, my mother tapped on the door to the bathroom, where our guest had locked himself in, and we celebrated Shavuot. That night I started to let my hair grow.

"Hello, darling. My name is Nadine, I'm 25, with big boobs. I entertain you topless, in only the tiniest panties with garters. I like to make love to gentlemen and to give erotic massage. Agamemnonstraat, Mondays to Fridays."

I hadn't read this ad before. There was no telephone number, so I'd have to go there and try my luck. A friend of mine had once lived in Achillesstraat. Agamemnonstraat couldn't be far away.

I peed twice in the bushes in Olympiaplein because it was better not to arrive with a full bladder. The first time I walked past, I didn't ring the doorbell. I just gave the place the once-over. It looked like all the other houses in the street except that the curtains were of some thick turquoise material. I walked on and finished up on the quay, where I went and stood on the bridge, looking down at the dark water and at the gulls and the people fishing. Normally I don't bother to look at water or at gulls but this time I did. The gulls weren't bad-looking and the water was also better than you might expect, though nothing to write home about. In a snack bar on the next street I ordered a Coke because all the saliva seemed to have drained from my mouth. A man beside me was reading the paper, and I wondered if he, too, was waiting for something or somebody. Even after I had emptied my glass there was still no saliva in my mouth.

Farther down Agamemnonstraat a man was washing his car. He looked at me but I went on looking straight at the front door, waiting for it to open.

"Are you the new driver?"

I was hoping she wasn't Nadine but, if she was, it wouldn't have made any difference anyway. She reminded me of the little flower woman who used to stand in Maasstraat and give me a friendly greeting every Saturday as I walked past her in my yarmulke.

"No, I'm not the new driver. I've come about your ad."

She shut the door. We were standing in the hallway, which was wide enough for a couple of bicycles.

"You see, sometimes we get our drivers from the paper too."

"I guess you do," I said.

"I have a girl for you, though. Blond, slim—"

"Fine," I said.

"Don't you want to know any more?"

"That's OK."

"Then you'll have to settle up with me first. It's 125 guilders."

"I don't have it exactly. I only have 150."

"We have plenty of change," she said, and laughed.

We came into a sort of sunken sitting area, what could have been the living room of a family with too many children. There were two sofas, and the TV was on. Plates of food that nobody seemed likely to finish were on the table, there were empty cans all over the place, and a girl sat staring into space on a sofa in front of the window.

The one I called the little flower woman to myself said, "That's her."

I went up to the girl. She held her hand out to me and the little flower woman said, "That's Astrid."

Everything about her was white. Her hair, her short skirt, her boots, her plastic jacket; even her skin looked as if it had white makeup on.

"What would you like to drink?" asked the little flower woman.

"Coke," I said.

"We have beer too."

"That would be even better."

There was a movie on TV, but Astrid wasn't watching it. I couldn't really tell what she was looking at. The room smelled the way the packed synagogue can smell on the Day of Atonement just before the closing prayer is said and the congregation asks God for the very last time to enter them in the Book of Life.

I was given a can of beer. I thanked the little flower woman profusely because I felt like having a beer, like having a lot of beer. Perhaps the little flower woman was beginning to take to me; in any case, she gave my arm a squeeze and said, "You're very welcome, young man."

"Let's go," Astrid said suddenly. I started to follow her, holding my can of beer.

"Do you have any condoms?" asked Astrid.

She was asking not me but the little flower woman, who said, "Which ones do you want?"

We went into a room and Astrid said she would be back in a moment, she just had to go to the bathroom. It struck me that her voice matched her looks perfectly, as if she had powdered her vocal cords too. She spoke with a drawl but it didn't sound unpleasant. The way she looked, she couldn't have spoken any other way.

I sat down on the first bed I saw; there was another one near it. On the floor lay an umbrella. The last visitor must have left it behind, I thought. When I looked more closely I realized that it was a parasol, presumably put there for decoration. Except that the room was too small for a parasol and you had to be careful not to trip over it. A plant stood next to the parasol, and next to the plant a small lamp cast a glow like old red wine. Just above the parasol hung a photograph of someone about to dive off a diving board. There was a pile of towels on a small white shelf nailed to the wall. I opened my can of beer and Astrid came back into the room.

I looked again at her white hair and her smooth white skirt, which, like her ankle-high boots, shone with a curious brightness in the semidarkness of the room. She reminded me of a character in a movie about ancient Egypt I had once seen. It had been a pretty old movie and I knew that they hadn't made movies like that for about thirty years, but she looked as if she had just walked out of one. She also spoke as if she were playing the part of a princess for whom even talking was too much of an effort.

She took her boots off and I untied my shoes, and I asked, "How old are you?" because you have to ask something, after all.

"I haven't seen eighteen for nearly ten years," she said.

"And where are you from?"

She looked at me with her blue eyes. It wouldn't have surprised me if their color had been artificial—contact lenses maybe.

"Why do you want to know?"

"No particular reason."

"I come from Schiedam."

"I come from Amsterdam," I said. Except for her panties she was completely naked now. Her round breasts stuck straight out, as if they were being pulled up by invisible wires.

"Let's have a nice cuddle now," she said. "Nice and cozy. That's how I like it."

"Yes," I said, "me too." I pushed my can of beer between the towels and took off my underpants and laid them on top of my other clothes. I already had an erection, and I always feel embarrassed when I have an erection before it's time. But you get

used to overheated rooms, you get used to the girls, just the way
you get used to other things, and finally you forget to feel embarrassed about any of it.

"Would you like a quick wash?"

"No, don't bother," I said. "I just had a good one."

"Could you get that condom?" She pointed to the white shelf.

She was sitting on the bed. I could see now that the staircase
leading to the next floor ran over the bed, so it was like being in
an attic. When you got up you had to be careful not to bump
your head.

"You can put it on yourself," said Astrid.

The others had always done that for me, and as far as I knew
that was the usual thing. Still, I told her it was no problem. I tore
the packet open but because of the heat, the poor light, and my
shaking hands I didn't get much farther than the tip. So I asked,
"Can you help me a little?"

I didn't actually hear her sigh, but I'm pretty sure she did, and
then she crawled toward me. She pulled it on with a quick tug.
"I'm not very practical," I said. "I never fix anything at home. I
can't even paint."

"That makes you smell."

"What? What does?"

"Paint."

I was sitting cross-legged next to her on the bed drinking my
beer, and I thought that what she really meant was I stank but
that she was being very subtle about it, a girl with tact.

"Let me have that," she said, "and we'll have a nice cuddle.
Nice and cozy." She took the can of beer from my hand and put
it on the floor. Only now did I see that her face was covered with
freckles. The freckles were faded, as if they were halfhearted about
wanting to be freckles at all, or perhaps it was because they were
hidden under white powder. She reminded me again of a woman
in some black-and-white movie, the kind they made dozens of
just after the war.

She took something from the little shelf and started to fumble around on top of me but I was looking at her freckles, and it was only when I asked, "What are you doing?" that I realized that she had put a second condom on me.

Not only did she think I stank, but she was disgusted by all of me. That's why I was now wearing two condoms, one over the other, and I wondered if my cock could expect a third one as well. I reached for the can of beer she had put on the floor. "No, leave it alone," she said. "We're going to have a nice, cozy cuddle now."

I pulled my hand back and lay down with my head beside the pillow, right under the bottom step of the staircase.

She sat on top of me, and I could feel that she still had her panties on. She would first try it like that, of course. I would have done the same if I were her. She smelled nice and she was warm and white but just as distant as that girl in the movie.

When she realized that nothing was happening she took her white panties off and put them somewhere by the pillow. She sat on top of me again and I stroked her buttocks, which were a little rougher than the rest of her skin. Her face was close to mine. I could see that she didn't have any powder on. Her skin was naturally white. The light had something to do with it, too, of course, but even in the sunlight her skin would have looked like flour and her freckles would have remained as faded as a dying sunbeam.

It felt like entering a pail of soapsuds.

I stroked her hair and asked if she dyed it.

"It's a wig," she said, "can't you tell?"

For the first time I heard something like indignation in her voice, as if I had insulted her by failing to notice that she wore a wig. I didn't know all that many people who wore wigs, and wig hair felt pretty much like real hair with too much gel in it.

She was lying on top of me and neither of us was moving. I

couldn't move, because of her weight, and she probably had a good reason for lying still too.

"Hey, come on, how about some action?" she said after a while. "A nice cuddle and a nice come, that's what I like."

"All right," I said, and placed my hand on her white throat. I wondered if her eyebrows and eyelashes had come from a wig.

"I'll give you my number in a minute," she whispered, "then you'll be able to come over to my place and we'll be nice and cozy together. I'll cook for you and after that we'll watch a video and then we'll have a nice, cozy cuddle."

Her cheek was next to mine. Had I wanted to, I could have counted her freckles. Suddenly I wanted nothing more than to have her cook for me, to watch a video with her, and to have a nice, cozy time with her, and I wanted to ask her what the price of such an arrangement would be. But then I felt that it wasn't right to talk about money while we were lying on top of each other.

I moved my fingers over her lips and her cheek and asked if she was a good cook and what her specialty was.

"Steak," she said. "And now it's your turn to lie on top of me."

She settled in the corner of the bed. There wasn't much room, with the staircase just four inches above my head. It was a little while before she opened her legs. Then she took hold of me as I have been taken hold of quite a few times before. Only she didn't say, "Come on!" or "Let's go!" or "Shoot!"

"I'll give you my number in a minute," she whispered. "I'm really enjoying myself."

"Yes, me too," I said.

I was holding her head tight. When I lie on top of a girl I tend to grasp her head and press it to me, to my chest or my neck or my shoulder, because that feels right to me. She said, "You're hurting me a little, because of the wig."

"Sorry," I said.

She pointed to where I could put my hands, on her temples. She looked at the staircase above her or at the wall to her right, and I held on to her head as if I were high up in a tree and afraid of falling.

It took longer than usual. I noticed that she was getting irritated because it was taking so long, so I started to talk to her. In waiting rooms, too, I always start up a conversation, but she said nothing back. She obviously felt we ought to finish up in silence. I wondered what her hair was like under the wig and realized that I wouldn't recognize her if I ran into her on the street.

"Hush, hush," she said after another few minutes had passed, although I had said nothing. I was still lying there on top of her and I was holding her head and she was acting as if she were swooning. Then I began to get irritated myself. Surely she couldn't blame me for having the feeling I was churning a pail of soapsuds or for my having to wear two condoms because she was too lazy to wash me. I made another few thrusting movements and she stared at the staircase as if her husband lived on the floor above us.

I thought, Nothing more is going to happen today. So I made a few more quick thrusts and got off her. "That was nice," she said, and I agreed.

I looked for my beer and she looked for her panties, which she found under the pillow. Sitting on the bed, she put them on.

"Can you take the condom off yourself?" she asked.

"Yes," I said, and took both of them off and put them on the white shelf.

"I just have to go to the bathroom."

"Will you be coming back?" I asked.

"Yes," she said.

I got dressed. I searched my mind for the name of the movie in which the girl had looked so much like her. I could hear people talking in the living room but couldn't hear her voice.

She came back with a paper towel.

I wrapped the condoms in it and followed her to the shower, which had been built into a clothes closet. A wastebasket stood in front of the shower, exactly the same as I had in my own bathroom. It was filled to the brim with condoms wrapped in paper towels. I added my offering, and for the first time that day I felt relieved, as if I had done a good deed. That was a sight to see, a used-condom museum.

We went back to the room and I sat on the bed again and drank my beer. She stood in front of me doing something to her face.

"Do you have wigs in other colors too?"

"It's about time you stopped asking questions. You've asked enough." Her voice was no longer drawling and distant but clear and very close, and I could smell chewing gum on her breath.

"Sorry," I said. "I didn't mean to be rude."

"You shouldn't talk so much. I'm only telling you for your own good."

"I realize that."

She came up to me and placed a finger on my lips.

"A wise man holds his tongue," she said.

I put on my shoes. "You don't like talking very much, that's for sure."

"It drives me crazy, all that talking." Her voice sounded clear and close again.

There's a song, a German sailors' chantey, I think, that goes something like, "She knew what she was saying when she held her tongue." My father sang it occasionally, but I couldn't remember the words or the melody and he wasn't around to ask any longer.

"We'll have to get a move on. Somebody else is waiting."

"I've still got some beer."

"You can take it with you."

I didn't want to leave the house clutching a can of beer, so I left it behind.

"You were going to give me your telephone number."

"Oh yes," she said. She took out a small vanity case and gave me a folded piece of pink paper. I could see that there were three pieces of paper left in the case, next to the makeup. Rosie, too, had kept her makeup in a case like that, except that Rosie's case had been blue, not white.

"We have to go," she said.

"All right," I said.

In the living room the little flower woman sat talking to a man. I couldn't tell if he was a customer or just an acquaintance who had come in to chat. They sounded as if they were enjoying themselves, anyway.

As I walked past, she called out, "Was everything to your liking, sir?" And I called back, "Excellent." I noticed now that there was a microwave in the sitting area and that the whole place smelled of food. If you can have an office in your home these days, you can have a brothel there too.

We were standing in the foyer.

"So long," I said.

"That's our little secret," she said, pointing to the piece of paper I was holding in my hand. I quickly shoved it into my pants pocket.

"It'll remain our little secret," I promised. Again I tried to picture her without her white wig and without the short white suit, but I would never be able to see her like that.

Even here, in a light that hid nothing, her skin was the color of buttermilk.

"Ciao," I said, and she said, "Take care." A few houses farther up I peed against a tree and then I went to a café where I had some more beer.

"Two sexy girls in naughty lingerie. Anything goes. Call for further information," I read on the piece of paper she had given me. And above that, "Personal attention at no. 26, great relax-ation for you and your business acquaintances." I turned the paper over and found two telephone numbers written in a large childish hand. Next to them someone had used a rubber stamp. It said "Astrid" in red and had three little hearts around it. I'd been given a stamp like that by my sister when I was eight or nine. My stamp had been blue and had said "Sheriff," not "Astrid."

I thought of her white wig. I already knew that I would call her to make use of her arrangements. I thought of her and all the others. You could say what you liked about them, but at least none of them had bothered me with questions that I couldn't answer or that I refused to find answers to, because I didn't want to spend the rest of my life thinking about them. Of course, we always met in darkened rooms where the idea wasn't to get to know each other too closely. It's just as well we meet each other in places like that.

"Two sexy girls in naughty lingerie. Anything goes." I sat there with the piece of paper in my hand and studied it as if it carried a message from another planet.

Only when somebody sat down at my table did I put the paper back in my pocket and order another beer. It was a woman with short fair hair and a khaki shirt. Both of us stared at our glasses until she said, "How about a game of snooker?" She pointed to the billiard table, and I realized that she had spoken Dutch with a heavy American accent.

I had never played snooker, but I agreed. She said that she was only interested in playing for money and that we both had to put up a twenty-five-guilder stake. I still had some money, so I handed her twenty-five guilders and walked over to the table to pick up a cue. She explained the rules to me and I looked at the little chain with a cross dangling around her neck.

"My name is Joan," she said, and she talked about a dog of hers that she was very fond of, which was why she had to hurry. Ten minutes later she put my bill in her purse and treated me to a beer.

"Like a rematch?" she asked.

Definitely. It was better playing snooker with her than sitting at a table looking at the empty street and thinking of Astrid or of two sexy girls in naughty lingerie, anything goes.

I had to give her another twenty-five guilders. She told me then that she always played for money. She was a professional snooker player, traveling through Europe playing snooker for money in all the big cities.

"Great," I said. "Maybe I should do that too."

We played again and drank beer. She told me to be careful not to let the black ball drop into the pocket, because then my opponent would win. Once again she made twenty-five guilders inside ten minutes.

"Another one?" she asked.

"No, thanks," I said.

"Run out of money?"

"That's not the problem. Sufficient unto the day, you know?"

We sat down. Joan told me that Amsterdam had a real snooker hall and that I ought to go there sometime.

"Great," I said.

I treated her to some of the small round meatballs they served as appetizers. When we'd each had five she asked me to lend her some money. She put her hand on mine and said that she was in trouble. She started to tell me a story, in English, about her boy-friend who was in the US Army and had to get back to Berlin but didn't have the fare, and how if he wasn't in Berlin the next morning, all hell would break loose. Although I felt I'd really had enough to drink, for the sake of being companionable I decided I might as well carry on for a while. There was still one meatball on the plate; her story was taking a long time to tell. At one point I interrupted her. "Don't give me that shit," I said in English. "I've heard it a thousand times before." That wasn't actually true. I'd only heard it a few times, but that had been enough for it to remain engraved in my mind so that I never wanted to hear it again.

I looked at the cross dangling over her breasts, and I thought of her dog and that they could all go to hell for all I cared.

She said she knew I didn't believe her, but that it was nothing but the truth and that she could prove it. She didn't talk loudly, just urgently. For me, too, the day had been long and hard. I said in English, "Don't fuck my mind, don't fuck my mind." Apparently I shouted it, because the bartender came over and said that this was a café for respectable people.

I don't know whether it was because of the bartender or whether it was the meatballs or what, but I took out my last fifty-guilder bill and told Joan not to worry. Then she started telling another story, but I had stopped listening. I was reminded of an aunt of mine from New York who always reeked of perfume and who talked about the camps whenever she visited us, as if she had only just been let out of one. It made even my mother feel like puking. To me that aunt always used to say, in English, "Make it a masterpiece, make it a masterpiece."

I watched Joan tuck my last bill into her jeans pocket and thought to myself that it had been a good day. You have to be able to shell out money from time to time without expecting them to take off their clothes and deliver the goods then and there.

Joan insisted that we be friends, that I'd have to believe she'd pay it all back to me, even what I'd shelled out for the meatballs. I knew I wouldn't see a red cent from her, ever. Even so we walked together to the streetcar. For the first time that day I was starting to feel the lack of a night's sleep, and by the time we finally reached Bilderdijkstraat I felt as if I hadn't slept for a week.

We went into a café I had never gone to before and won't ever be going to again. A man with an almost completely shaven head was sitting at the bar, and she said, "That's him."

He looked at me as if my semen were still between her legs, but that could have been my imagination. Whether he was really a GI I couldn't tell, nor for that matter whether he was really her boyfriend, but it was pretty clear that he was an expert at three types of unarmed combat at the very least.

I didn't want to drink anymore or to go on somewhere nice to dance.

"So long," I said.

"Yeah," said her friend. She took me outside, kissed me on the mouth, and promised again to pay me back for everything.

All I said was not to forget her dog. I can't remember if I got home by streetcar or taxi or on foot. I don't really think it can have been by taxi.

A letter was lying on my doormat. "I'll pick up your old newspapers," it said. "Call me." I folded the letter in four and dropped it in the wastebasket. I remembered again that my mother was waiting for me with herring salad. I called her but it was too late. She was already sleeping, or maybe she had hanged herself.

"I'll pick up your old newspapers. In naughty lingerie. Any-thing goes," I said to the sink I was bending over. For the first time that day I was looking at everything in a rosy light.

It was still Monday night when I woke up. I started to shave but quickly stopped. There was no need for it any longer. I called my mother again but she didn't answer. The piece of pink paper was lying on my desk. In naughty lingerie. Anything goes. Call for further information.

I turned the paper over and looked at Astrid's two telephone numbers. Much as I imagine an alcoholic thirsts for his next glass before the glass in front of him is empty, so I thirsted after those girls.

The first number was busy and stayed busy. I tried the second.

"Stijns here," said a man.

"Hello," I said. "Is this Astrid's number?" I thought of her white wig and wondered if she had taken it off by now.

"Astrid who?"

"I don't know. I only know her first name. Astrid."

"Who's speaking, anyway?" It was impossible to tell how old the guy was. He spoke with a slight nasal twang.

"Arnon," I said. "A–r—"

"Don't bother. Astrid isn't here."

"When can I reach her?"

"Try tomorrow morning, about nine o'clock."

"Thanks," I said.

I got undressed and lay down on the bed to sleep.

I woke up at eight-thirty. I went to the bathroom to wash and shave and thought of her halfhearted faded freckles.

In Sergius's kitchen the grease in the pan had turned a different color and so had the batter I hadn't used—a thin film had now formed over it. I remembered how we had sat here at the poorly scrubbed wooden table, eating cheese rolls in the middle of the night while he told me how he'd become a boxing champion in an old movie theater.

I threw the batter away. Before I went to the telephone I looked at myself in the mirror. Anything goes. Call for further information. I turned the piece of paper over, saw the stamp, and was again reminded of my own stamp saying "Sheriff." Perhaps it was still lying around the place somewhere in one of the boxes I had crammed with the useless objects I had been too chicken to throw out.

"Hello."

"Hello," I said. "Arnon here. Is that Astrid?"

"Yes." I could hear her lazy voice. From the way she spoke I could tell she was wearing her white wig and had her white boots on again too.

"I was at your place yesterday. I'm the one who talked so much. The one with curly hair."

Silence.

"The one who talked so much? Do you remember?"

"Yes," she said. It wasn't the "yes" of someone who remembered anything but the "yes" of someone who wanted to encourage you to go on. I thought of her breasts, which had looked as if they had been pulled up by wires, and the slightly rougher skin on her buttocks.

"You said you'd like to cook for me."

"Let me think," she said.

Two sexy girls in naughty lingerie. Anything goes. Call for further information. I knew right away that it had been a mistake to call her and felt the need for a drink to wash away the sharp corners of the day.

"Today?" she asked.

"Yes, fine. Great."

"Three o'clock?"

"OK."

"You'll have to come to Agamemnonstraat," said Astrid, "A g–a–m–e–m–n–o–n."

While she was spelling it out for me, which she didn't do particularly easily, I could see that whole home-brothel in my mind's eye again and I knew that what happened today would be exactly the same as yesterday.

"See you at three o'clock," I said.

"Nice," said Astrid, "cozy."

I folded the slip of paper and stuck it in my diary. I had never been back to a girl before. I had always wanted a new one. A face I didn't know and a smell I had never smelled, so that the hours I spent with them didn't seem the same and so I could remember each of them separately despite the short time we spent together, despite the poor light, and despite all the lies we told each other that didn't even have to be lies, although we would go on thinking they were or think nothing at all.

Vespuccistraat, Brederodestraat, Koninginneweg, Agamemnonstraat, Utrechtsedwaarstraat, Bilderdijkstraat, Frans van Mieriesstraat. Through Amsterdam ran a trail of girls and women with made-up names, all of whom I had been with. I had met them, and they had met me, in converted living rooms, on beds with bad springs, in clothes closets with built-in showers. I had never before been back to any of them. I may have walked down their streets afterward but I had never rung their doorbells; what was a one-night stand had to stay a one-night stand. I'd hardly closed the door of one behind me when invariably I went in search of the next. The mere time it took to walk home was enough to forget everything. Their wigs, their dyed hair, the sinks where they washed me, and above all the face of the one who was not there and who never would be there either. There was less and less time between one face and the next, for no matter whose bed I lay in, each of them made me want to fly to the next.

Yet here I was going back to Astrid, and I thought of her all morning. Of her thin, faraway voice and her aversion to all the talking that people do. Maybe she was right—maybe we all ought to stop trying to put love into words. Maybe we ought to stop driveling about love altogether and simply give out warmth in the only way we can, with our bodies, and for the rest hold our tongues.

That morning I read three books I was supposed to write reader's reports on, and I did my best to say favorable things about their imaginative power. I thought of that parasol and the bed I would be lying on again in a few hours and the little flower woman who would settle up with me in the hallway and call me her young man.

After eating a herring I took my second shower that day, rubbed extra gel into my hair, looked for a clean pair of socks, and put money in my pocket.

At the corner of Willemsparkweg a boy and a girl were standing behind a trestle table.

"Buy some plums, sir?"

I stopped. "Where are you from?"

"Near Tiel," said the boy. He was older than the girl, had a short, thick neck, and was solidly built. He'd be tough later on.

"Those plums come from your own garden?"

"One guilder twenty-five a pound," said the girl.

I stooped toward her. "What's your name?" I asked.

I couldn't understand what she said but it sounded a little like Diederikje.

"I'll be back in an hour and a half," I said. "Then I'll buy some of your plums."

"Oh, it's you," said the little flower woman.

"Yes, I have a date with Astrid."

"Come in," she said and shut the door.

"Astrid isn't in right now, she's on escort."

"I have a date with her at three o'clock."

"Have you come for an anal?"

"No, for Astrid."

"So you've come for an anal."

"No, for Astrid. I just said."

"You've come for straight, then?"

"Well, I suppose so, yes."

"Then follow me. You might as well take another slim one. But let's settle up first."

I gave her the 125 guilders; this time I had brought the exact amount. Again I followed her into the living room. Two women were sitting there.

"He came for Astrid but I told him that he might just as well take another slim one." She gave me a friendly little shove. "That's her," she said, and pointed to the girl sitting on the sofa by the window.

"Hello," I said. We shook hands. I didn't shake hands with the other girl, nor did she seem to want me to.

"Cold hands."

"It's cold outside," I explained.

"Some summer."

"What would you like to drink?" asked the little flower woman.

"Beer, if that's all right."

"I haven't been shopping. Will a Coke do?"

Coke was fine, I said.

"Go and sit down, young man, make yourself at home. Would you like a cushion?"

I said I didn't need a cushion and looked at the other girl. She had short blond hair, was wearing a white T-shirt and panties, and sat on the sofa with a bowl of nuts clasped between her knees. The girl I would be going with soon was wearing a kind of black playsuit. We said nothing, and all three of us watched the cartoon they were showing on RTL 4. Several dented plastic cups and plates that had been there yesterday were still lying on the coffee table. It was just like the class trip, shortly before bedtime.

"Do you know Astrid? Do you know her well?"

"Not well, actually. I only went with her once."

When the cartoon was over the one in the playsuit said, "I was just going to eat. When you're on your own, you eat when you're hungry. But then you turned up."

I nodded.

"So I'll just take it out of the microwave again."

"I'll look after it for you," said the little flower woman.

"I always buy frozen meals."

"Are they OK?" I asked.

"Not bad."

"Where's the TV guide?" It was the first thing the girl in the T-shirt had said but no one answered. She produced a bag of nuts from under the cushion and refilled her bowl.

"Let's go. Don't forget your Coke."

We went back into the room with the parasol. I sat down on the bed. She said she would be back in a moment. I heard a new cartoon start. I thought of Astrid. She had decided to specialize in anal intercourse, possibly because she felt like a pail of soapsuds inside. She, too, would be remaining a one-night stand.

"Look for the guide yourself. I can't go chasing after the guide for you all the time," I heard the little flower woman shouting.

The girl came inside and shut the door.

"I thought you'd be undressed by now."

"I was waiting for you."

"Would you like a wash?"

"I did that at home."

"My name's Maria, by the way. It's not made-up. It's my real name."

"I'm Arnon, not made-up either, so we're even."

Both of us were naked, except that I still had a glass of Coke in my hand.

"Here's the guide right in front of your nose, you dimwit. Why don't you keep your eyes open?" exclaimed the little flower woman, sounding right outside our door.

"We'll use that bed," said Maria.

It was the other one, not under the staircase but next to the window. It was bright there, brighter than usual. I didn't need all that light. She drew the curtain. Now I could no longer see my clothes, which I had put on the floor.

"Where are you from?"

"From Dortmund. Couldn't you tell by my accent?"

"No," I said. "My compliments."

"And you?"

"From Amsterdam. But my parents are from Berlin. They're Jewish, like me, but you've probably seen that for yourself."

"Doesn't matter," she said. "None of that matters. Just lie down."

I did. A mirror had been fixed to the wall the entire length of the bed. She laid her head on my chest. "Boom, boom, boom," she said.

I didn't think much of that. "What's wrong?" I asked.

"Your heart's going boom, boom, boom. It's going crazy."

"Of course it's going boom, boom, boom. If it wasn't I'd be lying here dead, and that wouldn't be very funny."

She lifted her head from my chest and started to massage me. Her reddish-brown hair hung down her back and over her face in untidy curls.

"What would you like me to do for you?"

"You think of something," I suggested, and began picturing a vodka with a beer chaser at some bar. I remembered that I had left *The Dog with the Blue Tongue* someplace, but I had no idea where. I didn't care either.

"French massage?"

"Great."

She started by jerking me off. I had been with a lot of them by now, but they all ended up jerking you off as if they were rinsing out glasses. I had never come across one who could do it as well as I could myself. Maybe I ought to go and make a living at it.

"I never knew there were orange condoms."

"Oh, they've been around for a while," she said. "They're better for French massage. The green ones can be quite bitter. They don't taste good at all."

I heard the doorbell ring somewhere and I wondered if that was Astrid.

"Do you come quickly?" she asked. "If you do I'll take that into account."

"That's nice of you," I said, "very nice. But what can I say? Sometimes I do, sometimes I don't. It sort of depends on my mood."

"I've just been to Leidschendam. On an escort job. I have my own car."

"I don't."

"Do you have a microwave?"

"No, I don't have one of those either."

"It's useful, you know, a microwave. Particularly if you live on your own. Do you live alone?"

"Yes."

Her back was full of moles.

"Me, too. So you know how it is."

I wasn't sure I did know how it was, but I asked no questions. The French massage continued.

"This is our last day here."

"What?"

"We're closing," said Maria. "We'll only be doing escort jobs from here in the future. We had a police raid last Friday and we aren't allowed to be a club anymore."

"Then I'm glad I wasn't here last Friday."

"It wasn't that bad, actually. The cops are usually OK to the customers."

Minutes went by. It was a good thing there was nothing to think about except the rest of the hour and the sounds of the TV coming through the thin walls. I wondered whether the girl on the sofa was still sitting there eating nuts and if the little flower woman had come back with her shopping so that she could give me a beer in place of my tepid Coke.

"That's better," said Maria, "that's how I like it to look." When she said that, it felt as if ages had passed, as if I had been lying on that bed all my life looking at the back of the head of a stranger giving me a French massage, both of us waiting for the moment when it would be over.

"You get on top of me now, then I can take a rest."

I climbed onto her. I could see the two of us in the mirror. I've never understood why people would want to look at themselves in a mirror at times like these.

"Is that a bird?" I asked, and pointed to a tattoo on her left breast.

"A butterfly," she said. "Imagine not being able to tell. Do you know what they used to call me? Madame Butterfly."

"Madame Butterfly," I said, and kissed her ear.

She grabbed hold of me and pushed me inside her. She looked at me and I looked at the butterfly, and the longer I looked at it the more it began to seem alive. I moved in the same rhythm as you use to rock babies to sleep. I felt as if I might drop off at any moment, as if I were getting a foretaste of all the hangovers in store for me and all the mornings they would fill. I watched myself lying on Madame Butterfly's body. I saw our knees, I saw our heads, her curls, which would probably remain curly for another week yet, I saw everything. I held her head tight, as I had held so many other heads tight, pressing it to me because that seemed to be the best thing to do now, and I looked at the butterfly, both in the mirror and on her breast, and after ten minutes all I wanted was to get away. To Astrid or to Marcella, to someone else anyway.

I rolled off her.

"Was that it?" she asked.

"Yes," I said.

She took hold of my cock. "Did you come? Surely not."

"Of course I did," I said. "No question."

She worked on it briefly with her hand.

"Well, just a little. It'll have to do then."

She said it in a consoling tone of voice and we got dressed.

"Would you like to freshen up?"

"No," I said. "I live around the corner."

"The customer is always right."

She asked me if I could guess how old she was. "Thirty-two," I said. She said, "Thirty-four." She intended to call it quits in a few years.

I watched her shake out the towel on the bed and turn it over. That towel must have been shaken out and turned over at least twenty times, but that was something I had stopped caring about months ago.

"Will you work in an office?" I asked.

"Are you crazy? I want to work in catering."

"That's good too."

She looked at herself in a tiny mirror. She put on some lipstick.

"Actually I'm a trained nurse, but I left because of my back.
I worked in a nursing home."

"That must be awful," I said, "working in a nursing home."

"Yes," she said, "there's nothing worse."

I picked up my keys from where I'd left them under the bed
and put them in my pocket. Madame Butterfly brushed a curl
from my forehead. "Well, that was a brief pleasure."

"Never mind," I said. "You did your best."

We walked to the front door. I looked for Astrid but she was
nowhere to be seen. I waved to the little flower woman, who was
on the telephone and waved back. We were standing in bright
sunlight now.

"I thought that was great," I said.

"Yes, me too," she said.

I walked toward Hectorstraat. The hour, which had lasted
fifteen minutes, was over.

I went and stood against a tree in a small square. I not only
opened my fly but pulled my pants down too. I leaned my head
against the trunk. A large purple patch, which looked very much
like a bruise, was the visible reminder of Madame Butterfly's
French massage.

SANDRA

*M*r. Dreese lived in the attic, and all the way up the stairs I kept thinking it might not have been a bad idea to have told someone where I was going or at least to have left a telephone number or an address.

On the third floor I passed a baby carriage, on the fourth floor a racing bike, and the next floor had a skylight letting in an unpleasant glare. I was probably getting worked up for nothing, since the worst that can happen will happen anyway. Yesterday I put a bet on Ajax to win tonight's game at the Olympic Stadium. I bet five hundred guilders, more than I did on the Parma-Antwerp final, when I put a hundred guilders on Parma. The day after that I walked around with two hundred guilders in my pocket like the smartest guy in town.

Mr. Dreese stood leaning over the banister, and as I climbed the stairs toward him I said, "Sorry I'm so late, but I couldn't find it."

"Stephen?" he said.

"Yes," I said.

His attic was furnished the way people do their apartments if they intend to rent them out furnished later on. It was even hotter inside than outside, where it wasn't exactly what you might call cold. The place smelled of buckskin. I had never actually smelled buckskin, but if you ask me buckskin smells the way it smelled in that attic.

"Here," he said.

We went into a small room off to one side that had a desk and two chairs. A fan hung from the wall, slowly rotating back and forth. You find fans like that everywhere in Israel—in living rooms, in cars, sometimes even in bathrooms.

Mr. Dreese had a square face and wore glasses. To judge from appearances he came from Indonesia or somewhere in that part of the world anyway. I thought of my last girl and wondered if she, too, had come up here and waited for the fan to swing back and blow across her face again. The little room looked like my principal's study. Except that the study had had no fan. At some point in their lives people have no choice but to throw in their lot with that of other people, or with that of a soccer team, or with that of the money they have spent and will never recoup. Then I thought of my last girl again and wondered if she'd worn something special for the occasion. I was wearing my green sweater, which still had two holes in it, and my white pants. I'd been wondering all day whether or not to go. I'd given it some thought at lunchtime, when I'd been trying to sell copies of Het Parool at South Station, and later on as well. I'd walked around in my Het Parool T-shirt trying to get the attention of people who could think of nothing but catching their trains. I'd shouted, "Het Parool, Het Parool," but even if I'd shouted, "For ten cents I'll bite my cock off," nobody would have stopped. By four-thirty I had sold three papers, so I took my T-shirt off and put on my sweater and left the other thirty papers lying right in front of the escalator leading to the platform where one caught the express streetcar for Amstelveen. I left the T-shirt lying there as well. Someone was sure to be happy to have it.

"With a *ph?*" asked Mr. Dreese. "Stephen with a *ph?*"

"Yes," I said.

"Why did you call me?" His hands lay on the desk, holding a ballpoint. Every time the fan blew across his face a few hairs on the side of his head rose.

"I need the money."

He nodded.

"I've run up debts all over the place. Things are getting a little out of hand and I don't feel like murdering my mother."

I laughed, but since I was the only one who did, I quickly stopped.

"We've been in business for eighteen months now," said Mr. Dreese, "and I'm glad to say that things are up to expectation. This is one of our ads, in fact."

He tapped his pen on the magazine lying in front of me but I wasn't looking. I could only think about how hot I was.

"I already went over one or two points with you on the phone, didn't I?"

I nodded and wondered again how many of them had sat here and what that girl would have said to all the questions she couldn't understand.

"I need your passport photograph. You'll be given at least one assignment. After that I'll want to see you again. I wash my hands of some people at that point, but all other things being equal, the ball can start rolling then as far as I'm concerned. OK?"

"Yes," I said.

He picked up a sheet of paper and I noticed that it had started raining again. The weather was getting hotter, but it went on raining anyway. Every time I looked at him I had to squint a little against the light pouring in through the small window behind him.

"Age?"

"Twenty-two."

"Height?"

"Five eight, roughly."

"Eyes—shall we say blue? Hair, dark blond. Is it naturally curly?"

"Yes."

"Nice."

"Thanks."

"What do you do?"

"What do you mean?"

Mr. Dreese took off his glasses and rubbed his eyes. The few hairs on the side of his head caught my eye every time the fan blew them up. The middle of his head was bald.

"What sort of work do you do?"

"I work on and off for the radio."

"Any hobbies?"

"Well, you could put art."

"What sort of art?"

On the way over I had eaten some fried fish fillets with cock-tail sauce. I could taste the sauce with every word I said.

"Any sort of art. It's all the same to me."

"That was my old job."

"What was?"

"I used to work a lot on old topographical maps but you can't make a living from that anymore."

"Really?"

Cosmo was still lying on the desk in front of me. Every time I bent forward to read the advertisement I felt a little dizzy.

"Sports?"

"Tennis." I thought of my mother and the coach, and in my mind I saw the whole of Karel Lotsylaan again and all those Wednesday afternoons I had made a mess of there.

"Men and women?"

"Women only."

"S and M?"

"No."

"Couples?"

"No."

"Age limit?"

"Oh, age means so little. Let's say seventy."

I regretted that as soon as it was out. I ought to have said forty, but I couldn't go back on it now. I really needed a drink, but he hadn't offered me anything.

"Stephen used to be my favorite saint."

"Excuse me?"

"He used to be my favorite saint. Stephen."

I wondered if the T-shirt and the newspapers had been taken away yet.

"I'm going to assign you a file number. All you have to do is let me know when you're available, and then as far as I'm concerned the ball can start rolling."

It was the second time he had gotten the ball rolling by now. Expressions like that drove me crazy. All sorts of expressions drove me absolutely crazy.

"Any questions?"

"When I get there, do I have to call you and say I've arrived?"

"No, we only do that with the girls. Anyway, there's not much point. It goes on in hotels most of the time."

"And does the driver do the settling up?"

"That's different from the girls too. You do it yourself. Once a week you come here and settle up with me. Do you have a suit?"

I said, "Yes," although I didn't.

"Is there anything you can refuse to do?" I asked.

"Sure. We don't allow excessive behavior of that sort."

I didn't know who "we" referred to or what sort of excessive behavior they didn't allow.

"You're told beforehand what arrangements have been made,"

he said. "For instance, if you're going out for something to eat first. And it doesn't always have to end with sex either."

"Do I get condoms from you?"

"You take care of those yourself. Otherwise I might as well set up shop selling condoms, and I'm pretty sure someone's done that already."

He laughed, so I laughed along with him. I thought of the girl who had told me she had started on a boat where they held singles nights. There were bound to be a lot of boats doing that.

Mr. Dreese tapped the back of his hand with his pen and told me there was no reason to be afraid of being saddled with Ma Flodder types. I remembered the man who had talked about the most beautiful place on earth.

"Will I be picked up at home?"

"I don't think you really expect that, do you?"

Then he stood up and said, "I'm a man of few words."

I stood up too. "So am I, come to think of it."

"You'll bring your photograph on Saturday?"

"In the morning?"

"The afternoon would be better. The nights are long enough for me as it is."

For me, too, I wanted to say, but I didn't.

"Till then," he said. "Hang on a minute—I'll give you my card."

I walked downstairs, past the racing bike and the baby carriage. "Dreese, Director-Owner," it said on the card in English. Under that: "Blue Moon, escorts, dinner-dating, sightseeing, guides for men and women."

Outside, those who weren't lying on a beach in Spain were busy shopping. I walked the whole way back through Hoofddorp-plein and Zeilstraat.

I was reminded of the time after I got kicked out of school when I was determined to become an actor and made the rounds of all the drama schools. In Amsterdam I even managed to get into a weekend course. Our instructor was someone we all knew from the Persil commercials. The first day he told us his name was Pollo and that *pollo* was Italian for chicken. We all had to do the same sort of thing with our names. The second day we had to turn up in sweatsuits. I didn't have a sweatsuit. I used to wear my father's fur coat at the time. Late on Sunday I had to do an improvisation with a woman who had hit on the bright idea of turning up practically topless. I don't remember what the improvisation was about; all I remember is that the Persil man kept shouting, "More intimate, more intimate!" followed by, "Take his shirt off now." I think we were playing a couple having a fight. Every time she bent forward, her breasts would slip out of her scoop-neck T-shirt and have to be pushed back in again. I got a hard-on just from feeling nervous. Every time she took a step toward me I took a step back because I thought, step forward one inch more and she'll be able to feel it. In the end I was standing up against the window. When it really looked as if, urged on by Pollo, she was about to undress me, I broke off the improvisation. Within half an hour I was told not to bother coming back to the drama school. And at the Maastricht drama school they told me not to bother coming back after just one day, but there, luckily, they kept their distance. After that I did some screen tests for commercials, but I was given the boot by those people, too, after six months.

I took a job in an office with a woman who had hair that hadn't been cut for twenty years and that must have taken her a good hour to put up every morning. Her name was Hanna, and she was particularly partial to cheese-and-egg rolls. She was very grand, which you could tell from the way she walked. She was well past retirement age but had come back to work. She made us all feel that the whole place would go to wrack and ruin without her.

A girl they had plucked from the meat counter of the nearest

Albert Heijn store sat next to me in the office. She was always good for a laugh. She had a very poor opinion of the meat she'd been cutting for the past four years. She told us what all of them would do with the meat when they were bored. She couldn't have cared less that there were only about twenty words she could spell correctly, nor did she care about the rest of her job, for that matter. People who don't give a damn about things like that can often be very funny. The two of us worked in the double-payments section. For a year and a half I had to see to customers who had paid their bills twice.

One week before Christmas they fired me, and Rosie finished with me on December 10, so December is usually a pretty bad time for me.

Whenever it was someone's birthday we would go downstairs for coffee. Hanna was always the first to get up from the cake, I was always the last.

We had a men's room and a women's room but I always used the women's because the stench in the men's room was unbearable. There was a guy in the office—I don't know exactly what he used to do in the men's room, but he must have thrown up in there at least three times a day as far as I could tell. He's gotten married since then, and it seems he throws up a whole lot less now. He and Hanna are the only ones still working there, I think. And Mrs. Tuynman is still there, too, of course, but I could write a whole book about Mrs. Tuynman, because she was hopelessly in love with her dog. Her dog had won every conceivable prize for best-looking dog. Whenever he'd win yet another one, she'd treat us all to a round of chocolate croissants. When I started at the office she had a father and a dog but when I left she had only the dog. Her father passed away on the sofa the day of our office party. The next day we all had to offer her our condolences, but I didn't. It isn't a principle with me, but I never offer anyone condolences. And I hate people who offer their condolences to me.

I always kept my distance from Mrs. Tuynman's dog. I'm not particularly fond of dogs anyway. The largest creature I've ever put out of its misery is a bumblebee, but that could easily change in the not-too-distant future.

One day I spoke to a sailor who told me he was going to work on an oil rig, because from an oil rig it wasn't all that far to paradise, and paradise, according to him, was the best place to grow old in.

At the bottom of Zeilstraat I went into a snack bar and ordered fries. Two men hanging around the slot machine looked Catholic enough to know everything about saints. "Do you happen to have any idea what sort of saint Stephen was?" I asked.

Neither appeared to. One of them said, "I'm a sales rep, I don't know anything about saints. Ask him." He pointed to the man behind the counter.

"Stephen was a saint," he said. "That's all I know about him. He died a horrible death. The Jews did him in. The old race, you know."

"Thanks," I said. "You've told me enough." I went outside with what was left of my fries. "Only he who has known his fellow men well does not succumb to everlasting loneliness," someone has written, I forget who. Anyway, I had begun to dislike people more and more. The only ones I didn't dislike were those who smiled at me because they thought I'd be good for fifty guilders. Most people aren't worth fifty guilders, if you ask me. That's why I don't smile at them.

I remember the evening I went into the café at the bottom of Lange Niezel. Everyone was saying it was the last hot day of the summer. I went and sat inside. After a couple of hours the man next to me asked if I could remember the first rock concert I'd ever been to. He had undone his tie and his face was wet with sweat. He had hamster cheeks, his hair was cropped short, and his nose was red and swollen. I had never been to a rock concert but I saw no reason to tell him that.

"What are you doing here?" he asked.

"I live nearby," I said.

"How do you manage to survive in this neighborhood?"

"I do all right. Don't worry about me."

"What's your name?"

"Stephen."

"Stephen. Frans. Stephen. Frans. I don't promise, but I might remember."

"And you?"

"Frans. I just told you."

An old woman was there and a girl who kept crying, whom they had told to go home. There was a black man with a moustache, too, who said nothing. Everyone else was sitting outside because people had been saying this would be the last hot day of the summer.

"My first rock concert was Pink Floyd," said Frans. "A third of the people here are regulars, a third are tourists, and a third are fools. For the time being I'll give you the benefit of the doubt and count you as a fool."

The old woman, who had trained her glasses on us, said, "Crocodile tears."

Ever since I had sat down, that girl had been standing there crying. First she had leaned against Frans, who had said, "There, there," and Karin, the girl behind the bar, had said, "Crying will make you feel better." One way or another I found the sight disgusting, her standing there with her red eyes and running mascara and wailing as if the world were coming to an end.

The jukebox played "Faces, Faces," a song I like, and the old woman said, "I don't feel sorry for her, you know."

"What do you do?" Frans asked me.

"I read manuscripts for a publisher."

"Definitely a fool."

"What about you?"

"I'm in debt collection. In Baarn. But I studied in Leiden. I'm a real Leidener. But this is the most beautiful place on earth. I've been almost everywhere, but this is the most beautiful place on earth."

The jukebox changed color from blue to yellow to green and back again. It did it over and over, and you could watch for hours if you were drinking beer.

"Crocodile tears," said the old woman. "You should never do it without a French letter. I don't feel sorry for her at all. There was a time when I'd feel sorry for just about everybody, but you get hard."

"Does it take long to get hard?" I asked.

She was sitting next to me, but only now did she look at me straight on, from head to toe and back again.

"Ah well, son," she said, "you get hard before you know it. It happens faster than you can possibly imagine." She turned to Karin behind the bar. "Which way looks better?" she asked. "With or without glasses?"

"Without," we all exclaimed.

The girl was sitting at a little table by the billiard table, still whimpering. Karin brought her a cup of tea with nine lumps of sugar. The black man, whose name was Willem, stood us all a round. "I can do that again now," he said, "seeing that the tourist season is over."

"There's really nothing like it," said Frans, "ice-cold beer like that. But I have to have it in a bottle. Then at least it's something like the right temperature. Mind you, you have to finish it quickly before it gets lukewarm. And then you sit there with your gut full of cold beer. I wish I could get it just right."

In the corner the crying had finally stopped.

He emptied his bottle and we emptied our glasses.

"She's not up to much, that one," said Frans, "on account of those calves."

I turned around. "You're right. She's not up to much."

"On account of those calves. It's a pity really, but we have to be blunt. Blunt but fair. Isn't that so, Annemiek?"

"Absolutely," said the old woman.

"What's the last movie you saw?" I asked.

"I don't remember," said Frans.

"Frans doesn't go to the movies," Karin explained, "because that's four beers he would miss out on." She winked at me. To make doubly sure, I took another look at the girl who wasn't up to much on account of her calves.

"Do you really have to go home now?"

"My chauffeur drives a train," said Frans. "How old are you?"

"Twenty-two."

"A kid. What have you got to worry about?"

"And you?"

"Twenty-nine."

He got his coat off the rack and ordered a glass of Dutch gin. His neck was covered with little red blotches.

"This here is the most beautiful place on earth," he said. "That's why I don't go on vacation anymore. You can eat here, drink here, and pick up a girl here if you want. Have you ever been to Den Bosch? You try going into a café there. There'll be four people in it and they'll look at you and think, What's that stranger doing here? Walk into that café twenty times, the same four will still be sitting there and they'll still look at you and think, What's that stranger doing here? Get home safely, Stephen."

We watched him disappear, with his umbrella and his raincoat, in the direction of the station. Now only Willem and I and the woman were left. And the girl at the little table, but she didn't count.

When I finally walked home, the streets were almost deserted. Even the snack bar owners and the whores were asleep. I thought of the man who took a return ticket every evening to the most beautiful place on earth.

The rain had washed the gravel on the path. There was no one in Vondel Park except a few cyclists. I sat down on a bench, ate the last of my fries, and looked across the houses and the water to the other side. I often used to sit here looking at the people lying on the grass. When I was sixteen, my greatest ambition had been to be able to sit in a café every morning and not to have to go anywhere. At Vossius they were forever asking you to tell your ambitions. When I was seventeen I spent an average of an hour and a half a day in the shower. They kicked me out of school just before Whitsun. The weather was fabulous. There was a coffee machine in the main hall that could be made to take Italian liras. At the end of that May the janitor caught me in the act. He'd been lying in wait for me since January. He was so mad he was frothing at the mouth. When my father was mad he frothed at the mouth too. But when he got sick he frothed at the mouth all day.

Here there was nothing but the water, the houses, the wet grass, and the raindrops on the trees, and I didn't give a damn about any of it. That's why I liked this place.

My favorite breakfast was a cup of coffee, a glass of water, and an aspirin. In a halfway decent café that didn't set you back more than two and a half guilders. Princess Coca worked in the Banana Bar. It wasn't her real name, but I called her that. I had breakfast with her once. She always carried an umbrella. It was because of her that I started reading *Laurel and Hardy's Journey around the World*. Sometimes they disappear and others come to take their place. Or they come back but no longer remember who you are. My father always said that our family numbered no kings of the underworld, only street princesses and newspaper vendors and chicken killers. My father would have made one of the world's best racketeers.

I thought of the letter I'd found yesterday evening when I came home. "Please contact me at the telephone number below any night after eleven o'clock."

It had been jotted down on the back of an invoice. The name on the invoice had been scratched out in black felt-tip pen. There were more and more people around these days who knew my address. I really appreciated it when they were original about the way they tried to make contact with me. That's why I didn't wait until eleven o'clock but called right away.

"I was asked to call this number," I said to the lady, whose name meant nothing to me.

"Hang on, I'll get my husband," she said.

For the first time I noticed the pungent smell in my room. When I came home late I would always pee into the plant. I thought of Sergius, who had told me that all his sailor friends pissed into the kitchen sink even long after they had last been to sea.

"I was asked to call you."

"Yes, I was over at your place yesterday evening. By mistake I took the yellow slip back with me and left you the two white ones. You should have had the yellow one and me the two white ones. All right if I come over this evening and change them?"

"Sure," I said, "I'll be at home all evening."

The man on the telephone had indeed been at my place the previous evening. He was small and squat, with hair as short as his nails. He'd said, "She's from Lithuania." He'd looked at me when he said that as if he expected me to say, "Then take her away again," but I said nothing. For a few seconds all you could hear was the ticking of the big clock, and then the man said, "Well, in that case we'd better settle up." I'd taken out my Postbank card. It was August. That month I paid for everything with my Postbank card; otherwise I wouldn't have been able to pay for

anything. I had specially checked with him that it was all right.
I looked at the girl, who was still half hidden behind the man in
his lumberjack's shirt. Her hair had been dyed carelessly, as if
she'd been in a great hurry, the way my ancestors had been when
they baked their bread before leaving Egypt.

"Sign here, please."

I signed.

"These cards drive me crazy."

I nodded.

"Please keep your eye on the time." He probably thought that
the girl from Lithuania couldn't tell time herself. "I will," I said.

I heard him bang the door behind him, and then once again
the ticking of the clock, which wasn't even my own. "Please, sit
down," I said to her in English.

She remained standing, so I sat down myself. She was wearing
black leggings that were slightly too short, a blue raincoat made
out of some sort of parachute material, and those shoes that people only wear on the beach in really good weather. She held a
yellow vanity case in her hand, an idiotically large vanity case,
as if she were planning to travel with it to the ends of the earth.
There she stood, and it didn't look as if sitting down was something she proposed doing.

I poured myself a glass of wine. "Please, sit down," I repeated,
and pointed to a chair. Finally she turned and sat down. She was
still holding her case in her hand. We talked in English.

"What's your name?"

"Sandra."

"What would you like to drink? Wine, water, brandy, vodka?"

"I don't know." She laughed, but I couldn't see what there
was to laugh at. I got a glass of water from the kitchen. If she
didn't know, she might as well have water.

"There's slivovitz too, if you want."

"No liquor. Thanks."

Her lipstick and eyeliner had been carelessly applied too. She was pale, slightly taller than me, but probably just as skinny. She had made an attempt to put her hair up at the back of her head with a sort of large hairpin. It was nearly one o'clock. I took a walnut out of a box that had been standing under the table for a few weeks now.

"Want one?"

She shook her head.

"So, what part of Lithuania are you from?"

"Vilnius."

"What did you do there?"

She laughed again. I don't really like people who keep laughing for no good reason. I cracked another walnut and filled my glass. "I don't understand," she said.

"How long have you been in Amsterdam?"

"One."

"One what? One week? One day?"

"One week."

"Are you here by yourself?"

"I'm here with a sister-in-work."

"A sister-in-work?"

I looked at the case on her lap and wondered what in God's name she had stuffed in it.

"Do you want to stay here in Amsterdam? Or do you want to go back?"

She laughed and said, "I don't understand."

"What do you speak? German?"

"Russian and Lithuanian."

"I don't speak Russian and I don't speak Lithuanian. So let's have a drink."

I saw that she hadn't drunk any of her water; no doubt she thought I was trying to poison her. So I poured myself another glass. We sat at the table like that without saying anything. I drank and she stared at one of the lychees lying on a plate. They had been lying there for six months. They had probably dried up inside, but I had left them where they were. Just like all the other things I left lying about, either because I forgot to clear them away or because I thought they might come in handy. Minutes passed. I took advantage of the opportunity to drink up the last dregs of the bottle.

The nights were already growing cold. I turned on the heat. It was almost fall. It wouldn't be long now until the High Holidays, seeing as they came around every fall. But this year wouldn't find me in a synagogue on Yom Kippur. It would make no difference to me if God inscribed me in the Book of Life or in the Book of Death. I'd be lying low that day in a club on Stadhouderskade where there'd be a girl I thought was particularly pretty who called herself Marielle. There, in that club, I would celebrate the holiest day of the year in a way it had not been celebrated in all the six thousand years of its existence.

I put my glass down on the table. "Let's go," I said.

We went into my bedroom. I looked for the Vladimir Vysotsky tape. When I found it, I played it very loud. It was the only tape in the house she'd be able to understand. I listened to him singing the song about all the things he didn't like, and I remembered how Sergius had tried to explain to me what it was all about. "I don't like cynicism, but I don't like sobstuff either. I hate it when people read my letters over my shoulder. I don't like riding schools, arenas, Peace and Prosperity: hurray for the Plan! And being told things are going to get better, that turns my stomach again."

"Do you know him?"

"Yes. Where is the shower?"

I showed her the bathroom. She put the vanity case on the washing machine and started to get undressed. I had never met one who wanted to shower first. When she was almost naked she turned away, so I left the bathroom. I found another can of beer under the hat rack. When that was empty, too, I remembered that she didn't have a towel. There were no clean ones, so I went to Sergius's place and borrowed one of his. He certainly wouldn't mind a girl drying herself with his towel. He had stopped minding most things.

When I went back into the bathroom she was standing there in her panties and a sort of stretchy top. She was spraying herself all over with deodorant, and not just herself: the whole bathroom smelled of it.

She was shivering. I handed her the towel.

Normally I don't take them into my bedroom, but she looked blue with cold, which is why I let her sit on my bed. She took some cigarettes out of her case, and I got a cup from the kitchen for her to use as an ashtray. She was smoking Dunhill Greens.

"Cold?"

"No."

Vladimir Vysotsky was still singing. I took off my shoes and lay down next to her. It was cold in the bedroom because I had forgotten to close the balcony doors. She took two packs of Bene-Luxe from her case and put them next to the cup that she would use to stub out her cigarettes.

There was a bottle of slivovitz next to the bed. "Want some?" I asked.

She shook her head. "Me neither," I said, and put the bottle back.

We were lying side by side, and after a while I kissed the hair above her ear. Her hair, too, smelled of deodorant. I could see her eyebrows, which were painted just as badly as the rest, and five little pimples between them, and I could see her gray-blue cat's eyes, which made her look pretty.

"Nineteen is a nice age," I said.

"I don't know."

"Me neither."

On the outside her mouth tasted of deodorant, and on the inside of Dunhill Greens. When I stopped kissing her, I could see her shiny nose with twenty thousand little black dots on it. I wondered what the combination of wine, beer, and vodka tasted like in my mouth. "I like you," I said, just what all the others must have said and what they would go on saying, only I meant it— just like all the others. Running my right hand back and forth along the side of the bed I felt for the bottle. Vysotsky was still singing his song. "She said, 'I do not love you.' He said, 'That cannot be.' She said, 'I will not drink with you.' He said, 'Have one with me.' And when the bottle was all gone, said she, 'My dearest one, please close the windows and the drapes.' To which he said, 'Now you can get the hell out of here.' "

The tape was nearly over. She took off what clothes she still had on, and I undressed completely too. When Vysotsky finally stopped singing, I could hear that she hadn't turned the shower off right, but I was too tired to get up. I looked at her body, still at the stage of growing into a woman's, and saw the way she was looking at me, her eyes half closed as if she had only just woken up and was surprised to find where she was. It was nice watching her with her half-closed eyes. Her narrow, pale face with the shiny nose and thin lips reminded me of something but I couldn't think what it was. As far as I was concerned she could stay with me forever. Most people think one night is nothing, but compared with one hour or fifteen minutes, a night is an eternity, which was exactly what I was after. If you're thinking the whole time about what your face will look like after it's been hit by a few bullets, you can't go back to the front, Sergius said. If you're thinking the whole time about the next morning, you can't go on drinking, and it's the same with eternity and all those promises. I was reminded of a joke Sergius told me about the Russian army. Sergius either told jokes or slept. When we lived together he bought an old Volvo. We drove around Amsterdam in it but within two weeks he had managed to wreck it.

Next to the cup lay the two packs of Bene-Luxe. She had a long neck and small breasts, and she said, "I work for my family. I go back in thirty days."

"Yes," I said, "yes."

It was nice kissing her. Gradually the sheet, too, began to smell of deodorant. Her hair felt stiff from the dye. She kept her eyes open, not looking at the wall but looking at me, one eye half closed, as if she were squinting into the sun.

She looked cute like that. Presumably that was the reason she was putting the look on; it was calculated. She knew exactly what she had to do to look so cute.

Sometimes when I come across somebody cute I suddenly think that you can ladle the eyes out of her face with a soup spoon.

I remembered Marielle, who had told me, "They cough up five hundred guilders for a quarter of an hour 'without,' and not just Arabs either." I remembered the man in the café I'd been drinking with all night who asked me if I knew why these were great times. "No," I said. "Because you no longer need a pistol to play Russian roulette," he explained.

I thought about all that only when she'd been back in the bathroom for a long time and I was running my right hand back and forth along the side of the bed. I had been thinking of nothing at all, perhaps of the five little pimples between her eyebrows and of the taste of Dunhill Greens and the smell of deodorant.

I put on my sweater while she got dressed in the bathroom. I spoke no Russian and no Lithuanian either, and at that moment my English was worse than ever. That's why I didn't speak at all. I knew that it wouldn't make any difference what I said anyway, even if she did understand it. What counts in the long run is what people do with each other and what they want to do with each other. Only they can never get enough of all the lies they tell each other, and there's nothing more left of those than of your piss, which right now looks like Mr. Kleen.

I gave her my telephone number and twenty-five guilders. Then I quickly drank another can of beer and thought how lucky it was that a few oil rigs lay on the road to paradise.

When I heard the car drive off, I was back in bed with my sweater on. You could gamble your life away. It was as simple as that. Come to think of it, everything was as simple as that. I ran my right hand along the side of my bed. Later I remembered that Sandra was working for her family and probably for her in-laws, too, and, who knows, perhaps for her whole street. That would get her a really fine funeral back in Lithuania. At least they'd be sure she hadn't died in vain, because they'd have gotten a good few years out of her.

I got up, turned the music up full blast, and opened one of the Bene-Luxe packs Sandra had left behind. Vysotsky sang that song again; he shouted that he didn't like cheap cynicism or sob-stuff either, and that he loathed himself when he was a coward.

Ever since I first started doing it around the age of twelve, I've always preferred jerking off to good music. Just then I was convinced that I'd smell of deodorant for the rest of my life and that my mouth would always taste of Dunhill Greens.

My mother said that you never forget certain smells, but it took me just five minutes to realize that even that isn't true. You think you will never forget something, just as some people think they love someone too much, but you forget smells as easily as you do faces and names and promises. Deodorant takes no more than a couple of hours to disappear.

The only letter from my father I still have is one he wrote when he was home for a few months in the summer. The letter consists of nothing but figures. I think they're stock quotations but I'm not sure. Actually, I also still have his season ticket for the streetcar.

It was at least twenty-two hours ago that the driver rang my door for the second time.

"Come in," I said.

"This yellow copy is yours and I have to have the white ones back. It's a bitch."

"Don't let it get you down. Would you like a glass of wine?"

He would, so we sat down. I gave him the two white receipts

he needed. "Take-Out Inc.," they said under the heading "Merchant."

"We're very discreet," he said.

"Good," I replied, "great."

"At twelve-thirty I have to pick up a girl at Schiphol Airport. She's been to Geneva with an Arab for a few days. They lead some life, our girls do."

"Your health," I said, and poured him a Chianti. "I didn't realize you could take them on vacation too."

"Anything goes, so long as you pay."

I thought of Sandra's ridiculous vanity case. "Have you been working for this agency long?"

"About eight years. We're one of the biggest, did you know that? We employ two hundred girls, easy. Of course they aren't all on duty at the same time. Our place is run just like the inland navigation office."

I didn't know what went on in the inland navigation office, nor was I all that interested.

"You have to figure on going out in the car about once an hour. You're left with no real time for a private life, but I earn as much as a family doctor. And once a year I go to the Antilles. My boss comes from the Antilles. He owns a house there and I take my wife there for three weeks."

"Do you drive all over Holland?"

"Yes, and sometimes as far as Germany or Belgium, though that takes longer than an hour, of course. Most of my runs are outside Amsterdam. Especially on Friday nights. The countryside is a madhouse then. There's nothing to do out there, and on Friday night they want to do the lot."

Friday night, good old Friday night, with two challahs, two candles, and a glass of cloyingly sweet wine.

I looked at the man sitting beside me and talking to me as if we'd been friends for years. He sat there, with almost no neck and his short, fat arms. They lay on the table like sausages, next to his glass of wine.

"I come from the Jordaan," he said. "We just used to walk into some bar, but in those small country towns . . . If you ever have any trouble there, the whole town knows about it. We have our regulars, too, of course, who don't know what to do with their money. There's one man who has a swimming pool. If the weather's good, he always says, tell her to bring her bathing suit."

He hadn't meant to say anything funny, that was for sure, but I began to laugh. And I couldn't stop, as if I'd just heard the joke of the century. I saw him looking at me but luckily he started laughing too.

"Does she also have to put those orange things on her feet?" I asked. "Flippers?"

"I have no idea," he said. "I never ask that sort of thing."

I tried to imagine Sandra in a bathing suit in some big empty swimming pool somewhere, but I couldn't do it.

"We have everything," he said, "we really do. We're one of the few agencies who have transvestites too. And we have gigolos. But I wouldn't do that myself, not even for ten thousand guilders a pop. And gigolos are much more expensive than girls. It's much more dangerous for men than for women. I've had gigolos in the car who've run away from the client screaming. Most of the guys are past caring, though."

I remembered Sergius telling me that in the desert every day is the same. When he came back, people looked the same too. Like sparrows, he said. You only think they're all different when you're young.

"We have every nationality, from Brazilians to Russians. We have one Russian girl who's been deported from this country more than twenty times. Five days later she's back on our doorstep. But we kicked out all the ones from Ghana. They're thieves. Every last one of them. We've heard it's the same in other agencies. Stealing from the client or from the owner. You can bet on it." He took a swig. "Look, you can keep a girl as long as you want. Which is why I told you to keep an eye on the time. Because you have to pay extra, of course. We once had a driver who told the girl, 'We'll split whatever the customer pays over the agreed rate.' You can pull that off once or twice, you can pull that off ten times, but the eleventh time you're going to run out of luck. That driver left us minus his teeth."

"Your health," I said and opened another bottle. "What happened to the girl?"

"We threw her out too, of course."

"With or without her teeth?"

"With. We're a respectable agency. My boss is tough but fair. It has to be like that, otherwise you can't keep your head above water in this business. I've rarely seen anyone work as hard as he does. He doesn't own just the agency; he has clubs, restaurants, late-night stores, and discos too. It's hard even to picture all the things he owns, and he works all day long. He practically lives in his car. Well, so do I, of course. When the girls are with the clients, I get a little shut-eye. You have to get your sleep somehow, don't you?"

"Yes," I said, "you'd be a wreck without sleep."

"Wrecks are something we can do without. If we find any of them on drugs, they're out on their ear. My boss loathes drugs. No joints in the car or in the clubs, he always says. I do martial arts twice a week myself; you have to in this business. If a client calls and says, 'I want five girls for three hours,' you're talking about three thousand guilders. And it can happen that a client keeps a girl for five hours and then just kicks her out in the street. So then we go and stand on his doorstep the next day with a couple of the martial arts guys. But there are some agencies where their immediate reaction is Molotov cocktails through the windows. Look, that's the difference. We're a respectable agency. My boss says, 'I'd sooner have a client who comes back than a client who can't ever come back.' "

It must have been a long time since he'd talked to anyone, if you ask me. After all, he spent the whole day sitting in a car driving around girls who'd already had to spend the whole night listening to other people's stories and presumably didn't feel like talking about what they'd just been up to.

"Whenever there's a cut in student grants, we notice it right away. They'll often say to us, 'We'd like to do it just once a month.' So the boss tells them, 'I'll put you down for just once a month.' "

When the wine was gone I wanted to give him a slivovitz, but he said he still had to go to Schiphol to pick up that girl.

I remembered the time Sergius didn't go out for five days and spent all day lying fully dressed on top of his sleeping bag. I'd knock on his door now and then, but he said there was nothing the matter with him. One evening I saw him in the kitchen wearing his coat and making beet soup. He said, "If you like, we could see a show tonight." He was half bald. What hair he had left was dark brown.

We walked into town. Sergius said he knew a place on War-moesstraat where you could get a decent meal. It had at least twenty strip lights, the tables were unfinished wood, and when you wanted to leave you had to buzz first so that they could open a small door for you. They were scared you would make off without paying. The food was rich and very good. The Chinese woman who served us was fat and cheerful. Sergius ordered a second helping and I ordered a couple more cans of beer. He said, "Sometimes I eat a lot and sometimes I eat nothing all day." I watched him eat, quickly and silently, concentrating. When he was finished, I pushed a can of beer toward him but he said, "Enough is enough. I'm tired of drinking, tired of fighting, tired of all those crazy things."

The place was called Kam Yin, which made me think of Come In, and a meal cost all of eight and a half guilders, which meant I would be coming back often.

A man in a suit, with a little white beard, was sitting next to us. He watched us eat with interest. His own plate hardly seemed to empty. I couldn't tell how old he was, but his eyes floated on his face like two drops of fat on an undersized chicken that hasn't survived the famine. When we got up to leave, he turned toward us as if he owed us an explanation. "I can't get these French beans down," he said. "So I'm going to ask them for a doggy bag in a minute. I'll be able to chew them better at home."

"Shall we go?" said Sergius.

We walked past the cafés and the budget hotels where you can get a good cheap breakfast. I had often walked that way before, only this time I was walking with Sergius and he was greeting all the people he knew.

It was almost twelve o'clock when the driver got up and said, "I really have to go to Schiphol now." I saw him to the front door. "If you like, I'll drop by with the book of photos."

"Yes," I said, "I'd like that." I remembered that I had to have passport photographs taken the next day.

"We have all kinds, except from Ghana. We kicked those ones out."

"No skin off my back."

"Just ask for Little Michael and I'll drop by with the book of photos."

"I'd like that," I repeated. When Little Michael had been gone for a while, I thought of Sergius again, the way he'd stood there confronting that short heavyset man in his yellow tie, and how I'd said to him, "Let's go." The man with the yellow tie had said, "I don't fight with old men." One of the bystanders asked if I didn't think I ought to stick up for my friend but I pretended not to hear him.

Later Sergius said that you must never think too much about what you might look like if you got the shit kicked out of you. There's no point. Once you've actually had the shit kicked out of you, there's plenty of time for you to think about it.

"The problem is that I keep thinking about it all the time."

"It'll pass. My trainer said that whenever I started bleeding I should wipe the blood off my face with my glove and smear it over my opponent's face. It's all a matter of strategy, of course, but a face covered with blood is less pleasant for the referee too. That's why it's better if you both look the same."

Then we went to that other show, where they gave us a discount, Sergius because he was bald and me because I had curly hair. We sat close to the platform and put our feet up on it, but the girl came over from the bar and said that we weren't allowed to put our feet there. Sergius asked what we were supposed to do with our feet. Would she please tell him what in God's name we were supposed to do with our feet?

In front of us, at an angle below the platform, was a small shelf with holes in it for our glasses. The first girl danced to "The Best." Sergius said he'd been there a few times but he hadn't seen her before.

She was wearing a wispy black dress and knee-length boots. She didn't dance too badly. Later she took a candle from the little bag she had put down on the platform behind her, next to the mirror. Then she looked for a member of the audience to light the candle. It took quite a while before she found someone who had a light on him.

Tina Turner started "The Best" for the third time. By then the burning candle was sticking out of the girl's body, and she danced like that for a little while longer, which I thought was quite an achievement.

After that we went and sat at the bar. We ordered beer, which cost four guilders. The people in the room were waiting for the next dancer. One of the barmaids walked around collecting empty glasses. "When we finished fighting," said Sergius, "and were sent back home, I didn't feel like working anymore. My job was laying electric cables, but after rushing around in the desert for six months I thought it was time to move on. I wanted to go to Canada but I wound up in Norway. After a while my money was gone and I looked for work on a fishing boat, but they don't like taking on foreigners over there. I hitchhiked even farther north. A woman lived in one of the villages with her son; they told me I might be able to get a room with her. Her name was Anna Larsen. I went around to see her. She was pretty old and she said she'd give me room and board if I did repairs around the place and shoveled the snow. Her son was named Alfred and he spent most of the day walking around the house singing. The people in the village said that Alfred was crazy, but Anna Larsen said that her son was her son and he'd been perfectly sane the whole thirty-five years. A ship's captain who wasn't a ship's captain anymore lived there too. They had taken away his license because he'd put out to sea drunk in bad weather and wrecked his ship. I don't remember what his name was or whether he was Anna Larsen's husband or friend or just a lodger, because they never talked about that sort of thing. Anna Larsen said that she liked having me in the house. I could understand that. When Lapps drink, they go nuts. They make their own drink. It's the worst stuff on earth. Sometimes I would drink with them. Afterward I would stick my finger down my throat because I didn't want the stuff in my body any longer than was absolutely necessary. I was the only foreigner in the village and soon everyone knew where I was staying and who I was. One night I heard someone bang on the door and shout in English, 'Come out and I'll make you eat your own prick.' I could tell he was talking to me, so I shouted back at him to shut up. But the man kept yelling, 'Come out and I'll make you eat your own prick.' I was in a good mood, so I yelled back, 'I'll eat my prick but first you'll eat yours.' Then the man started to kick the door with his boots. I knew it was childish of me but I went outside. When he started to kick me, I broke his nose, and then he hit me so hard that I could hardly see out of one of my eyes for the next couple of months. I left that same morning because I didn't feel safe in the village anymore. I would have left anyway, even if none of that had happened, because Alfred's singing was driving me crazy."

Meanwhile we had seen all five dancers. We had also seen a woman being screwed by a black man with a blue cap and blue suspenders. We realized now that the program was repeated every hour and that we could stay on until they closed. The people in the room were waiting for more of the same. The smoke from the smoke machine wafted in front of the mirrors, and a Japanese man sat there the whole time in the corner.

We watched the dancer with the wide mouth and the reddish-brown hair again and saw her do exactly what she had done an hour before. Again she placed her knee in a visitor's lap, and after her it would be the turn of the dancer who would stick a pen up between her legs at the end of her act and write "I love you" on the bare chest of a man she had picked to go lie on the platform. Most of the people in the room looked as if they had seen it all twenty thousand times before. At least the men's room was spotless.

"First you experiment with life and then life experiments with you," said Sergius, but I wasn't sure anymore whom he was saying it to.

The woman with the reddish-brown hair had sat down in a corner near the exit. Now she had on jeans and a checkered shirt. Sergius went up to her first, and five minutes later I followed. "This is Amanda," he said. She smelled of shaving cream.

"Hello," I said.

We asked her what she wanted to drink. We could hardly hear her. They had turned up the music because the next act was about to start. I couldn't conceive of memories other than these, of places other than this one, where you could while away your evening and part of the night.

"What are you two doing here?" asked Amanda.

"It's a great place, isn't it?" I said. "I like the red-light district. We weren't meant to live in the sunlight."

"I like the sun," said Amanda. She probably said a whole lot more, but I couldn't make out any of it because Sergius was sitting between us. Later he asked me to lend him ten guilders so we could get Amanda another drink. When she got up to go pee, I said, "Forget her—she smells of shaving cream. She isn't interested in me, or in you, for that matter."

"Youth is insane. Later on you'll still be insane, but without the benefit of youth," Sergius said, and grinned.

In the corner the next dancer stood waiting her turn. I looked at the moving spotlight projected onto the platform and at the people still sitting in the room, who seemed as if they were ready to stay there for the rest of their lives. I thought it didn't make much difference whether you locked yourself up all your life in some room to study the Mishna or walked through the red-light district every day and studied faces and bodies and even haggled about the price when you knew you didn't have any money on you. Either way you could imagine that you were part of something greater than your miserable life, which had started to stink before it had even begun. If you read books, rocked your upper body back and forth, and spent weeks pondering the question of what you must do if you find an article of clothing in the street, you knew that you were part of the nation of Israel; and all the answers to all the questions, the consolation of the whole world, lay in those three words.

I could also imagine that I was part of the woman who let me inside her and that I would receive from her everything one human being can receive from another, that it was important to remember her and that even weeks later I would still know that the water from the faucet in her room tasted of liquid soap. I didn't give a damn for nations; sometimes I didn't even know if I gave a damn for individuals.

I remembered my teachers. I remembered how my mother would take me to Lekstraat on Sunday and Wednesday evenings, to the Hamashmidim yeshiva, where they taught you what you must do when you and someone else pick up an article of clothing

in the street together. They also taught me that it somehow mattered what you did and what you failed to do with your life, that
there were such things as objective truths. At about that time we
went to Zurich, where a European Mishna festival was being held.
Just the way you have the Eurovision song contest, you have the
European Mishna contest. Each of us had to learn a section of
the Mishna by heart. As a reward we were given books. The more
Mishna you could rattle off by heart, the more books you were
given. I knew very little of it by heart. I think the piece I had to
say was about the way in which you have to build a tabernacle.
The festival was held in the biggest synagogue in Zurich. There
were scribes all over the place. You had to wait until they called
you up. Then you had to go up to one of them and recite your
portion of the Mishna. Luckily my turn never came. Too few
scribes and too many children had turned up for this particular
Mishna contest. I saw all those tzitzis dangling in the urinal in
the men's room, and I was ashamed because I wasn't wearing any.
Back in the bus we all had to sing *"Yeshivas Hamashmidim Amsterdam, chay, chay, vekayam."* One of the rabbis had to be sent
home in a state of nervous collapse after he drew blood scratching
a pupil's arm. We also went swimming, in a swimming pool they
had rented for us alone since we males had to keep to ourselves.

Now here I was, sitting half listening to Amanda as she told
us that she had a son in Brazil, whom she kept calling "my baby."

I knew that nobody could care less what you did and that
nobody gave a damn either whether or not you dropped dead.
People are as disposable as plastic bags. They are alone in believing themselves to be special and unique, and their children even
more special yet. That's something you have to believe, too, if
you want to continue in the land of the living. And for as long
as you want that, you're going to have to keep your mouth shut
about plastic bags. I know from the time I worked in an office,
and from later on, too, that there is almost nothing worse than
people who think they are indispensable. I'm aware that I'm as

dispensable as the starlings in Central Station, who do nothing but shit. And a few people I like are aware of the same thing about themselves.

In the end you don't miss other people, just the time you spent with them, of which a few memories are all that remain. If you don't talk about those memories, they'll be no more than the water my mother left to boil on the stove all day on Saturdays; just a little steam remained by the evening, which mingled later that night with the smell of the fresh wash. Then, thank God, it was all over again for another week.

People are like an old newspaper to one another, for wiping their rear ends with if they happen to have run out of toilet paper. Somebody told me in the streetcar recently that the Pope blesses all the pregnant women in the world every day, even those who are anything but Catholic.

The fat black woman had been dancing again now for about ten minutes. Sergius had climbed onto the platform and was dancing beside her. I liked watching him dance. I sat at the bar waiting for something to happen. I didn't have even the vaguest idea what that something would be like; all I knew was that I had to sit there a while longer and wait. I used to think that all the waiting in the whole world could be fitted into those forty-five minutes on an ordinary weekday when some people are already saying good morning to you and others are still saying good night, when the telephone girl says, "The lady will be with you in forty-five minutes, Mr. Van Grinbergen." You spend those forty-five minutes walking around your house, and you no longer know why you called in the first place, or where that snot in your nose came from, or why it's so damn quiet everywhere. All you can think of is how she'll look and what she'll say and what kind of clothes she'll be wearing, and you wonder whether she'll be the type who'll take a ride to paradise for a couple of hundred guilders extra.

Amanda went downstairs because she had to do her number again in a few minutes. For the next-to-last time that night.

"I'm leaving," I said to Sergius.

"Don't you want to wait for Amanda?"

"I feel like some chocolate ice cream."

I walked to the stairs, to the exit, over the small polished tiles.

She was standing in front of the pita stall. She was wearing a turtleneck sweater.

"How're you doing?"

"Fine," she said. "How are you?"

"OK."

They were busy in the stall making pita and falafel sandwiches. Two houses down was the café where the woman worked who said whenever she saw me, "Yes, my boy, all things will pass." I have no idea why she said that. Maybe she was slightly crazy. She just started saying it one day and then she couldn't stop.

"How much?"

"Fifty, plus fifteen for the room."

"I never pay for the room."

"Then beat it. I don't have time for small talk."

"Me neither, but I do feel like an ice cream. I could buy you one too."

"I have to work."

"I'd do something about my teeth, if I were you. My mother always said, 'My teeth came through the war very well because I cleaned them every day with a rag.' I'd do the same if I were you."

"Fuck off."

"I'm only telling you because I think you're nice."

She turned away. I walked on to the café, where Jeanet was playing a slot machine. Jeanet has white hair and her dresses always end a long way above her knees. The only thing she drinks is whisky with a lot of water, and if you ask her how old she is she says she has eternal life. She likes to dance when she's won. Sometimes she dances with me. She's been wearing the same dress for months, but you can do that if you have eternal life.

When she's won a lot, she lifts up her dress so we can see her panties and her round belly. Then she says, in half English, half Dutch, "We are lovers, we all have our brief encounters." And then she slaps her knees, which are so full of water that the whole café could quench their thirst with it.

When I walked in I could see right away that Jeanet would not be dancing with me this time. What's more, if she did, the night would not be better for it.

Even before I sat down, a beer had been put in front of me.

"I saw you hanging around," said Karin.

"I've been hanging around here almost the whole week, and from today I'll be hanging around here every day, so you'll have to get used to my face."

"I've gotten used to worse things."

Jeanet had gone over to the billiard table. When I looked out the window I could see the girl with the ponytail, the one who had no time for small talk.

A boy in a blue raincoat and a hood with a couple of lengths of cord dangling from it sat in the corner, in the strategic spot against the wall. He was drinking from a bottle. "I've let myself be fucked for fifty guilders," he said without talking to anyone in particular.

"But with a rubber, I hope," said Karin.

"Does he want us to feel sorry for him now?" said the old woman. "I wouldn't do it for fifty guilders."

The boy had a perfect face, with straight blond hair, and the rest of him was impeccably turned out as well. The old girl wanted a hot chocolate, the boy another bottle, and the other man a young Dutch gin with ice.

"Whenever I look outside I see the girls calling me," said the man next to me. His arms were brown and hung from his shoulders as if carrying a couple of weights. A poodle was tied to his bar stool.

"Just look straight ahead," I said.

"Then the beer calls me." He tossed off the small glass of gin. "I want to be your underwear," he sang off-key.

The boy with the hood got up. "I'm off again," he said.

"Bye," we all said.

"And who's calling you now?" said Annemiek, in her hoarse voice and with a mouth full of meatballs.

"Just you," I said, "only you. Surely you know that."

It wouldn't be long now before it was Yom Kippur again. "All the vows" was what Kol Nidre meant but I didn't know anything else about the prayer they said on the most sacred night of the year. I would be back here on that night, the most sacred night of the year, as I was every night, and just like all those people sitting there in their white shrouds mumbling the Kol Nidre, so too I wanted nothing more than to forget all my vows. I would keep hanging around here, the most beautiful place on earth, until I had forgotten everything and only the beer I had drunk still existed, and the money in my pocket, and the one whom I could never find but for whom I had been searching for weeks because she was the most beautiful in the whole district.

At twelve-thirty I went outside. The woman in the turtle-neck sweater was standing under the awning of the pita stall. "It's fifty now," she said. "Great," I said, "only I'm not in a fucking mood anymore. Maybe tomorrow. *Ciao, bella.*"

The way I was going now, I'd be able to go for years. Here and in other cities. Lots of people had asked me what I was looking for. You might as well ask a tree what it's looking for in the ground or vodka what it's looking for in the bottle. I found such questions particularly tiresome. I had long since ceased to hope for great answers to great questions. She was standing on the other side of the bridge. She wore the usual white blouse and had nice brown eyes. She was missing a couple of front teeth, but otherwise she still looked pretty good. I had eaten french fries with her once in the Febo. I had treated her to an ice cream, but when she'd pressed me, I'd said, "Sorry, I don't mix business with pleasure." That's one of the few things I still feel good about.

Soon we'd be eating little apples and honey again. Only this time without me. The warmth you found among the apples and honey, the candles and the challahs—the solace and the warmth they promised you if only you were prepared to be part of the chosen people—was all thousands of times phonier than the warmth you could get from your first visit to a toothless whore.

I walked back the way I had come and smiled at anyone who smiled at me. The street was barely five feet wide and less than fifty yards long. I remembered that someone in a wheelchair had got stuck there one night and caused a huge traffic jam. I was walking through the blond section. The district was made up of all sorts of smaller districts. In the black section they were a bit friendlier and more inclined to tap on the windows. The black ones are fifteen guilders less than the blonds, but the ones from South America are just as expensive. In this particular alleyway, which was no wider than a condemned man's cell, they were very young, no older than I was, anyway. I had already been to bed with my fill of women old enough to be my grandmother.

She opened the door even before I stopped.

"Fifty," she said in English.

"OK," I said.

I followed her up the stairs, past the woman who had been sitting next to her. The tiles were light blue, as if we were in a swimming pool.

Her name was Alissa. I undressed. She just took off her panties. She kept her stockings on. She had brown eyes, a pinched face, and short brown hair. When I was completely naked, she said, "Now please pay." I picked my pants up from the floor again and looked for some money.

"Where are you from?" I asked. We spoke in English.

"Budapest."

She lay down.

"Please don't kiss me."

"Don't worry, I won't kiss you."

I did hold her head tight, though. I'm used to holding their heads tight now when I fuck them.

"Will you be going back to Budapest?"

"I come from nowhere and I go to nowhere, and now please shut up. I'm trying to do my work."

After that we had nothing more to say to each other. When I left, though, I saluted good-bye and blew her a kiss. Out of habit.

Part Five

IN THE EMPLOY OF THE BLUE MOON

That Saturday at four o'clock I was standing outside Mr. Dreese's building. Once more I climbed past the baby carriage and the racing bike. Mr. Dreese's face appeared above them under the skylight and he called, "Stephen?"

The TV in the living room was on the movie channel, and I could see Robert De Niro's face. The fan rotated slowly back and forth just as it had the last time, although it wasn't hot today. *Cosmo* and all the papers that had been lying on the table the last time were still there.

"Have you brought your passport photograph?" he asked.

I handed him the passport photograph. He stapled it to the questionnaire he had filled out for me the last time.

"Your file number is 31F. It would be helpful if you mentioned it at the beginning when you call, then I won't have to hunt around for it."

He had on the same olive-green sweater he'd had on two days

before. It had something printed on it but I couldn't make out what.

"Do you know yet when you'll be available?"

"Mondays."

"Any other days?"

"Wednesdays to Saturdays."

"We'll call you as soon as we have anything for you. Things are a little on the quiet side right now."

He stood up.

"As far as I'm concerned the ball can start rolling now."

That must have been the twentieth time he said it.

"We'd appreciate it if you wore a suit when you go out to work."

"A suit," I said.

A Moroccan was sitting on the sofa; the way he looked he could have spent most of the past few months in a cardboard box. Robert De Niro was still busy beating somebody up on TV.

Mr. Dreese saw me to the stairs. "Thanks for coming. See you soon."

I went into the store across the street and bought an ice cream. I am Stephen and my number is 31F, I thought, but I am also Arnon, curator of the used-condom museum, to be found adjacent to the empty-bottle museum. Admission is free, just like the wine. I had hung the condoms on a washing line in my room and had written names on them with a felt-tip pen so that I could tell which was which. Some were light red, others transparent; some still had pieces of toilet paper sticking to them; and a couple were not quite dry yet.

I walked to my mother's house.

"Where do you keep Papa's suits?" I asked.

"Why?"

"I need one. I've been invited to a party."

They smelled of old man's deodorant and they fitted me. The pants kept slipping down, that was all, but they could be made right. I took two suits.

"What sort of party is it?" she wanted to know.

"Just a party. Like any other party."

I walked back through Minervalaan. It was nighttime and there was no one around. A few years before, I had been determined to become king of the Amsterdam underworld. There was still a café at the time where they would give me credit, and I thought that one day everyone would be called on to become one of the things people had been called on to become for thousands of years. There aren't any more cafés in Amsterdam where I can get credit now. Except for the Jericho grill, where the hunchback will spot me three lagers a night, but that doesn't get you very far.

I thought of Sergius, who often said, "I'm tired of fighting." Yet I also remembered spending a few nights with him at the Lijnbaansgracht police station testifying that the boy with the long blond hair had gone for him first, that Sergius hadn't been the one to start it. The biggest drag about the whole thing had been all the friends of those drunken idiots who'd been there as well, yelling that I hadn't seen a thing and that they knew how to deal with jerks like me, if necessary right there at the station. The first time you hear that, you shit your pants. The third time you go there, because they want to ask you some more questions, you realize that those drunks are shitting their pants as well and that they find it just as much of a drag as you do. Even the cops seem bored stiff. Those maniacs can yell as much as they like that they won't be treated like dogs or that they're pissing blood and have to see a doctor; no one pays them any attention.

"Go and piss blood at home, you wacko," yells the police-woman behind the counter, and to us she says that this is what she has to put up with week after week.

The boys say they'll be waiting for you outside and that they'll be making that lovely nose of yours look even lovelier. On Saturday nights the station is staffed mainly by idiots, so that when your turn finally comes to sign your statement it's almost light out and the streets are deserted. Sergius said you had to be insane to spend your evenings at the Lijnbaansgracht station. But some people obviously cannot let well enough alone. Then they write books or fight or play soccer. Or they become singers. That happens too.

"A hospital is the best place to finish off a real evening," Sergius would say, laughing. Actually I was through with that kind of evening, as well as with the kind of people who wear sunglasses all the time because they spend their lives walking around with a black eye.

At seven o'clock that Monday evening I took a shower. I put on my father's suit. I polished my shoes. In one of the suit pockets I found a roll of peppermints. At least three years old but still edible. I remembered somebody once told me that peppermints are made from methanol. I went and stood in front of the mirror. Mr. Dreese had said that he thought my curly hair was nice. I hoped my clients would think so too. I put on aftershave, got a bottle of slivovitz from the kitchen, and sat down beside the telephone.

At eleven I called the Blue Moon.

"I've been waiting all evening," I said.

"That goes with the job," said Mr. Dreese. "We'll call you the moment something turns up."

I went to a store that stayed open late and bought some beer.

"Are you getting married?" they asked.

"No," I said, "I'm not getting married."

Back at home I took off my father's suit and put on a T-shirt. I walked past the bowl of mussel shells on the table. They'd been there for days. Since Ajax played Barcelona and I was the only customer in the café.

I had sat at the bar watching the TV. Ajax were down 4–2 and there were only two minutes left. I ordered another drink and thought of the five hundred guilders I had lost. It's always harder work not thinking about something, because more and more comes into your head that you shouldn't be thinking about.

I remembered the time I'd wanted to become a publisher and walked around the Book Fair making the acquaintance of all sorts of people who were behaving as if they'd never been drunk before and as if it were the first time they'd been allowed out on their own. Everyone tried to put you off with the same garbage—publishers, writers, and soccer players. I followed Wim Kieft for a while. He always starts by cursing and swearing at the linesman. After that, he has a go at the referee. Then he turns to the other team, and when he's finished with them he swears bloody murder at his teammates. By that time the match is as good as over. He can also play normal soccer, of course, it's just that he knows his way around. I once heard Wim Kieft yell at the linesman, "I'll stick that flag right up your ass." I'd yell that sort of thing myself if I had to slog my guts out on pitches like that with nothing but imbeciles everywhere I looked.

Then I lost interest in following Wim Kieft. I drank wine, tequila, buttermilk, and slivovitz one after the other. I ate sugar lumps and raw mushrooms and felt exceptionally good. Better, in any case, than on the sort of evening when you end up in a café with some pain in the ass and have to drink Belgian beer all night.

An old phone book makes an excellent substitute for toilet paper. The Amsterdam phone book lasts a good four months.

I looked at my father's suit hanging over the chair. Marielle had said that Old Spice turned her stomach. I suddenly felt like calling Mr. Dreese and telling him that as far as I was concerned he could stuff his file numbers and his whole escort and dating business. Not because I suddenly had second thoughts. For a few hundred guilders I was even prepared to let myself be fucked by some guy. Actually I'd sooner suck him off than let him screw my ass. Sucking someone off is something I would even do "without," provided I got a bundle for it. By morning you would have forgotten everything that had happened to you the night before. That's the good thing about mornings, they say.

Only I would rather be in business on my own. Then at least I wouldn't have to wear my father's suit or remember a file number or breathe in Mr. Dreese's cologne once a week.

I called the Blue Moon but they were busy and stayed busy. I waited another hour and a half. Eventually I threw the mussel shells away, put on a Vysotsky tape, and called the number Little Michael had given me. Money is there to be spent, especially when you have only two hundred guilders left. I asked if Sandra was working that night. "Yes," the girl said. I thought of that idiotically large vanity case of hers, then I thought of Wim Kieft, and after that I thought of all the people who had gone on at me about love. Incidentally, Wim Kieft doesn't live very far from here. I've stood next to him in the neighborhood Albert Heijn a couple of times.

When I was fifteen I acted in *Antigone*. I was a member of the chorus. Ismene was played by the woman with the biggest ass in Amsterdam. I can't remember who played Antigone. I wore a black sheet made by a woman who taught math and who stood in the dressing room just before the first night sobbing like one possessed. At the time Rosie was still wearing OshKosh outfits and writing me hundreds of letters.

When I was twelve I belonged to a Jewish youth club. In June we would commemorate the Six Day War and play a game in which we had to liberate the Wailing Wall. In October we would commemorate the Yom Kippur War, but I no longer remember what kind of game we played then.

The first pack of cigarettes I ever smoked were John Player Specials. For three and a half years I subscribed to *Football International*. As a premium for signing up they gave me a bag with

"Football International" printed on it. When I was eighteen I threw away all my *Football Internationals*. One Sunday morning in May I left my parents' place with a single suitcase. It wouldn't have done to fill it with *Football Internationals*. "You can't leave me like that," said my mother in the front yard.

"This is the way people do leave one another," I said. "Don't keep nagging me."

Later I said the same thing quite a few times to other people until there was no one left to say it to.

The suitcase was too heavy for me. I had left a fried egg and a tomato behind on the table.

I rented a room in Rombout Hogerbeetstraat from a flower seller. I lived mainly on rice wafers in Rombout Hogerbeetstraat. For two weeks when I was eighteen I had a sweet untouched girlfriend. She went crazy later.

I ate the last few mushrooms I had left and remembered that I had to hand over five hundred guilders the next day. When you're hungry, nothing beats raw mushrooms.

For quite a while I continued to walk around with *Laurel and Hardy's Journey around the World* in my pocket, but I couldn't find Princess Coca. I couldn't ask for her either, because as far as I know I'm the only one to have called her that.

Finally the girl called me back. They always call you back to check your number.

"Oh, it's you again," she said.

"Yes, it's me," I said.

"Sandra will be with you in thirty minutes."

"Fine. Great."

I thought of Sergius. Even when it was cold he would sit by the open window with his feet on the windowsill. He either looked out or looked at nothing at all. Sometimes he made money renovating houses. He owned an electric drill, five pairs of pants, five shirts, and the sorts of other clothes that most people have. He also had a sleeping bag.

I once spoke to a woman who told me that when you give

birth it feels the same as when you have to shit really badly but can't. I spoke to another woman who told me, "Everyone in my family is a garlic lover."

I had given Sandra my phone number. But even as I gave it to her, I knew she would never call me.

My father is buried three hundred yards above the freeway to Tel Aviv. He had false teeth but he was ashamed of them. Whenever he cleaned them he would lock himself in the bathroom. He would stay there for an hour, and if anyone wanted to come in, he'd start bellowing his head off. He had lived in an attic once. A doctor had lived next to him, a Dr. Landsmann. He was a pediatrician, and he'd been made to perform all sorts of experiments in order to save his life. When he came out, he said, "I can never be a doctor again." He'd gone to work in a store where they sold belts, ladies' handbags, and that sort of thing. My father also worked there. One morning ten years later the people downstairs found Dr. Landsmann's body in their garden. "After ten years no one could have expected it," said my father. He spoke of Dr. Landsmann with great respect but he loathed doctors otherwise. Jeanet, incidentally, was the same. They'd done her knees in, she said.

There are still a few things I want to do. I want to go on working for Mr. Dreese's escort agency. If that isn't successful, I'll try it out on my own, but not for less than a hundred guilders a time. Eventually I'll set up my own escort agency. I used to want a girlfriend who would think everything I wrote was fantastic. Since then I've discovered that writers all have friends and girlfriends who swoon over every last *the* they put down on paper. It's easy to tell that from their books. Once I asked a girl if she would teach me how to finger her. She was from Zeeland.

Kol Nidre is the only night when the synagogue gets at all crowded. It's the night for declaring all your vows null and void, for dismissing them as if they had always been no more than dust. You have to put on a shroud that night. I don't have a shroud. I know a lot of unsuccessful small-time crooks, though, who wouldn't think twice about robbing your grave for one.

I like a good striptease. In fact it cheers me up. My father told us, "Dr. Landsmann liked a good ham sandwich with two eggs on top." Everyone needs something to cheer them up.

"Hi," said Little Michael.

"Hi," I said.

Sandra had her large yellow vanity case with her again. Her hair had been dyed a second time. A little better this time.

"Here we are again."

"So I see."

"Look," said Little Michael, "her girlfriend's sick. There's something wrong with her jaw. Is there a hospital around here?"

"Take her to a dentist."

"I'd rather go to a hospital. She has no papers, nothing. We have to pay cash on the spot for everything."

"Try the Free University," I suggested, "it's the closest."

"You can pay me for just an hour but I'll probably be gone for longer. A bit of a lucky break for you, OK?"

"OK," I said.

He said something to Sandra that I couldn't make out because he was whispering. She held her head close to his ear. Finally he said, "It's your friend."

He slammed the door behind him.

I realized that Sandra was wearing new jeans. They were a little too big in the bottom.

"Did you buy those in Amsterdam?" I pointed to her pants.

She nodded. We spoke in English.

"So your sister-in-work is sick?"

"Yes."

"OK. Let's have a drink."

I hated people telling me about illnesses. Her vanity case was on the table. She was drinking wine. She had too much lipstick on. You couldn't see the real color of her hair—dark blond— anymore. She was smoking.

I asked her what she did in Lithuania. She studied Lithuanian history, she said. That conversation took about fifteen minutes.

She smoked and I drank. She used one of my dirty glasses as an ashtray. After six cigarettes she went to take a shower. This time I gave her a towel before she went into the bathroom. She closed the door. I sat on a pile of books in the hallway. As far as I could tell, her English consisted of just two sentences: "Where is the shower?" and "I don't understand." You didn't actually need much more.

After ten minutes she came out. She held her case clasped under her arm.

We lay down on the bed. She smoked and I drank. Vysotsky was singing, but when the tape stopped I didn't turn it over.

I kissed her a few times. Now and then I stroked her long neck and her back with its small bumps. Her vanity case, which was even fuller than last time, stood at the foot of the bed. I wondered if she had brought anything else over from Lithuania.

When I turned around, I saw that we had tipped over the ashtray. The left side of my bed was covered with butts and black streaks and smudges. The two of us going up in flames was all I needed that night.

I stroked her belly and felt her hair, which was just as stiff as the hair on her head.

"I'm not well," said Sandra. She looked at the wall but there was nothing to see there.

I ought to have shouted, "Stop playing games, you filthy little slut." I ought to have pulled her floral panties off, and her undershirt, but I didn't move. Not because I had suddenly seen the light and wanted to behave like a decent human being. It was just that I was dog-tired. I thought it was just as well. Her sister-in-work had an infected jaw. Sandra was unwell and so was I. It was cold in my room because the doors had been left open all day. I turned toward her, felt how warm she was—all living people are warm—and fell asleep against her.

She was the first to say "shit" when the doorbell rang. It was almost two-thirty. I put on my sweater, went to the window, and called out that I was coming.

"Did you manage all right?" I asked Little Michael. Sandra stood next to him with her little bottom in the jeans and her vanity case, which she held as if it were her baby.

"No, I have to go back tomorrow," said Little Michael. "But you got at least half an hour extra."

"That's true," I said.

"And I don't think she minded too much either."

"You're right."

I held out my hand to Sandra.

"*Ciao*," I said.

She nodded.

She followed him out.

At the door, Little Michael said, "Until next time then."

"Yes," I said.

I walked upstairs. I held on to the banister firmly. Sandra's towel lay on the floor. A hair that couldn't have been mine was stuck to the soap. The tub was stained with light brown and dark red specks like freshly laid eggs or mushrooms. In the light I couldn't tell if it was shit or blood.

Tomorrow, I thought, tomorrow I'll clean it up. Tomorrow I was also due to pay five hundred guilders and to call Mr. Dreese. I would be a model employee. I would have to become a little less choosy, perhaps, so that they'd have more work for me, since hanging around was worse than anything. It's a good thing choosiness wears off quickly, they told me, just like everything else.

Once I thought up a way to swindle banks.

Sergius and I had had a plan for sticking Chanel labels onto cheap perfume from Poland. Later he promised to become my driver if I ever got my escort service off the ground. That was just before he left.

When you're old, you'll get your own place at the bar and you'll say about the person who's just left, "In the old days that one'd still fuck you every now and then for a hundred guilders."

Then Jeanet will say, "We all have our brief encounters," and pinch me softly in the crotch. One thing I can promise, and I promise it to you all: the whole underworld will come and dance at my wedding.